LOST
Somewhere

GERALD WOLFE

WESTBOW
PRESS®
A DIVISION OF THOMAS NELSON
& ZONDERVAN

WestBow Press books may be ordered through booksellers or by contacting:

WestBow Press
A Division of Thomas Nelson & Zondervan
1663 Liberty Drive
Bloomington, IN 47403
www.westbowpress.com
844-714-3454

ISBN: 978-1-6642-2422-3 (sc)
ISBN: 978-1-6642-2424-7 (hc)
ISBN: 978-1-6642-2423-0 (e)

Library of Congress Control Number: 2021903343

Print information available on the last page.

WestBow Press rev. date: 03/04/2021

CHAPTER 1

Terry wasn't at all sure he knew where he was or how he got there. He decided to ask a local for directions, if he could find someone. After all it was too easy to get lost in the vastness of Wyoming. Just then he realized he was entering a town and saw a weathered sign that read, "Somewhere, WY, pop 75." *Now just where is Somewhere?* he thought, chuckling. "Somewhere," he said as he drove into the nearly deserted town. "Now to find a shower and a room for the night."

He spotted a general store and parked his tired S10 beside an equally tired Suburban. As he entered the nearly bare general store, the people inside all stared at him, no one saying a word. One of them finally approached and offered his hand. "Hi, I'm Jess Martin. Welcome to Somewhere." Then the others warmed up and welcomed him too.

"Are you just passing through?" asked one of the women.

"Well, sort of. I was hoping for a room and a hot shower for the night." Terry answered.

"No such place in Somewhere," Jess answered. "But Molly and me would be glad to offer our old bunkhouse for a night. Not much to look at, but it's warm, dry, and it has a reasonable bed."

"Thank you." said Terry.

After some small talk about where he was going and why he was in this part of the country, Jess suggested they head for home.

When they arrived at the ranch, Molly fixed up one of the bunks and said goodnight to Terry. Left alone with the kerosene lamp and the quiet of the night, Terry slumped into a chair by the wobbly table and wondered what brought him to this place.

He slept soundly for what seemed like just a few minutes before a rooster announced the dawn. Opening his eyes, he could see a thin sliver of light showing up over the distant mountains. He stretched and got up. He poured water from the pitcher into the wash basin and splashed it on his face. "That is cold!" he yelled, now very much awake.

Terry dressed, stuffed the rest of his clothes into his bag, took a look around the room, opened the door, and stepped outside. He started toward his pickup just as Jess came out of the house with a milk pail in his hand. "Hey, you're not running off without breakfast, are you?" Jess asked.

"Well, I understood it was a bed, not bed and breakfast."

"Come on down to the barn while I milk the cow, and you can earn that breakfast if you feel you're taking advantage of us." As they walked to the barn, Jess did most of the talking. He talked about the ranch, its size, the trials of ranching, the benefits of living way out in Somewhere, Wyoming, and the need for help they couldn't afford. But overall, he mentioned being satisfied with living here.

Terry had never heard of anyone with so many problems being content with their circumstances. He shared briefly about his family, Mother and Dad separated, an older sister who he said was a doctor, and a younger brother in high school. But he revealed as little about himself as possible.

As Jess milked the red cow, he told Terry to put some hay from a small pile in the corner into the stalls for the two saddle horses. Terry also noticed a bucket and went to the well. With a hand pump, he drew a bucket of water. He had learned how to make the hand pump work from a family camping trip to a ranch in Michigan. He filled the bucket a couple of times and gave water to the horses.

Finished with the milking, Jess stood up and motioned toward Terry to head to the house. The aroma of bacon and eggs from the wood stove greeted them as they entered. Molly welcomed Terry and told the men to sit down. She dished up a generous plate for each one and sat with them. Jess gave a rote blessing: "God is good, and we thank Him for this food." As Jess began to eat, Terry took the hint and dug into his generous helping. He tried not to look too eager, but the food was so good, and he hadn't had much since yesterday morning. It was quiet for some time, except for the sounds of eating.

"How did you come to be passing through Somewhere?" Molly asked after a while. "There aren't many people who take the turnoff out of Metteetse that you took. Or did you just get lost?"

"I was looking for a place to get lost, and that road seemed to call to me." Terry stammered something about the road less traveled, but he really didn't give a reason. He finally admitted he wasn't sure what happened and blushed slightly.

Molly didn't miss a beat. "Well you just about did it! There isn't much out this way, so I suppose it was as good a choice as any. At least you are near Somewhere," she said, laughing. That broke the ice and conversation came more easily. Jess and Molly asked about the weather back east, about the farms, about how people made a living, and just regular tourist information. Not once did either mention Terry taking this unlikely road and ending up here, for which he was thankful since he couldn't explain why.

"Where are you headed next?" Molly asked.

"No place in particular," Terry responded. "I don't have any idea or a reason to find one. Just moving on and trying to stay lost."

"Well now, ain't that a life filled with purpose!" Jess said. "But since you're here and don't have any place to go …" he hesitated briefly, "is it possible you would, uh, stay awhile and help us out here on the ranch? If you were to stay on a few months, we would be selling some livestock and could probably make it worth your while. Not twisting your arm in any way, and it ain't much of a proposition, but if you might …" Jess felt embarrassed and just stopped talking as though he were afraid of getting in deeper than he intended.

Terry pondered this during a long silence as breakfast was winding down. He considered the people who had taken him in, looking from Jess to Molly, and the generosity of their offer. How could he turn them down? But how could he stay since he didn't want to be tied to anything? It was an interesting offer, and since it was Somewhere, he wouldn't be found easily. No phone service, no TV, not many people. The isolation called him.

"I suppose I could do that."

Jess bolted out of his chair and shook Terry's hand. He acted as if he wanted to hug him, as if Terry were coming home rather than being a total stranger. Terry felt as though he had come home. The short time here felt warmer than it had ever been at his real home. What was it about this place? What was he getting himself into? He didn't know, but right now it felt good.

The next morning Terry was up just as early as the day before. He helped feed and water the horses. He cleaned out old straw from one of the stalls and tried to find other things he could do to help. Jess finished milking, and they headed for the house for Molly's breakfast. Something had stirred in Terry the night before. Something he couldn't quite remember but wanted to know, but he didn't know how or whom to ask. He just kind of blurted out the first thing that came to mind. "Jess, do you think God is interested in us at all?"

Jess hesitated. "That is an awfully big question to try to answer on an empty stomach!" So the question and the answer died. Terry wanted to ask again but wasn't sure how or if he should.

That morning the two of them took the ranch suburban out to the pasture to see the herd of cows and calves. It was about time to separate them and that would involve being on horseback most of the day. Jess wasn't sure Terry would be of any help since he hadn't mentioned ever being on a horse before.

"What kind of work did your father do that kept him away from home all the time?" Jess asked as they rode back in silence.

"Well, he was a traveling salesman for a western wear and tack company. He went to farm stores and large sports stores in six states. I never knew exactly what he did there, but he was apparently successful. He seldom came home, and when he did it was only for a day or two. He and Mom argued a lot and Dad left without saying goodbye most of the time."

"Did you have livestock?" Jess asked.

"No, we lived in a ritzy Cincinnati suburb that my mom said was good for us since there was a good school nearby. We did go to a stable once in a while when Dad was home. Sometimes we watched the trainers. Sometimes we would have a chance to ride the horses a little."

"How much have you ridden a horse?" Jess asked.

"A few times." Terry tentatively replied.

"Did you like it?"

"It was one of the worst experiences I had ever had, but I liked the horses."

After a long silence, Jess spoke quietly, "Would you be up to trying it again with a real cow horse?"

"Maybe. What did you have in mind?" Terry asked cautiously.

"Well you seem to get along well with that black stocking-footed pony in the stalls this morning. How about trying to see if you get along as well on him as around him?"

"Well I guess so," Terry responded tentatively.

Jess wanted to shout for joy but kept a straight face and drove a little faster, hoping Terry wouldn't change his mind.

CHAPTER 2

That night Terry lay awake a long time. He was troubled by the nagging question about being in Somewhere and if there was any purpose in it. Not that he cared, but it was troubling that he had even thought about God. Jess didn't appear to be any help in figuring it out, and Terry didn't know enough about what he had heard the few times he went to church to be of any help in answering the question. He eventually drifted off to sleep. Morning was only a short time away.

The cowpony was saddled and standing in the runway when Terry got to the barn. Jess was already milking, so without being told, Terry did the chores he had done the day before. Jess hid his smile but was excited to see Terry was smart enough to know things had to be done and willing to do even the simple things without being asked.

When he finished with the regular chores, Jess called to him, "Untie that black pony, and lead him around the barn and back again. He hasn't worked for a few days and needs to get the kinks out. And maybe you can get acquainted."

As Terry untied the reins, the horse snorted, which didn't help the butterflies in his stomach. But he knew enough not to let the horse know he was uneasy and led him out of the barn. Jess watched nervously. When they disappeared around the corner, Jess just held his breath until he heard the steady *clip-clop* returning to the barn. Terry took the horse toward the corner of the corral and then all the way around. They entered the runway, and he tied the horse back where they had started. It felt good.

Jess wanted to jump up and shout for joy as Terry tied the pony to the stall. It seemed right for Terry to be doing this. He believed things were going to work just fine.

That afternoon, Jess gave Terry his first lesson on the horse. The skilled cowpony performed most of the maneuvers by himself, but he didn't get false signals from Terry. It was better than Terry expected and the cowpony was so different from the tired horses he rode at the stable with his father.

Jess unsaddled the horse. Terry saw a curry comb and brushed the horse's back and long mane. Again he found himself wondering why he was there. Why the horse experience and especially this horse. The thoughts he had last night began to take a shape he couldn't explain. *Could this really be a place where I can fit in since I've never had one yet? Did Jess really mean the praise he gave me, or was he just doing it to get a helper for a few months?*

Sleep didn't come easy that night as Terry still wondered how choices and destinies fit in. Why and how did he happen to be in this unlikely place with these unlikely people and have this happen? He lay awake a long time, trying to figure it all out.

CHAPTER 3

The next morning Terry and Jess saddled up and rode out to the north pasture to find and count the cows. "We need to know how many we have to account for or find where they are hiding." There were four fewer than Jess expected. He rode one way and Terry the other around the pasture. Terry spotted two cows in a deep ravine. He called for Jess and waited as he rode up.

"That was smart not to go down there alone. I will circle around and come in behind them. You watch them come out, and keep them close," Jess said, more impressed with Terry for not trying to make a big show by going down there. It was a long ride around, but as Jess came in behind the two cows, the third cow got up from the grass, and three healthy calves followed them without trouble up the valley to the herd.

When Jess reached the pasture, they rode silently for a while before Jess said, "I've been thinking about your question, Terry. I don't know much about God, but I am convinced that there is something that keeps this world running. Maybe God gives us the chance to make our own way but puts up roadblocks that remind us we need to be careful and think seriously about our direction. Maybe He arranged for you to come to Somewhere. I don't really know, but I for one am glad you're here."

In the next few days, Terry rode the cowpony—Buck—several times. Once he even rode out to the pasture and back alone. He kept thinking about how much more fun it was to ride for a purpose than at the stable, where it seemed the owner only wanted his money. He became quite fond of Buck, and they struck up a good friendship. He talked to the horse and asked questions that were on his mind, even though Buck didn't answer. Terry began to feel he was going to fit in after all.

Jess had said they would be rounding up the cows and calves they had counted. Molly had an especially big breakfast ready by the time Jess and Terry came into the kitchen the next morning.

"Sit up and chow down," Molly advised. "You're gonna need all the strength you didn't know you had today. By the time we get all those cows in the corral and separate all the calves, you may be wishing you had never come to Somewhere."   T h a t didn't sound especially comforting, but Terry could sense the excitement and real pleasure in Molly's voice. She didn't often show much interest in the workings of the ranch, but today was different.

"Are you going on the roundup too?" Terry asked.

"You bet!" Molly replied. "I wouldn't miss it. And besides, I have chuckwagon duties, and that is as important as getting out there is."

About that time a couple of pickups with stock trailers came into the yard. The men unloaded their horses, and the women began unloading coolers and boxes of food and drinks. Things started to heat up when Jess yelled, "Let's mount up!"

The riders and horses moved out at a walking pace. No need to tire the horses now. There could be harder riding later keeping the herd together and moving them into the corral. Terry felt a thrill he had never known before. This was real work with a real purpose. Nothing he had done before seemed anywhere near the satisfaction he was feeling right then. He had ridden Buck many times since the day they did the count and felt more comfortable in the saddle. He began to wonder if this was his purpose in life. How had this happened? He had tried to escape all he had known from his past, but he never expected to end up on a cattle ranch. What he thought he knew before didn't fit with today. He just didn't know what it was. He thought of the things he had heard about a plan for our lives, but it hadn't made sense. Was it here in the simple life on a ranch in Somewhere, Wyoming? Terry wanted to find out. How could he be sure? Or was it merely another dead-end street like ones he had traveled before? Terry wanted to know but was afraid of the answer. So he turned his thoughts to what the day would hold and prepared to work harder than he ever thought possible.

CHAPTER 4

N o day in Terry's life had ever been so tiring, or humiliating. But no day had ever turned out so rewarding and filled with the satisfaction of having worked so hard and helped so much. The cattle seemed more restless. They resisted being herded together; they especially didn't like being driven toward the corrals. They seemed to have memories that they didn't like, though they probably didn't know just what was going to happen. As Terry was resting comfortably in the saddle, one of the cows and her calf bolted from the herd. It was right in from of him, but he wasn't sure just what to do. Buck wheeled, nearly losing Terry, and raced after the runaway. The single cow just kept running, and Buck raced after her. Caught by surprise, Terry wasn't prepared for what happened next. They headed toward the fence at breakneck speed. As the cow and her calf reached the fence, they saw a broken portion and bolted through. Buck saw what was coming and sat down in a quick stop, launching Terry into the air and over the fence. He landed in an open space, framed by two of the largest cacti he had ever seen. Terry sat there stunned as the others rode up, fearing the worst. When they saw that Terry wasn't hurt, they began to laugh. The men jumped off their mounts and went to the rescue, relief in every action.

"Ain't no better place you could have landed," one said. "Them cactus plants ain't very soft."

After getting the cows back in the pasture and mending the fence, everyone mounted up again and kept the herd close together. Jess rode up beside Terry, slapped him on the back, and told him how proud he was of him.

With the herd in the big round corral at the ranch, it was time to separate the cows and the calves. Jess took Terry aside. "You are riding the best cutting horse in this territory, and the only one that I own. If you don't want to take this responsibility, I can get one of the others to ride for us today. But I would like to have you up today. You are lighter than any the rest of us, and you have built a special bond with this special horse. What do you say?"

Terry hesitated for no more than an instant and replied, "I would be honored to try, but you saw what happened out there. And I wouldn't know the first thing about what to do."

Jess gave him a firm slap on the back. "Let's get to work then. First you have to know how to get your horse to lock on to the calf you want. Then you have to hang on because you will have the ride of your life, watching him match wits and deception. Let's start with the basics on how to identify the calf you want."

After a half hour of instruction, Terry rode into the corral. He wasn't totally sure just what to expect, but he felt he was ready. Jess told him which calf he wanted, and Terry rode slowly into the herd. When he spotted the calf, he eased the reins forward and pressed his knees just lightly. Buck moved forward confidently and easily moved the calf away from his mother. But then the calf realized that Mama wasn't by his side anymore and made a beeline to get back to her. Buck slid into place to block the retreat, nearly unseating Terry, who had a firm hold on the saddle horn with reins loosely looped but still was barely able to recover.

"Nice work," one of the neighbors told him. He knew Terry was new at this and the compliment was genuine. "Not many fellers aren't upset on their first try with a good cuttin' horse."

13

Terry gained confidence and worked well most of the morning. Jess asked for one calf that was probably the biggest one in the herd, and his momma was very protective. As Terry approached, she moved in. Buck already knew the calf was spotted and made the cow look foolish as he cut her away from her calf. But Momma wasn't finished. She charged the enemy with her head down. Terry didn't see her coming, and she hit Buck in the shoulder, making him lose his footing and leaped aside to avoid falling. It was all Terry could do to stay aboard. And just as fast, Buck moved to cut her off from another run. He cut out her calf again without Momma ever knowing he was gone. Buck seemed to know how to handle ornery critters and drove the angry cow back into the herd.

The rest of the morning was routine. All the calves were branded, doctored, and separated from their mothers. The bawling from one pen to the other was deafening, so Jess called for a break. Everyone went up to the house, where the women had set up plank tables to serve dinner. The hearty meal was necessary for hard work on the ranch.

Terry was exhausted. He went to the bunkhouse and washed up. He thought he could rest few minutes, but he dropped on his bunk and instantly went to sleep. If it hadn't been for Paul Young, Jess's neighbor, who told him he was doing a good job, he would probably still have been asleep the next morning.

"Best come up and get some victuals," Paul yelled as he shook Terry awake. "The day isn't over." Terry jumped. He was embarrassed but glad Paul didn't tell everyone else where he had gone.

Finishing up in the afternoon was easy. They drove the herd back to the pasture and watched as the cows and calves were reunited. The ornery cow was delighted to see her calf again, even as she bellowed her objection loudly for such cruel and unusual treatment.

CHAPTER 5

R anch life settled into a routine of fences to fix, horses to tend, and haying equipment to repair. There were also trips to town for supplies, and they checked on the cows at least once a day. Of course, there was eating and sleeping, and sometimes they played checkers in the evening.

One morning Jess came to the bunkhouse early. Terry had been up for a while, but it was unusual for Jess even to come to the bunkhouse. He seemed hesitant and unsure of just what to say and asked Terry to sit at the table. Terry felt the uneasiness of the situation and reluctantly agreed.

As they sat across from each other, Jess began. "You've been with us nearly three months. You have worked hard and never complained about getting up early or working late. You haven't ever questioned why you should do a dirty job when I went to town and didn't help. I have never had a hired hand work harder than you do, and you aren't even hired. You drifted into Somewhere with what seemed to be nothing and have lived and worked with us ever since. Why?"

Terry didn't know what to say. He had been wondering why they allowed him to stay but didn't want to ruin what had been some of the best times of his life. He knew Jess and Molly probably deserved to know why this unlikely drifter had taken their hospitality along with the work so easily.

"Well it's a bit of a surprise to me too," Terry began hesitantly. "I'm nineteen, nearly twenty, and have never worked harder or liked it more than here with you. I grew up in Ohio and didn't do well in school, barely squeaking by in high school to get a diploma that doesn't mean much to me since I barely learned enough to say I was a graduate." Terry choked back a sob before continuing. "My dad left us a long time ago. Mom has worked at various jobs as an accountant to keep food in the house. I never really appreciated any of her sacrifices, and perhaps Mom didn't really deserve my respect. She didn't get it from me either. Some of the money she earned wasn't done admirably, but she never held back anything that me, my brother, or my sister really needed. I didn't know what I wanted to do after high school. I just left in the middle of the night, never communicated in any way, and ended up here. My sister is involved with some bad company. She is a senior in high school, not a doctor as I told you before. But just like me, that doesn't mean much. I'm not sure what my brother is doing now, but if I were to guess, he isn't making very good choices either. I never had a job that I liked or stayed with more than a few days. I always felt I was being taken advantage of, even when it was probably obvious I was getting more than I was giving. I saved enough money to buy my pickup and planned to leave as soon as I had enough saved to leave. Ohio isn't the best place to live. I had heard of Wyoming and thought it would be a good place to get lost, or at least never found.

"When I came into Somewhere that evening, I was running short on just about everything, including self-assurance, worth, and yes, money. Everything, that is, but fear. I had a lot of that. But I had learned how to hide most of my feelings, so I decided I could probably bluff these backwater dummies into a place to stay and a few gallons of gas. So when you offered to give me a place, I took it without caring. I thought I could easily steal some gas, and I wouldn't have to be here long enough to answer for it. What I didn't reckon with was that you 'backwater dummies' were able to spot a loser better than most Ohio dudes. So I was surprised as I got to know you and your neighbors. I have always wondered why you have let me stay."

Jess had listened quietly. He had suspected as much the first time he saw Terry. But he had also felt he saw something else buried in that guarded attitude. He sat quietly for a few moments after Terry stopped talking, choking back emotion, and wished he had a simple answer. Nothing he heard surprised him. Jess had heard this story many times over from other young men wanting to throw off their pasts. He had tried to do it himself when he was young and fortunately had met Molly and found something he couldn't treat carelessly as he had his own family and life. So Jess felt he knew what was churning in Terry.

"Terry, I didn't come out here this morning to put you on the spot. Molly and I have thought about your being here and the strange way in which we were handed the help we needed on this ranch. We aren't really able to hire someone to work here, but when you showed up, it just seemed right to offer this bunkhouse. No one has ever stayed in it but Molly and me as long as we have owned it. But the previous rancher owned the land that included all the smaller ranches around here, was all in one piece at one time, and a working crew lived in this bunkhouse. When Molly and me were married a couple of years ago, we bought this piece of land off the old BarJ Ranch and struggled to make the payments. But that is in the past. Knowing we needed help to develop the place didn't stop us from trying. We built the house room by room. Little by little we scraped together what you see here now. You came along, and somehow we both felt that giving you a few days in our bunkhouse, eating at our table, and just caring was what we should do. We never expected or intended to have a 'hired man,' especially one who didn't cost us anything. So the reason I came out this morning was to offer you a job working here at our place. We don't know what to offer for pay, or how we could even give it. I had offered you something when we sold the calves this fall. Anyway, I don't know what I am really offering, but I just want you to know how much we need you, how much we have appreciated you, and how foolish we feel for not offering to pay you sooner. So you think about it, get washed up, and come up to the house for breakfast. Okay?"

Terry didn't know what to say. He couldn't have said it if he knew because there was a lump in his throat and fear in his heart. He began to feel something new. He believed he loved these simple people. No one else had ever shown him the kindness he felt from Jess and Molly. Jess had said more about respect and need than anyone he had ever known. He just nodded to Jess and watched him close the door on the way out.

Breakfast was the best Terry had ever tasted, even though it was the same as every other day. The eggs, pancakes, and sausage as common as the coffee they had before. But today it had a meaning he hadn't expected.

CHAPTER 6

The day progressed as usual—milking the cow, feeding the horses, fixing fences, getting the swather ready for haying, and catching up with the weeds around the place. In the afternoon a rain shower came up and put a stop to all outside activity.

Terry cleaned out the stalls and the moldy hay from the unused mangers. He went up into the loft and moved the last of the hay into the front of the loft. He didn't need to, but he thought it would be faster to feed it in the morning when he came out to take care of Buck and Babe, the other horse, and the milk cow.

It was pleasant to hear the rain falling lightly on the roof. He had never known it could sound so comforting. But it also made him think of his mom, sister, and brother back in Ohio. He started to wonder if he had made the right decision and if he should at least tell them he was okay and still thought of them. But that thought left sooner than it came.

Late in the afternoon, the storm seemed to let up. But black clouds still seemed to hang over the mountains to the northwest. Jess said he didn't like what he saw, but he didn't seem too worried as they ate supper and headed for bed a little early.

Terry dropped on his bunk and was asleep about as fast. He dreamed of home and what he had left behind. About 1:00 in the morning, he heard a crash of lightning, and the whole world seemed to light up. He jumped out of bed and raced to the window.

Flames were coming out of the end of the barn. He pulled on his clothes as fast as he could and raced to the house. After pounding on the door, it took only a few seconds to see Jess, who sleepily asked, "What—" He never finishing the sentence.

"Get the cow and the horses out as fast as you can," he yelled, disappearing into the house.

Terry ran to the barn, which was filled with smoke, the horses squealing, cow bawling, and chickens clucking, he opened the doors and gates, and chased out the animals. As he emerged, he realized Buck wasn't with the other horse. He raced back inside, now thick with smoke. Terry could hear the frightened horse trying to find its way out. He dove into the stall and grabbed the halter. Buck reacted and reared, taking Terry off the ground. Terry started to scream but held it, realizing it would only make matters worse. When they came down, he talked quietly to Buck. "Easy now. Just come with me. Let's go." Stroking Buck's neck, he eased the horse out of the stall and into the runway. It was nearly black, and fire was leaping out from the grain bin. Terry held firm to Buck's halter, talking softly to him all the time. Finally they emerged just as the far end of the barn crashed to the ground, sending a shower of sparks into the night air and falling on him and Buck. Buck reacted to the sting of the sparks with a wild scream and plunged away from the barn with Terry hanging onto the halter for dear life. It was only a few minutes of frantic running, but it felt like hours. When they were nearly out of the yard, Terry was able to get Buck to stop. The seasoned cowpony just stood there, trembling and huffing. They turned away from the fire but could feel the heat from the intense flames making short work of finishing off the rest of the barn.

«At least no livestock was lost, and everyone is safe," Terry said aloud. "I don't know if I could have done that if I had been thinking about the danger." He heard his name being frantically called from what was left of the smoldering barn. When he realized Jess didn't know if he got out, he released Buck, went back into the yard, and called out. Molly ran to him and smothered him in her arms as Jess ran up and embraced them both, crying and talking all at once. Buck just stood there as if saying, "Doesn't anyone care about me?"

No one knew what to say. They just stood quietly, sobbing in joy and relief.

"Oh, God," Jess said, "I haven't paid much attention to you for a long time, but tonight I am so thankful to you for your protection and for making it possible to be here with those I love so much. I am sorry for ignoring you and for taking everything so carelessly and thanklessly. Molly and me want you to know that coming close to losing Terry has made us realize just how terrible that would have been. I want you to know that I want to be the kind of husband I should have been all along and …" A heart-wrenching sob escaped from Jess's throat, and all three stood there crying as if they had lost everything.

As the emotion of the moment began to go away, they looked at the loss. Light was coming over the eastern ridge, and the smoldering barn became more visible. They could see the cow, and one of the horses was calmly munching grass at the edge of the pasture as if nothing had happened. The rooster began to crow, and Buck snorted and ran up and stood beside Babe. Jess, Molly, and Terry realized that the terror of the night would soon go away with the coming of the morning.

CHAPTER 7

As they slowly walked back toward the house, two pickups careened around the corner and came to a sliding stop. Neighbors jumped out and began asking if everyone was okay. They could see the barn was gone, but they were first and foremost concerned for their dear neighbors and their livestock. Jess assured them that everyone was just fine though tired, sooty, hungry, and thirsty. Just then two more pickups came into the yard. It was more than Jess and Molly had seen since the roundup. After telling the story over and over, the men looked through the ashes for hot spots, and the ladies began to pull coolers and grills out of the trucks to make the biggest breakfast that Somewhere had ever seen.

After everyone had eaten more that their fill, one of the ranchers, John Fisher, stood up. "My precious neighbors," he began. But couldn't go on for the sob that erupted from him. When he regained is voice, he continued. "I think we are here for more purpose than to make Jess and Molly feel supported. It isn't often we have such an opportunity to see where we have been and where we are going. For some time I have been having dreams that frightened me into remembering my long-forgotten past. I can't say that what I done has been all that bad, but I can say that it hasn't been all that good either. Me and Veda Mae have been thinking it would be good if we was to begin getting together and recognizing that God is still is around, and that He still wants us to worship Him and see that He really has made it possible to be as prosperous as we all are. It ain't just the work we done, and it sure ain't the money we have. But we have truly benefitted from His land. We just think, 'We done it,' when all the time, He did. I ain't much in talking, but—" He was interrupted by hearty laughs from all those present. "But it strikes me that we ought to give God thanks for Him taking care of Jess, Molly, and, and—" "Terry," someone yelled. "Terry," John continued. "So, dear God, I hope You remember me from way back, and I just want to tell You thanks for taking care of our neighbors and keeping them from being hurt in this tragic night. I don't know what You had in mind for this fire, but maybe right here we have discovered it. Amen." With his hat in his hand, John sat down.

It was very quiet for some time. Then timidly one of the women began to sing, "What a Friend We Have in Jesus," and most everyone else joined in.

Then they all set to work cleaning up the charred remains of the barn and rounding up the livestock. They all promised they would be back to help with a shelter for the animals.

Terry fell into his bunk exhausted that night, thankful that the bunkhouse had been spared since it was close to the barn. Before he went to sleep, a nagging memory of having gone to church when he was quite young began to fill him with a sense of longing and wonder. *Did it really mean anything then? Does it have anything to do with being here in Somewhere, Wyoming? What was it that I was told?* He couldn't quite remember, and he didn't have much of a chance to think about it as he drifted into a sleep of deep exhaustion.

The next morning, the sun was up and filled the bunkhouse with light when Terry woke up. He quickly dressed and hurried to the house. It was quiet, but there was a note on the table: "Gone to town, will be back later. Some breakfast in the icebox, can eat it cold or heat it up. Glad you are still here. Love, Molly!"

"Love, Molly?" Terry asked out loud. What did it mean? He was a hired man. Terry looked in the icebox and found the plate of sausage and eggs as promised. He found a frying pan and heated it up on the wood stove, being careful not to set anything else on fire. It was good, but it was different not having Jess and Molly there.

Going outside he looked at the remains of the barn. Buck came to the corral fence and gave him a, "Good morning," greeting. Terry knew what he wanted but wasn't sure he would get his measure of grain. Looking around, he found a charred sack by one of the posts of the barn. It was burned on top, but the grain was still there. He scooped some into a sooty pail for Buck and Babe. It was obvious they liked it as they ate noisily. He looked around and found an old washtub without too many holes. He used some twigs to stop up the holes as much as he could. Then pumped water and filled the tub. It still leaked but not so fast that the horses couldn't get a good drink. Trying to think of anything else he could do, he sat in the shade of the bunkhouse as Jess and Molly drove into the yard. At first they just sat in the pickup, talking. Then they got out and came over to Terry. They pulled up a bench without saying a word and just sat down. The rather large package they carried sat on the ground beside them. It was an awkward moment. Nothing was said. No greeting. No recognition. Just silence. Terry shifted uneasily on the old bench, not knowing what to do. Finally Jess spoke up.

"You're probably wondering what is going on," he offered tentatively. It was true, but Terry said nothing, just listened. Finally Molly handed him the bag from the General Store in Meeteetse. Terry took it but was unsure what to do. Looking inside, he saw the logo on the box and knew it was boots. Genuine cowboy boots. And the right size too. He grinned sheepishly, took the box out, and held it for some time.

"Well they won't do you any good if you don't get them out and try them on," Jess said.

The boots fit perfectly but felt rather strange compared to the worn running shoes he had been wearing. He got up and tried to walk. The boots' heels made balance a real challenge. Taking a few steps toward the corral, the boots began to settle on his feet, and Terry liked what he felt.

"Now you look like a real ranch hand," Jess exclaimed.

Terry liked it and knew it was a sacrifice for Jess and Molly to provide. He knew for sure he had found a real family, and that felt even better than the boots.

"I better get some more water for the horses," Terry said. He turned quickly so they wouldn't see the tears in his eyes. He grabbed the bucket, pumped some water, and hurried as fast as he could toward the corral. Partly so there would be some water left, but mostly so no one would see or hear him crying. They must not know how much it had touched his heart. It made Jess and Molly so much more than the people he worked for. A prayer of thanksgiving erupted from his lips, surprising him but renewing more thoughts he had forgotten and were hidden under the junk of a compromising past. And God smiled.

The next morning everything was back to as normal as it could be. The regular chores were done, and Jess was filing the sickle blade for the swather. As Terry came up, Jess looked up and casually announced that today they would start cutting some of the grass to be stored for the winter feed supply. This was new to Terry, but he welcomed the news and pitched in, asking how he could help.

"You could get some water bags from Molly and fill them. And find out how long it would be 'till she has our lunch ready."

Terry hurried off to the house, got the water bags, and was informed that the lunches would be ready in about half an hour. Filling the canvass water bags at the pump and hanging them on the side of the suburban, Terry wondered how lukewarm water tasted when you are really thirsty. Loading a gas can and tools finished the rest of the preparations. Molly called that lunches were ready. Jess handed the keys to the Suburban to Terry, and he climbed on the swather, turned the key, started the engine, and yelled, "Follow me." Terry moved in behind the swather, and they were off for a day of fieldwork.

The sun was high in the morning sky as they came to the field. Terry opened the gate, and Jess pulled into the thigh-high prairie grass, threw the sickle into gear, and moved off down the field, leaving a neat window of bright green prairie grass in its wake.

Terry was watching as more of the field of grass was being deposited in rows when he heard a loud bang coming for the direction of the swather. He saw Jess wave at him, and he drove the Suburban through the grass to the swather.

Jess wasn't sure what happened, but as they inspected the machine, they found the driveshaft had come loose, and that stopped everything. It didn't look like a real serious breakdown, but parts of the U-joint were lying on the ground under the hay.

"Wouldn't you know it,'" Jess said, fuming. "Just when everything was going nicely, something has to happen to mess it up!"

Terry started to search for bolts and other pieces in the dust and found some of the parts. With what they could find and the other things in the Suburban, they put the driveshaft back together, though it didn't look quite right. Fortunately it was not one of the high-speed shafts that had come loose, but it was essential since it drove the machine forward.

Jess started up the swather and shifted into low gear. He held his as he slowly let out the clutch. The swather moved forward smoothly but slowly. As he saw everything working well, Jess shifted to a higher gear and was able to cut about half the field before waving Terry over again.

"What happened?" Terry asked anxiously.

"Well, the sun came up and reached noontime, so I figured we need some grub to finish the rest of the day. What say we drive over there by those trees and have some lunch?" Relieved, Terry grinned and relaxed.

Lunch was almost as good as home cooking in the kitchen, and the water was almost cold. Jess explained that it was cooled by evaporation, which didn't seem possible. It was good anyway. They got back to swathing shortly after lunch, and about 4:30, they finished the field. As they drove home, Terry asked where they would put the hay since there was no barn and no hayloft.

"We have to let it dry for a couple of days first. Then maybe we will stack it in the corner of the field until we need it at home. We can't stack it too soon, or it will rot if it's too green. And it could even start another fire."

They drove into the yard about 5:30, and Molly came out to see how it had worked out. After Jess explained what happened she told him about a visitor she had just after they left that morning.

Between her tears and struggling with emotion, Molly explained. "He asked if we had a deed for our property. I assured him I thought we did and that we received a paid-in-full receipt for the loan we took out to buy our half section. I didn't give any details other than what he asked for. He gave me this business card, stating he was from a law firm in Ohio that was looking into the legality of the ranchers in the Somewhere area who may have stolen land from the BarJ Ranch. I assured him it was not stolen and that we had entered into an agreement with Otis Linderman, who had originally homesteaded nearly eighteen square miles in this area. I didn't know what to think, but he menacingly noted that we would be hearing from his firm in the near future."

Jess stared at Molly and said nothing. It was startling news. The worst of it was that he knew they did not have a deed for the ranch. They had done business with a handshake and goodwill, which wasn't the way it was done anymore. Jess wrapped his arms around Molly as she sobbed out her fear and helplessness. He felt the same way but controlled himself and just whispered words of hope and comfort.

"We will get by this too," Jess said quietly. "We have faced other real problems and have been able to solve them, so I believe this will be the same." But inside he felt no confidence and no room to turn around.

Terry felt sick and slowly moved away from the distressed couple he had come to love and respect. *It just isn't fair,* he thought. *How can this be? What can I do to help?*

That evening the three of them sat around the supper table a long time trying to map out a plan. But nothing seemed right.

"Who was the loan company?" Terry asked.

"First State Bank in Cody," Jess replied.

"They must have some records of your buying and who was selling, and the agreement you both must have signed. That might be the best place to start," Terry suggested. "Maybe we could talk to an attorney after we have some information and see if there is cause to worry."

Terry suddenly felt like he had overstepped his welcome and apologized for butting into their personal affairs. But they all agreed and made plans to go to Cody in the morning.

There wasn't much sleeping that night, but Terry fell into a deep sleep with wild dreams and strange solutions.

CHAPTER 8

Wednesday morning dawned with a slight drizzle. It fit the mood around the breakfast table. The rain dripping off the eves sang an ominous song. No one wanted to talk very much. As they finished up and Molly washed the dishes, Jess was looking over the papers they had collected, which they hoped would be enough to prove ownership of the 320-acre ranch they called home. There were cancelled checks from a bank in Cody and some descriptions of the boundaries, but nothing that said a deed was issued or that there had been anything like a survey of the property. Jess was certain there had been a description of the land given to them, but he couldn't find it in the few papers kept in their file. He felt fear rising in himself as he tried to remember how it was they had come into contact with Otis Linderman. But he couldn't even recall the situation that made it possible to consider buying this small portion of the BarJ Ranch when it was still more than 18 sections, 11,520 acres. Half a section was a such small part, but it seemed to Jess and Molly they had purchased all of Wyoming, not just this little ranch in the western part of the state.

"I just can't remember how it all began and where the agreement we must have signed with Linderman could even be," Jess said followed by a groan. "I just can't remember, but it has been nine years. After the last payment, we should have received a bill of sale or some kind of receipt saying paid in full, but I don't remember anything."

Molly was finishing the dishes when she brightened up and asked if Jess had looked in the top drawer of the dresser in the bedroom. "We kept our important papers there before we found that old desk. Maybe it is in there."

Jess searched the dresser from the top drawer to the bottom drawer but found nothing. Not having more to go on than their recollections, Jess and Molly decided to get ready and go on into Cody and talk with the banker. Maybe he had filed a bill of sale or some other document when they applied for their loan.

The three of them piled into the Suburban and headed to Cody. Just as they were about to go out the gate, Terry asked if they had the card and notice of the man from Ohio who had started all this panic. Molly let out a yelp and said that she had left it on the table. so back to the house. A frantic search found it on the top of the cabinet. Then back into the Suburban and off to Cody.

It was a quiet ride into Metteetse, where they stopped for gas. Terry had taken some of the money he still had and bought each of them a candy bar for the trip. It was the sweetest peanut bar he had ever eaten. He felt like part of a family and was accepted as one. Nothing he could have imagined compared with the peace and satisfaction he felt that rainy day in western Wyoming.

Metteetse wasn't a big town, but it was large enough to have a farm store that had just about anything a regular rancher could need. There were shovels, pitchforks, baler twine, thousands of nuts and bolts in a variety of sizes, paint, and nails. If it was needed on the ranch, the Metteetse farm store had it. Terry recognized some of brands of tack from his dad's sale catalogs, and he knew what every piece was used for. It was the first time he ever thought about how much his dad must have helped small towns like this one in his traveling sales career. When Jess called him to get going, reality came back, as did the uncertainty they were all feeling.

As they got closer to Cody, more farms were evident. Terry was thinking about what they would find at Cody National Bank. He suddenly had an idea about the representative who started all the turmoil. "Could I see the card that guy left with you, Molly? My mom once worked for a large legal firm in Cincinnati, and it just may be the same one." He didn't know how it would make any difference, but maybe they could find out if this was a legitimate claim or something much more sinister. The card was well done, and the man's name was identified as a claims detective for the Cincinnati Legal Department of Bushner and Welch Associates, specializing in boundary and property disputes. Terry looked at the card a long time. The address was in the heart of the financial and banking district. He did not recognize this law firm, but it looked as though it could be legitimate.

As they drove into town, Terry suggested they have the banker call this firm just to find out if it even existed. Everyone thought that was a good starting place. "Maybe they could give us information on where Mr. Linderman or his heirs are located. Then we might be able to contact them too," Jess suggested. Having this much of a plan was encouraging to all three as they parked in front of the Cody National Bank.

CHAPTER 9

As they entered the bank, Molly tripped on the doormat and fell, hitting her head on the inside door and landing flat on her face. She lay there without moving as Terry and Jess knelt to help her. They could do nothing to arouse her, and customers and tellers crowded around them.

"Can someone call a doctor?" Jess asked.

No one moved. One of the observers, Christen, finally said she was a nurse at the local hospital and knelt to help. Christen held Molly's wrist to check for pulse and said it was very weak. She carefully turned Molly's head and pulled her eyelid back to see her bloodshot eye. An ambulance arrived at the door, and paramedics rushed in. The examination was quick and thorough, but it didn't help when they said Molly must be taken to the hospital. Jess just stared into the EMT's face. No words could come from his throat as the tears flowed down his cheeks. Terry put his arm around him and tried to encourage him as the ambulance crew readied to leave. Jess ran out to follow in the Suburban.

Terry just stood there in shock. Not knowing anyone in Cody, he wasn't sure just what to do. He finally sat down at one of the sitting areas and cried. He even prayed for God to make everything right again. To his surprise, he began to feel as though everything would turn out all right. The same people who had merely stared at them started to come over to comfort him and assure him that "Your mom will be okay." He tried to explain, but they weren't listening.

As Terry was trying to figure out just what to do, a young man came and sat in a chair across the table from him. He was reading a book and occasionally looked up and studied Terry with a look of compassion. When he couldn't keep quiet any longer, he moved to Terry's side of the table and quietly asked, "What happened that makes you so sad?"

Terry recounted the entrance to the bank and the accident that sent Molly to the hospital. He made it clear that she was not his mom but that he had been working for Jess and Molly almost eight months. "It has been the best time of my life, and I don't know what to do." A sob escaped from somewhere deep inside.

Rob asked why they were in Cody at the bank. Terry didn't know just what to say but finally felt it was right to share the reason. The story came out in a jumble. "They just can't lose their ranch after working so hard all these years. With the lightning destroying their barn and the hay crop still in the field, Molly in the hospital … it just isn't fair or right!" Terry sobbed. "It just isn't right!" He said it so loudly that a number of the others in the bank looked his way.

"I don't know what to say," Rob answered. "My name is Robert Evans. I am a local attorney, and I am curious why you all came to the bank. You could have gone to the courthouse to see if there had been deed or ownership documents filed."

" I don't know if I should tell you anything," Terry answered. "I don't have any connection that gives me any rights. You would have to ask Jess about that."

"Well then, we should go to the hospital and ask Jess. I suppose you would like to go there anyway. I can take you there and see if there is something I can do to help. Besides, I like to help people who are in trouble when more just seems to be piled on."

Terry smiled through his tears for the first time since the accident. *Maybe this is help and maybe it can solve both problems,* he thought.

"Well I would like to go. Thank you for offering."

As they left the bank, the sun broke through the overcast sky, just in that very spot. It seemed to say that everything would work out for the best way, even though the rest of the sky was still overcast and threatening.

CHAPTER 10

As Rob and Terry drove through Cody toward the hospital, Rob was a veritable tourist guide. Terry didn't know how historically significant Cody was. The past had formed and hardened the people into the fiercely independent pioneers Terry had only read about in western novels and some history books. It was interesting, and he hoped to visit again and see some of the significant sights Rob was telling him about.

As the hospital came into view, fear rose in Terry's heart. *How badly is Molly injured? Is it dangerous? Does it mean she won't be able to go home?* And on and on he worried.

Nothing prepared Terry for the sight that met him as he and Rob entered the waiting room. There were Molly and Jess, signing the release papers at the desk. Nothing seemed to be wrong at all. Molly's face had the look of perfect health Terry was used to, except for a huge black eye.

As Jess turned around to leave, he nearly ran into Terry and gripped him in the tightest bear hug ever. Both of them were surprised to see each other there. Since Molly was ready to leave, the questions flew between them. "How did you get here?"

"What happened to Molly?"

"Why didn't you come with me?"

Terry tried to explain what happened after the ambulance left. He introduced Robert Evans and explained that he brought him here. Terry didn't tell Jess that he had discussed their problem with a stranger and found out that Rob was an attorney.

"I would like to treat all of you to lunch at the greatest little eating place west of the Mississippi," Rob insisted. "You have never had western food like Jimmy fixes it. There isn't anything that doesn't taste wonderful, and it would please me to treat you with a special experience in Cody. And there is nothing you can do or say to change my mind!"

Everyone just stood there until Jess said, "Well let's go then!"

After settling at the table at the Rusty Stirrup Cafe and giving the waitress their orders, Rob asked the question that had bothered him ever since meeting Terry. "When I asked what brought you to Cody, Terry said you were having some kind of land dispute. I am a local attorney specializing in land disputes, and I would be most honored to look into the problem for you."

No one spoke. They sat there dazed and a little uncertain of what to say. Had Terry told too much to this stranger? What if he is really the one behind the problem and is looking for a quick and harmful solution. How would they know? Jess looked at Terry. He didn't accuse him, but it was close.

Rob finally broke the silence. "I don't know anything about the particulars of this problem. Terry only said that you had come to Cody for information about your land. He would not say what you were looking for or what you hoped to find because he knew he didn't have any right to meddle in your affairs. But I sensed the situation may be serious and has enormous implications. The bank will close in about thirty minutes, so I would like you to stay here in Cody at least overnight.

"We can't do that," Molly blurted out.

"Why not if it won't cost you? And you can stay as long as you need to free of charge. If you say no, you will have robbed my wife and me of a great opportunity to serve someone in need.

I do not need your business in my law practice. God has seen fit to make me as prosperous as I need to be in order to help anyone, regardless of their circumstances. So please, if I can help, I would be honored!"

Before anyone had a chance to say anything, the waitress brought the best looking meal with the best smelling aroma. The hungry bunch around that table just sat there as Rob gave a short and passionate prayer of thanksgiving for the food and this wonderful family. It didn't take any encouragement to get started eating at the sound of the "Amen." And nothing they had eaten for a long time had tasted better.

As the meal progressed, Jess asked Rob, "Why would you be interested in our problem? You don't know anything about us."

"I know that we met under very difficult circumstances, but it is often that when there is no opportunity to plan our meeting, the best chance of honesty exists. I met Terry there in the Cody Bank and offered to help to get him here because he needed help that I could give. I am willing to take the chance because I sense you have nowhere to turn, and you aren't sure if there is any solution to your problem, even though I don't have the faintest idea exactly what it is," Rob replied. "I also sense that it is nearly a make-or-break situation, especially since you made the effort to come to Cody and try to find out something that could save your ranch. That much I know. But that is all. So are you willing to give me the opportunity to try to help?"

After a long silence, Molly said, "Jess and I are not all we could be, but we work hard, and Terry came out our way in unusual circumstances. He has been such a help and has given us more encouragement than we have had in a long time. The fire in the barn made us begin to wonder why this happened. Perhaps you are the way of helping us find out." Turning to Jess, she continued,

"I think we should take the chance on Rob and try to settle ownership of the ranch straight out."

No one noticed, but Rob sent up a silent prayer for wisdom and the ability to make this a truly profitable trip for these special people.

CHAPTER 11

After they finished their meal, they sat around the table for a long time talking about what had happened. Suddenly, Terry spoke up. "I want to know what happened to Molly in the bank. No one has said anything about it and if it is a problem or what. How come you look okay after the scare you gave us all?" He looked straight at Molly.

She returned his gaze with a look of pure compassion and shared what the hospital staff told them. "It looks like I just collapsed under the load of anxiety and from not having eaten or drunk anything since breakfast. And tripping on the floor mat didn't help. They checked me out, but after I had some orange juice, it seemed that I was okay again, so they let me check out. If I have any more problems, they told me to call them immediately. But this dinner was just what the doctor ordered. Thanks, Rob. We are all very glad you happened to come along."

"Well if we are ready to go, let's see about a place for you to stay. Then maybe we can talk about this problem. It won't solve itself." He laughed.

They followed Rob in the Suburban to the outskirts of Cody. As they turned into the lane that looked like it came out of a picture book, everyone was sure they could not afford such a nice place. Rob came to the end of the driveway of a modest home and got out. He walked over to the Suburban and asked them to come in to meet his wife. As they entered, Lottie Evans greeted them.

"This is my wife, Lottie," Rob said. "She will show you where you can stay and give you the schedule for dinner. We can talk after you are settled and have some time to just rest and get your thoughts in order."

"It is my pleasure to have you in our home," Lottie said. "Your rooms are out back, so let's walk out there and get you settled." As they left the house through the patio door, they saw where they would be staying. The neat little house set back into the trees was so inviting they just couldn't imagine that they were going to stay there.

"There are towels under the sink in the bathroom. Each room has two full beds, so you can use as many as you want. There is a small kitchen to make coffee or get a snack from the refrigerator as you want. Just make yourselves completely at home. I will come out and call you for dinner at about 6:30," Lottie said. "See you then." She left them standing in the kitchen.

"What is going on, Jess?" Molly sobbed as the weight of their circumstances and the uncertainty of the future came crashing down on her.

Jess just held her close and tried to explain. "I don't know, but it sure seems to be pretty nice so far."

CHAPTER 12

After they had rested for a while, there was knock on the door. When Molly opened it, Rob came in with a notepad in hand and a plate of cookies.

"Let's sit at the kitchen table and write down the story from the beginning. I mean from the time you first came to Somewhere and how you found out that there was a problem."

Jess explained about hearing that the BarJ would sell pieces of land to interested folks if they wanted to farm or ranch. "We shook hands and began to be ranchers. When we finished the loan payment at the bank, they sent us a paid in full notice. But as far as the land, we really didn't have anything in writing." Molly gave Rob the business card the man had left.

"This is interesting," Rob said thoughtfully. "Now we need to figure out just what has happened to make this law firm think it has any claim to your land. And who is behind it."

Terry interrupted with a question that no one had seemed to consider. "How will the cow get milked tomorrow, and who will feed and water the horses? We left early this morning and only gave them all enough water and feed for the day. But they must already be wondering what it going on." Everyone sat in stunned silence. It wasn't even a distant thought, but they all knew that it was an important consideration.

When no one said anything, Terry offered, "I could go back

to the ranch and take care of the chores and maybe arrange for one of the other ranchers to take the horses, maybe even the cow to their place for a day or two. It isn't the best idea, but we can't contact them any other way." Silence still reined.

Jess spoke first. "Are you sure of this idea, Terry? It is more than seventy miles back and then you have to come back here to get us. That is a lot to ask, even if I don't have any other solution but for all of us to leave now and go home."

Rob finally broke the silence. "Lottie and I have never been in the Somewhere area; we really haven't heard of it before. But it could be helpful to get the lay of the land and talk to others who were in the initial land deal like you were. Let's get some preliminary idea of what has happened and get you on your way. Then we will set a time when I can come down and look over the situation. You have already shared how this problem came to your attention Why do you have cause to question your ownership? There must be some paid in full bill of sale or something."

Molly began. "Well the men were out in the hayfield swathing when this late-model, fancy SUV drove in the yard. I went out, and the man introduced himself by handing me a business card. You have the card from a law firm in Ohio. He asked if we had a deed to the property, and I said I believed we did. When he just stood there waiting, I got a little frightened but told him I would be able to show him when the men got back this noon. He hesitated but finally said that we would be hearing from him in a few weeks. Then he got in his car and left. It left me very upset. I was standing in the middle of the yard when the guys drove in from the field saying they had finished cutting and couldn't do anymore that day."

"I remember how she dove into my arms and sobbed out the story," Jess recalled. "Later we decided to come to the Bank in Cody to see if they had a paid in full notice for our property.

That is where you found Terry, at the bank. We hadn't talked to anyone yet. The accident with Molly happened, and we went to the hospital. That pretty much fills you in. We negotiated with Otis Linderman, owner of the BarJ Ranch, who told us that he was selling off part of his spread because he was getting older and wasn't able to manage it all. Other people, the friends and neighbors we have now, did the same thing. We aren't the only ones who feel this could be a real problem. Anyway, that is the story. If you want to help us, we will do the best to pay for your services but ..." he left the sentence hanging in midair.

"I'm not interested in making money here. This just feels like a truly unjustified and possibly a criminal situation. Here is what I want you to do. Stop at the bank again. And be careful not to trip, Molly." Rod chuckled. "See if they have any records of your loan, sale, anything than may help. Leave word with them that I will be along tomorrow and pick up the information. I will try to contact this firm to see if it is legitimate and who is behind their inquiry. What I find out will help us get started on untangling this situation. I feel very confident that you have done what you agreed on with Mr. Linderman, but we just aren't able to do business with a handshake anymore. That is truly sad, but there are people in this world who will do anything for a fast buck. So let's just see where this leads. Before you leave, would you mind if I prayed for you, your trip home, and for a good resolution to the problem?" Molly and Jess just nodded and Rob offered a short, passionate prayer.

CHAPTER 13

As Jess, Molly, and Terry were getting into the Suburban, Lottie came out with a large bag. She pushed in through the window, saying, "This will help tide you over until you get home." With that she turned and went back into the house.

When Molly opened the bag, her tears began to flow. "This is enough food to last two days!" she exclaimed. "No wonder she didn't let us say anything. I would have objected. It looks like we got the right person to help us after all. No one else would be so thoughtful. How can we ever repay them for their help?"

"I wouldn't worry about it now," Jess responded. "Just be glad that for once we were in the right place at the right time."

Everyone was silent as they pulled up in front of the bank. When they passed the front door, Molly laughed at how easy it was to get in. The bank president was in his office, and they were ushered in. Jess told in as much detail as they could what happened and why they were there.

"I remember something about Linderman selling off part of his spread. Let me look into this, and I will get the information we have here ready for when Rob comes to get it. And by the way, you couldn't have chosen a better attorney. He is a knight in shining armor to a lot of people in Cody. If this can be settled, Rob will do it. And my guess is you won't owe him a thin dime. He is just that way. So let me work on it."

As the trio left the bank, they felt hope for the first time. The banker's endorsement of Rob helped too. So with lighter hearts they piled into the Suburban and headed home.

"It is going to be a little late when we get home," Jess said. "So we will just do the chores and get some rest." There wasn't much talking the rest of the way home, except to enjoy a magnificent sunset.

CHAPTER 14

It was nearly dark when they pulled into the yard. There was the cow standing by the corral and one of the horses, but they didn't see Buck anywhere.

"He is probably around someplace and will come in to get some grain and water later. Let's just feed, water, milk the cow and then get to bed. I for one am running on empty," Jess said.

It didn't take long to get going on the chores and to finish the bare necessities. Jess put the cow and Babe in the coral and shut the gate. Looking over the charred remains of the barn brought a sadness he didn't expect. It wasn't so much the barn but the dream that was on the edge of being shattered. He and Molly had wanted to have a ranch of their own for a long time, and now to have it but the uncertainty of how this would all turn out was a burden he did not want to bear. Tears came to his eyes at the prospect. He wiped them away, checked on the chickens in back of the old bunkhouse, closed the door securely, and started toward the house. Suddenly he heard a horse galloping in from the direction of the cow pasture. Sure enough it was Buck. Jess didn't wipe away the tears but let them flow as he went to the pump and drew more water, got some grain from the shed, and was greeted by the most welcome nicker he had ever heard. Maybe everything would turn out okay after all.

Molly heard the muffled call of the old rooster just at daybreak. She got up, started a fire in the cookstove, pulled on ranch work clothes and went out to let the chickens out of the bunkhouse coop. It wasn't until then that she saw Buck in the corral and whispered a prayer of thanks. It surprised her so much that tears came to her eyes. As she entered the kitchen, Jess and Terry were slicing potatoes, cracking eggs, and frying bacon. Nothing prepared her for the warm greeting she received from Jess as she felt his strong arms and the comfort of this special person who had gone through so much with her. Looking over Jess's shoulder through teary eyes at Terry, who was trying not to notice, she invited him into the family embrace. He hesitated, but when Jess opened his arms, too, he could not resist. The three just stood there in the middle of the kitchen and cried tears of joy, apprehension, and anticipation. It seemed as though it would go on forever when Molly let out a yelp and rushed toward the stove as the bacon grease had caught fire and seemed determined to burn down all the rest of their dreams. Clamping a lid on the pan, everything returned to normal.

As they sat down to breakfast, Jess was overcome as he began the usual, "Bless this food, Amen." Instead, through his tears he poured out his heart: "God, You ain't heard much from me for a long time. And I am not sure if you want to anymore. I just want to say that some of the things that have happened in the last few weeks have been hard, but they have also been pretty amazin'. I don't know how we will set everything straight again, or if we can, but we need Your help. So thanks for taking care of us in such an unexpected way and for our food. Amen."

As he looked up his eyes were again filled with tears. But shining through was his love for Molly and Terry. Everyone just sat there in stunned silence until Molly blurted out, "If we don't eat it'll be cold!"

During this most unusual breakfast, some plans were coming together. "I think we need to go to all our neighbors and see if they have had a visitor. It just may be that they have, and if we stand together, we have a better chance to survive. And we need to talk again about getting some communication in the area around Somewhere," Jess said. "If we could have called Paul or John, they would have watered the cow and horses, and it wouldn't have been such a dreadful time to come home. There are only five ranchers in this area."

CHAPTER 15

Everyone talking at once. Terry asked, "What was the guy's name who started this whole thing and where did you say he came from?"

Molly looked up and replied, "I don't remember. I had the business card he gave me, but I don't know if his name was even on the card. The law firm was from Ohio, I think Cincinnati, but I'm not sure. It had something about boundary disputes and other land ownership problems, but I don't remember noticing anything else."

"Hopefully Rob will be able to find out just what they are trying to do," Jess added. "He has the card and probably has connections that will give him information. I suppose even the sheriff in Cody may be able to help. So let's go visiting today and see if others are having the same problem. I know we have work to do and hay down that needs to be taken care of, but if we don't have a ranch in a few weeks, it won't matter. If we can't get some kind of shelter for the livestock and the hay, we will just have to stack it by hand and hope for the best."

As Jess and Terry got into the Suburban, Molly came out to join them with a notebook in hand. "It will be best if we can keep a record of what each rancher says. There are only four others around here, but I won't be able to remember everything."

Driving past the General Store in Somewhere, Molly let out a yelp. "Hey, that's the car the guy was driving the day he stopped at our place. Let's see, the license is WY 1-3487." She wrote it down in the notebook. "That is a Casper license number, so it could just be a rental. But it is funny that here it is a week later in Somewhere."

"Sure is a big vehicle for one person on such a trip. But I suppose if you don't have to pay for it, you may as well drive a four-wheel drive Ford Excursion. At least you would be able to get through if it snowed," Jess said and laughed.

The first family they visited was Jim and Leona McNerny. As they drove up, their dogs came out to give them a proper welcome. Leona stood on the porch and waved. Leona issued an order to the dogs, and they all went back in the shade and watched.

"Hi, neighbors," she called. "It's good to see someone around once in a while. It seems like we just work, work, work and eat and sleep. Come on in for some lemonade. And I just finished baking some cookies."

As everyone settled around the big kitchen table, Molly explained why they were there. A frown crossed Leona's face that would have been missed if you weren't looking. "I saw Jim talking to someone out by the corral just last week. I think it was the kind of outfit you describe, but he left after a short time."

"Where was he from, and what did he want?" Molly blurted out.

"He wanted to know if we had papers for our place and who we bought it from. I don't know what Jim told him, but he got into his outfit and left. Jim didn't say much about it but seemed troubled by his visit. I don't think we have legal papers for our ranch, but we have been here the longest, so it must have been an okay deal."

"Was he driving a big SUV?" Jess asked.

"I think so," she replied. "Didn't pay a lot of attention but it was big and not a pickup. Why are you asking? Is there a problem?"

Jim McNerny entered the kitchen and greeted everyone. He was big man with a lot of hard miles on him. His leathered face was so tan you couldn't tell just what color it really was. "Well, howdy neighbors," he greeted them. "To what do we owe this unexpected visit?"

Jess answered, "We were just asking about a guy that had come to our place and asked about our legal right to own our ranch. It seemed strange at the time and as we thought about it, we wondered if any of our neighbors had the same visitor and if they had legal documents for their land. So we are out visiting today and stopped here first."

"Well, to tell the truth, there was a guy here a while back. Seemed like he was snooping for something and didn't tell me much, but he wanted to know if we had a deed to our place. I can't remember anything about that since we bought from the BarJ on a handshake from, what was his name? Oh, yeah, Linderman."

"That's just how we felt too," Jess replied. "So we decided to ask our neighbors if they had the same experience."

As he finished, Molly started to say something, but Jess gave her a, don't-say-anything-yet look, so she just said, "We don't want to take anymore of your time, but let's keep in touch. If you hear or see anything more, let's stick together."

"I like the sound of that," Jim said loudly. "Can't be too careful these days."

"It's been so nice just to see someone else from the valley," Leona shared. "The last time we seen each other was when the barn burned down. We really need to get together more often."

They shook hands and got into the Suburban. With the doors closed and heading down the drive, Terry spoke up. "This doesn't look good. I hope Rob finds something convincing.

"Where should we go next?" Jess asked.

"Let's stop at Youngs' next. They're just up the road around the corner. Let's hope they have something better to offer, but I can't imagine how," Molly replied, fear showing in her voice.

CHAPTER 16

On the way to see Paul, he approached in his pickup and stopped along the road. As country neighbors do, Jess stopped, and the windows came down to talk.

"Hi, Jess," Paul said. "Say, I was going to ask you the next time I saw you if a man, from who knows where, stopped by your place a while back asking if you had a bill of sale for your land. What is going here? Each of us got our land the same way, with a handshake and the goodwill of neighbors, us and Linderman. It isn't like we held him up to have him sign over this little piece of a big spread. He offered it while we were living in town. What do you think is going on?"

"That's just why we were headed to your place," Jess replied. "We don't know either but were wondering if anyone else was being asked the same question. It looks pretty suspicious."

"Do you suppose we should get a lawyer to look into it for us?" Paul asked.

Jess hesitated before replying, "Well, we went to the bank in Cody that held our note in those days, but they didn't have current information and are going to look into it. Maybe we all should be doing the same thing."

"I'm kinda bothered by it," Paul said quietly.

"We were going around asking everyone else to help us get over the jitters about it and find out if others had the same problem,"

Jess said. "We thought we would ask the owners right around here, and you were second on our list. We just came from McNernys' and they had the same thing happen. You know Jim. He didn't act as if it was a big deal, but Molly and me are a little nervous about it."

"So am I," Paul said. "Let's keep in touch, but I gotta get to Metteetse before this afternoon, and Sally probably has dinner ready, so I better get movin'."

As Jess turned around, the atmosphere in the Suburban was tense. Not much was said on the way to see the Fishers, who were next on the list. They lived across from the Martins', north of town, so they had to go through Somewhere again. The SUV was still parked in front of the General Store. The mission gained importance, and Jess drove faster than he normally would toward John and Veda Mae Fisher's ranch. They had one the largest of the ranches that included a full section, 640 acres, but had more mountains and a little less farmable land. Who knows, maybe they weren't bothered by this mysterious troublemaker.

Turning into the lane that led to the house set back into the valley, Molly felt a fear she could only feel but not express. "This is weird," she said. "Something is wrong here."

As the house came into view, they could see the horses running up the valley followed by the milk cow. Chickens were scattered all over the yard. It looked chaotic and frightening.

Jess noticed John's pickup was not there. *Where were they, and what is going on?* he wondered. They jumped out of the Suburban and tried to herd the chickens into the pen by the barn. Jess ran to see if there was a horse left in the barn and found John's prize roping horse in the stall. He calmly entered, talking softly as he untied the halter rope and led the horse into the alley way. A saddle and bridle hung on the stall, so he slipped the bridle on slowly. This horse didn't react, so Jess knew the bridle was familiar. He saddled and mounted. The cowpony nickered but didn't fight the gentle reining out of the barn. "I'm going to see if I can round up some of the stock. I'll be back soon," he shouted to Terry, and left the yard in a gallop after the stock he had seen go up the valley.

It wasn't long until he saw a bunch of cows milling around in a small meadow. He slowed and rode quietly, thankful that this cowpony was familiar with the move he was about to try. He rode around the outer edge, spooking a couple of calves that were down in the brush alongside the small stream. Stopping, Jess held his breath. Hopefully they wouldn't spook the rest of the livestock. But kids will be kids seemed to let the cows know that nothing was wrong. As he circled the cows, one of the other horses snorted, and Jess's mount replied. *Good,* he thought, *they know this horse and aren't spooking.*

Slowly Jess nudged them down the valley toward the corrals. Everything looked like he had succeeded in rounding up most of the livestock, but one older draft horse suddenly shied and snorted. Jess stopped and held his breath. What had happened? He couldn't see any reason, so he pushed the herd to pass the spot. One or two older cows finally went on and most followed, some shying away from something in the weeds beside the trail.

As he approached, Jess spotted a red bandana waiving from a bush. It was typical of those worn by rodeo performers or in a parade in the western towns. His curiosity at full bore, Jess stopped to see why it was there and discovered more than he bargained for. There below the creek bank lay John Fisher. A bruise covered the entire left side of his face, and his arm was twisted behind him. As Jess approached, he feared the worst, until John groaned a little. Jess plunged down the bank and reached John's side, talking softly.

"John, can you hear me?" A flicker of John's eyes told him what he most wanted to know. He was still alive, but it wasn't all he wanted to see. Covered with mud from the creek and mostly soaked, there seemed to be little life left in John. Jess didn't know what to do. He looked down the trail and saw, with relief, that the herd was still moving toward the corrals. He hoped Terry and Molly would know what to do about getting them in the coral.

Moving slowly, Jess tried to get his arm under John to move him up the bank and out of the water. John moaned when Jess started to lift him gently but didn't resist. Laying John on some dry leaves, he took his jacket and covered him the best he could. Climbing up the bank to the pony, which was obediently ground-hitched where he had left him, he vaulted into the saddle and raced toward the ranch. He didn't see any livestock on the trail, so he assumed, and rightly so, that everything was in the corral. Rounding the last bend, he yelled to Molly to get the Suburban turned around. Skidding to a stop, he asked where Verda Mae was.

"I don't know," Terry replied. "I knocked on the door, but there was no answer. I didn't know if I should go in since I thought you might find them up the trail. What happened up there?"

Jess hurriedly recounted finding the horses and cattle, and then finding John in the creek, alive but with a beaten-up face and an arm that didn't look good. "Molly, we got to get some help. Take the Suburban and hightail it into Metteetse for the sheriff and ambulance. Terry and I will look around here and try to figure out what happened and possibly find Veda Mae, hopefully unhurt!"

Molly, white-faced, was rooted to the ground. "Get going!" Jess yelled. "There isn't any time to waste."

Coming to her senses, Molly raced for the Suburban. As it roared into life, she sent gravel flying on the way down the lane. Nothing could stop her now. They must not let their precious neighbors down. At the corner, just before the gate, she saw Ronnie Moore's pickup turning in. Stopping, she quickly related what had happened and said she was on her way for help.

"Let me go," Ronnie yelled. "I like to drive fast. See you asap."

Ninety miles an hour was nothing to Ronnie. He had been a race car driver before the accident that cut short his career. Now, with life and death in the balance, he had a purpose that couldn't wait. It was only 28 miles from Fishers's to town, but it felt like 180. Coming to Metteetse, he raced to the firehouse with the sheriff on his tail, siren blaring. Ronnie was thankful for that for the first time in his life. Most of the time he was in the wrong, but now, the more the better. Screeching to a halt at the firehouse, he jumped from his pickup and raced inside with the sheriff in hot pursuit.

"Chief, there has been an injury out at the Fisher place. John is down in a creek when Jess found him. They need help as soon as you can get it to them," he yelled.

The fire chief jumped into action. "If it had to happen, it couldn't be at a better time. The fire crew just brought in their helicopter for fuel, and they are ready to boogie."

The sheriff, who chased Ronnie inside, was on his radio, asking for all available help at the Fisher place out by Somewhere. After he was assured that someone was on the way, he turned to Ronnie. "You know, I ought to give you jail time for the speed you went through town, but today I will give you a medal for drawing me into this mess. John Fisher is a personal friend. I will be going out there as soon as we are sure this crew is taking off." When he heard the chopper lift off, he yelled, "Let's go, Ronnie!"

Ronnie couldn't believe how fast they were going on the road to the Fisher ranch, but he had no problem keeping up with Sheriff Parks. With siren blaring they didn't have to worry much about traffic and had clear sailing all the way to the ranch.

Meanwhile, Jess and Terry started looking for Veda Mae. They finally decided she must be in the house. Out in the country, doors were seldom locked. Such was the case now. Calling out loudly, Jess began going from room to room. He sent Terry to check the kitchen and the porch. It wasn't long until Jess located Veda Mae, hiding in a closet with the business end of a 12 gauge shotgun peeking out from between the hanging clothes.

"You come any closer, and I'll blow you to kingdom come!" Veda Mae shrieked. "You ain't gonna get away with your stealing ways, so just get down on the floor and spread you hands!"

"Veda Mae, it's Jess, and I ain't about to cause any trouble. I'm here to find out what is going on."

The 12 gauge clattered to the floor, and Jess found himself with a frightened and thankful sobbing woman in his arms. "It's going to be all right," he comforted Veda Mae. "Help is on the way, and I found John. Not good, mind you, but still alive. We should be hearing from help soon."

As they were talking they heard the faint *chop-chop* of the helicopter. Jess called to Terry, and they ran out to the yard just as the Forest Service chopper was setting down and Sheriff Parks drove up to the house. Two EMTs jumped from the idling chopper and ran toward them. "Where is the injured?" they yelled. Jess pointed toward the trail. "He is about a half mile up the trail, alongside the creek. He is was pretty well beaten up and looks like a broken arm, and he's barely alive. I will ride up the trail to help you locate him." Jess raced for the horse, leaped into the saddle, and galloped up the trail. The chopper lifted off just behind him and followed. The red bandana was still visible as Jess rounded the last bend. He motioned to the chopper crew, and they came in low, signaling they had located John. Jess's heart raced, and his horse was going crazy with the noise.

The chopper set down in the field on the other side of the creek. The EMTs were on the ground running before the chopper was fully settled. Coming over the bank they saw John and exchanged fearful looks. Plunging down the bank and wading through the stream, they set the stretcher down and examined John.

"What do you think?" Jess asked as he came closer.

"He's in bad condition, but his heart is strong, and his vitals seem to be pretty good. We'll know more when we get him aboard so we can hook up with the hospital. How old did you say he is. And a name wouldn't hurt."

"I'm not sure about age, but he has been here longer than any of the rest of us ranchers, so I'm guessing he's in his sixties. His name is John Fisher. His wife is Veda Mae. I just about got blown to pieces by her 12 gauge when I found her in the house, so something rotten has gone on here," Jess called.

Having completed their exam and with John loaded on the stretcher, they radioed the chopper and it hovered over them lowering a hoist. Hooking up the stretcher, they watched as the crew pulled John into the hold. Grabbing the lowered line the two EMTs lifted into the helicopter, and they headed toward Cody. Seeing this Jess knew it was much more serious than he had feared.

Returning to his frightened pony, Jess climbed on and slowly walked back toward the ranch house. Troubling thoughts raced through his mind. He didn't want to think about the consequences, but he was thankful that he was able to get there in time. A chuckle escaped him as he thought of Veda Mae in the closet, and again he was thankful. He wasn't sure who should get the thanks, but as he rode back down the trail, he met the others coming up with Sheriff Parks and shared the latest news from the chopper. As they talked quietly in the yard, an awareness that something was missing in the situation began to take over Jess's thoughts. After a discussion of what they needed to do and decisions made, everyone got ready to leave.

CHAPTER 17

When Jess, Molly, Terry, and Veda Mae were all settled in the Suburban, they headed toward home. This had been enough of a day for all of them, and they needed some quiet reflection to sort out their feelings, their fears, and their plan.

"I don't know just what I would have done if you folks hadn't come along when you did. This whole day has been a nightmare, and one I don't want to repeat. A while back a man in a big, black SUV came into the yard about chore time. He talked to John, mostly asking if we have legal papers for the land we farmed and ranched. John had told him he wasn't sure, but that a handshake with Otis Linderman was good enough for him any day. It got us to thinking that we were the only ones without any legal document showing our ownership. We trusted Mr. Linderman but, he isn't around here anymore. We kept thinking we should see if there was anything we could do, but you know how easy it is to put it off because this or that needs to be done right away. Yesterday a different man came by and told us if we weren't willing to give up this illegally occupied land, we would pay the consequences. John told him to leave, not turn around and not to come back if he valued his life. That was it! They came again this morning, opened the gate to the corral, and chased the cows up the trail. Then they left. But they must have been around somewhere because when John went up the trail, he didn't come back. And now I guess we know why. The horses started coming back just before you drove in. Something must have spooked them, and they ran off again. You know the rest. I am afraid to stay out there by myself now." She sobbed. "I couldn't get help if I needed it."

"Well, you just stay with us for a day or two," Jess said. "We will go into Meeteetse tomorrow and see where they took John and if you can go see him there. I am going to sneak back into the place tonight, take care of the saddle horse, and do a little 'night watchman' duty. Is that 12 gauge still in the bedroom and with more than one shot?"

"I assume it is right where I dropped it. There are two more boxes of shells in the nightstand," Veda Mae replied. "Be careful. I'm sure those people aren't to be trusted."

At lunch Terry offered to take care of all the chores here and at the Fisher's and sleep on the back porch so that Veda Mae could have his room. Plans were made and arrangements put in place for the night. All next afternoon, Jess plotted just how he would get back into the John's place without being seen. Finally he decided that they would drive on down to Ronnie Moore's and talk to him about his land. Then on the way back, Terry would drive and let Jess off near a place where the trees came right down to the road. It was a short walk over the hill to the Fisher house, and he could come in from the back.

Late that afternoon, they all loaded up and drove down to Moore's to hear the same story as each of the others told about their ownership. As they left and neared the drop-off place, an unfamiliar car sped by going the opposite way. Terry stopped, and Jess quickly ran into the trees.

Going down the hill toward the back of the house, Jess slowed and kept a sharp lookout for anything strange. He got into the house by the back door, avoided any windows, and went to the bedroom to retrieve the shotgun and the extra shells. He loaded the magazine, put the extra shells in his jacket pocket, locked the front door, and pulled down the shades. He went out the back again and into the trees and circled around to come out near the barn. As he slid into the side door, he heard a shuffling noise. Peeking through the slats of a stall, he saw the cowpony trying to get close enough to a bale of hay to get a bite. Relieved but cautious, Jess kept the shotgun at ready and eased up to the horse, speaking softly. When the horse heard Jess's voice, he calmed down, and all noise in the barn was gone. Unsaddling the horse, Jess found some grain and a little hay, put them in the stall, and led the horse in. He found some water in a jug at the end of the runway and filled the water pan. Then he went to find a place where he could hide. The loft would be ideal if he could still see the yard. He discovered a window that looked out over the corral and part of the house and driveway. The window, covered with dust, so seeing in would be impossible, but seeing out worked just fine. Jess stacked some hay near the window so he could have a comfortable place to sit and a good view and settled in for the night.

CHAPTER 18

Waking with a start, Jess realized he had slept most of the night. Had he missed something by sleeping? He heard a sound and saw the ATV come around the side of the hill.

Why are they up there, where did they come from and who are they? he wondered. Two men on the ATV, both dressed for being outdoors overnight, came into view.

Jess hurried down as quietly as possible, slipped out the back door of the barn, and came around to where the ATV was parked. Carrying the 12 gauge loosely but ready, he called to the men and they hopped off the vehicle. Both approached and held out their hands. John was unsure what to do when he saw what he thought was a sheriff's badge on both the men.

"We have been camped out just up that bluff, watching this place since we got the call yesterday from the patrol. They said some strange things have been going on out here. We couldn't take any chances. So how do you fit in?"

With a sigh of relief, Jess shook their hands and explained he had come back to take care of the horse he had used yesterday and to keep an eye out for his neighbor.

"I am John and Veda Mae's neighbor, Jess Martin. Veda Mae is staying over at our place for a few days. This is pretty upsetting for her."

"Understand," the older man responded. I'm Chuck, and this

is my deputy, Bill. It sounds real fishy from the stories we have heard from HQ. Maybe you could fill me in."

"Are you from Meeteetse?" Jess asked.

"Actually, we are from the state patrol. We had a tip that stuff was going on here that needed some answers, so here we are," Chuck answered as he pulled out his official ID. "We are working with the local sheriff to see if we can get some answers. You can talk to him, and he can fill you in better, but we aren't authorized to reveal more than that."

"I really can't tell you much more either. Did you find anything that looked suspicious in the hills around this place?" Jess asked.

"Well, nothing to write home about. But tell me more about the situation around here. It looks like something or someone is trying to run all the folks out of here so they can have some privacy. That's not the kind of privacy you are accustomed to. You like to live in the daylight, and the kind of hoodlums we are looking for like to live at night."

Jess hesitated but shared a little of the fear they had that someone was trying get their land. He mentioned that they had talked with an attorney in Cody about it but gave no details. "As a matter of fact, there was a big black SUV just like the one that has come to every rancher in Somewhere Valley at the General Store for a long time just yesterday. It had a Casper license plate, so it must have been a rental. It was troubling to see it there," Jess shared.

"Good tip," both men replied. "We'll check it out. Well, we ought to be going. Thanks for not using that scatter gun on us."

Jess laughed, as did the other two, and they left in the side-by-side as quickly as they had appeared.

Jess went back into the barn and took up his post in the loft to keep an eye on the yard and house. As time wore on, he became sleepy and took a short nap. Looking out it appeared nothing had moved so he stood and stretched. Just as his eyes came to window again, he saw some movement near the corral. He slipped quietly down the ladder and moved toward the back door. As he reached for the latch to open it, he heard voices and stopped. He didn't recognize either voice, so he waited until it seemed they had moved around the corner.

Slipping out quietly, he went the other way, shotgun at the ready. Rounding the corner of the barn he was face-to-face with Sheriff Parks and Ronnie Moore. "Am I glad to see you two!" Jess yelled, letting out a big sigh of relief. "I was sure my visitors had returned for a not too good reason."

"Visitors?" the sheriff answered. "You had visitors?"

"Early this morning. A couple of guys who said they were from the State Patrol were here looking around. They said you had contacted them to look into some strange circumstances around here," Jess replied.

"My office did contact the patrol. I didn't hear them say anything either, so I wonder what is going on," Sheriff Parks said thoughtfully.

"I hope I didn't tell them something I shouldn't have, but I told them about the black SUV at the General Store in Somewhere yesterday morning. They seemed interested but no reply, saying they would check it out. And then they left."

"Let me see what I can find out," Sheriff Parks said. "It just may be they were on the level with you, but it may mean they aren't either. What do you think is behind this land ownership question?"

"I think they want our land because it must be valuable," Ronnie said. "Judging from the hay crop this year, it just might be profitable enough to break even. But I am not sure about valuable. No one would want to live in this valley if they had some other place to go. That is probably why we all live here. It was a start and quiet. We all love our neighbors and the freedom," Ronnie trailed off in thought.

"So what are we supposed to do about these mysterious visits from strangers asking questions about our ownership?" Jess asked. "Isn't John's situation enough to find out? What do you think we should do?"

Ronnie and the Sheriff drove off, leaving Jess standing in the yard, puzzled, afraid, and looking for answers.

CHAPTER 19

F riday morning dawned bright and cool. A hint of a rain was in the air along with the promise of a beautiful day. Jess had walked home from the Fisher place the evening before, needing time to think and to try to put some pieces together. It just didn't make sense about the patrol guys and what this was all about. He shuddered when he thought of John Fisher and wished he had a way of finding out how he was doing. All the way home the troubling pieces of the puzzle just wouldn't fit. Why the threat or at least the question about ownership? Where would it all lead? How he had met Robert Evans and what he said, as well as how he had offered to help, puzzled him. What was going on?

Jess awoke with a jerk. He thought he had heard something. He had, in fact, heard Molly starting a fire and beginning to get breakfast ready. Terry was out doing the chores, milking the cow, feeding and watering the horses, letting the chickens out of the bunkhouse coop, and just generally taking care of things like a real ranch hand.

At breakfast Terry asked how they planned on getting the hay out of the field and to the yard in order to stack it there. Jess had been wondering the same thing. "I guess we will just have to use your pickup and get as much as we can on each load."

"It isn't the best, but I don't know how else to do it," Terry answered. "Unless you have another idea …"

The rest of breakfast was rather quiet. Veda Mae hadn't said anything all morning. She just didn't feel like talking and continued to worry about John and what was happening to him.

"Jess, maybe you could take Veda Mae to Cody tomorrow morning and find out what Rob discovered. It would be nice if she were to be able to be closer and maybe talk with John. I wouldn't want to be away from you that long if you were in the hospital under such circumstances," Molly said.

"That's a good idea. Let Terry and me get something figured out for the hay, and then maybe even this afternoon Veda Mae and I could go to Cody. I could sleep in the Suburban or maybe just drive through tonight to get back home. We really need to know if we are on the right track here," Jess responded.

"John has an old hay rack that we haven't used in years, but I think it is still in good condition. I'm sure you could use it. And Terry's little pickup could surely pull it," Veda Mae said. "I really would like to go to Cody. I miss John so much and am worried about his condition." A muffled sob escaped from her as she excused herself and quickly went to the bedroom.

When Terry and Jess pulled into the Fisher yard, nothing looked like it had been disturbed. The livestock needed water and some hay, so they set out to correct the situation. Jess found the hay wagon and looked it over. It had steel wheels, which would make it harder to pull with a load, but otherwise it seemed okay. Jess and Terry pushed it out into the yard and hitched up the S10. Terry laughed at the comparative size but agreed that it would probably work. The loads may have to be smaller than they would be with more horsepower, but it would do the job just the same.

After checking the doors on the house and the barn and watering and feeding all the stock, they began a slow ride home. The men were both quiet most of the way. Terry broke the silence,

"What do you think is going on with this land ownership problem, Jess?"

"I really don't know, but it is real scary. What if we lose the ranch? We would have to sell all we have built up in livestock. I am at a loss to understand why anyone wants this part of Wyoming anyway. It is probably some of the poorest land, even if it is beautiful, and the rewards of the surroundings are unlimited. Molly and I are just scraping by, even since we made the last payment. It just seems we can't get ahead. And to leave here" …

An unwelcome catch in his throat cut the conversation short.

Pulling into the yard, they began planning where they would put the haystack. "I think it would be best behind where the old barn was since there is more room there between it and the fence. We can build a pretty good-size stack and be able to put the second cutting on the same stack, maybe," Jess said.

"I don't know much about doing this, but I agree that is a good location," Terry replied. "Let's get going. It's almost noon and getting a load in now would get the stack started, and I could work on it while you are gone to Cody."

"I'll fill the pickup with gas. You go see if Molly could get a water bag and maybe a snack for us. We could get a load in a short time for the first one. Then I better get going."

It all worked out very well for the first load. The S10 did a good job of pulling the heavy wagon and the first load of hay. As they unloaded and defined the size of the stack, Jess instructed Terry on how to build the stack. "Be sure you get your next load out as far as possible on the edges. If you don't, the stack will just keep getting smaller and smaller, and we won't have anymore room. Try to build the sides like a wall. Then move into the middle to close the stack. Be sure to tramp the hay down as much as possible to build a firmer foundation. But whatever you do, don't fall off or stab yourself with a fork. I think you will figure out how to do it, and I expect you will do a fine job too. Well, I better get going. Thanks, Terry!" With that Jess turned and went to the house.

As Jess was going down the drive, Terry started toward the field but stopped when he heard his name. Molly, in work clothes with a pitchfork and lunch bag, was running toward the S10. She climbed in without a word and turned to Terry. "Well aren't we going to pick up some hay? If so, let's get going," she instructed.

Off they went. They both enjoyed the afternoon, working harder than Terry had ever worked and liking it more than all the loafing he had done at home.

The thought of home hit Terry with emotions he thought were gone. He really missed his mom and sister and younger brother. Thinking about them reminded him about the business card from the men. His mom had worked for a law firm for quite some time, but he couldn't remember which one. Maybe she would know if this Buschner, Welsh outfit was legitimate. He wished he had a telephone, and homesickness hit him more than he would have imagined as angry as he was when he left home. He wanted to talk about it but was afraid of saying something that would make his relationship with Jess and Molly strained or even come to an end. So he jusset his thoughts on stacking hay.

The haystack began to take shape with the third load they brought in. The loads weren't very big, since neither of them knew how to pitch the hay high enough to top a larger load. But it looked like the sides were growing pretty straight and not starting to slant in too much. Terry was pleased and about to start out for another load when Molly came out of the house and called him in for supper. It was 6:30 already but it seemed earlier. The satisfying feel of a job well done couldn't have been sweeter. Terry washed up at the pump and went to the house.

Molly had fixed a good-looking supper, and both she and Terry were hungry. It was a good combination. The conversation started about the haying and patting themselves on the back for such a good job for amateurs. It moved to the cattle but drifted into wondering about Jess, the trip to Cody, seeing John Fisher, how Veda Mae was doing, if there was a place for her in Cody, and what Jess found out from Robert Evans. It was a big list of unknowns, but every one of them felt so important. Sleep came slowly for both weary farmers that night in spite of being very tired. They just couldn't park their apprehension.

CHAPTER 20

The trip to Cody seemed longer than it did the last time Jess had gone there. The same weight of fear settled on him again, but this time it was heavier with concern for John Fisher. Veda Mae sat quietly for the most part, but occasionally she remarked about the mountains or other scenery along the way. It was obvious that she was trying not to think the worst for John.

At about halfway, Veda asked, "Who did you say that attorney was that you met here in Cody?"

"His name is Robert Evans, but everyone calls him Rob," Jess replied. "He is one nice guy and very generous. As a matter of fact, I am hoping he can steer us to a good place for you to stay. I am sure he will be anxious to help if he can."

Silence returned to the Suburban. It was so thick, as they say, that you could cut it with a knife. But silent it was, and silent it stayed. A few miles later, Veda Mae asked, "Do you think John is in trouble?"

"With what?" Jess asked.

"That he was doing something illegal and got caught or something like that."

"Not in a million years!" Jess answered too loudly. "He may have found something troubling on the place, I have no way of knowing that either. His injuries didn't look very good, but he would never do anything wrong or foolish that I can think of.

Can't see worrying about that. I just hope he is making a good recovery. And your coming up will speed that up. I'm sure of it." A slight smile crossed Veda Mae's face as Jess glanced over to see her reaction. He heaved a sigh of relief and smiled toward her.

"What say we stop at that little diner up ahead for a bite to eat before we go on. It would be good to stretch a bit, too, I suppose," Jess suggested.

"That would be a good idea," Veda Mae replied. "It is a long way up here isn't it?"

After the snack at the lunch counter, they returned to the highway. They were just entering Cody as the sun was setting. The clouds gave them a most spectacular view, and they enjoyed the display.

Jess remembered, at least he thought he did, the way to the hospital and drove with confidence past the bank and to the hospital. It was right where he expected it to be.

Jess entered the reception area and asked what room John Fisher was in. The receptionist told him that John was no longer in the hospital but had been moved to a nursing home nearby for recovery.

When he told Veda Mae that John had been moved to another facility for recovery, her face lit up, and a tear rolled down her cheek. Jess just put his arms around her and let her cry for a few minutes in relief. It was good news.

They went to Riverside Recovery Center, just a block away. As they entered, they were greeted by a man in a wheelchair who looked quite familiar. The bandages on his face and arm hid his identity, but the voice revealed they had found who they were looking for. John's good arm reached for Veda Mae, and they cried tears of relief and joy for long enough to make Jess think he should leave. Just as he backed away, John reached for Jess's hand and drew him closer.

"I can't thank you enough for coming. You're a good friend, and I don't know how to thank you for all you are doing for us. This isn't what I expected last week when I saw something strange down by the creek, but here I am. I don't want to talk about it now. Before you leave, I want to tell you what happened and see if I can find a good lawyer I can consult. And for bringing Veda Mae …" He couldn't go on as emotion erupted in his throat.

"Well I just may have the answer to your problem of an attorney," Jess said. "I am going to call him this evening and try to find a place where Veda Mae can stay as long as you are here. He is a wonderful person I believe you will like him. He has a heart of gold, as big as Wyoming. He will be glad to hear your story and help if he can. I'm sure. Where can I find a phone I can use?"

"Just ask there at the desk. They are very helpful around here," John replied.

As Jess dialed Rob's number, he wondered if he had been too generous with Rob's time. *Can't hurt to ask,* he thought. A familiar voice answered, "Hello."

"Hello, this is Jess Martin. We met a couple of weeks ago. I am in Cody with a problem, and I was wondering if I could speak to Rob."

"Why of course. Let me call him," Lottie said.

"Hello, this is Rob Evans. How may I be of help to you?"

"This is Jess Martin, Rob, from Somewhere. We had an unfortunate situation down there last week, and I am here checking on my neighbor. He will need to stay for a time, and his wife would like to find a suitable place to stay for that time. Could you help us find a good place?"

"Of course I will. You only needed to ask. Where are you now?"

"We are at Riverside Recovery Center," Jess answered.

"We'll be there in about fifteen minutes. Would it be good if Lottie were to come along?"

"That would be wonderful. We will see you soon."

"Fine. Goodbye then."

As Jess returned to find John, he smiled. *There is something I need to find out about Rob. I just need to know what it is that makes him so generous and so caring, especially to strangers.* John and Veda Mae had gone to John's private room, just down the hall, the receptionist indicated. They were talking softly as Terry came in.

"Am I interrupting something?" Jess asked.

"No, come on in. We were just catching up on where we left off and what has happened. Veda Mae told me how she held you up with the shotgun. We had a good laugh about it, but the memory of the whole incident is still very disturbing," John answered. "Is you friend coming here?"

"Yes. And his wife, Lottie, is coming too. They will be here in a few minutes, so I'll wait up front and bring them down when they come. They are wonderful people, and I'm sure you will find real help."

CHAPTER 21

Waiting near the reception desk, Jess tried to figure out just how to fill Rob in before they went to John's room. It would be helpful to have some of the background information so he could get a better idea of how to proceed. Jess looked up just as Rob and Lottie came through the door. They rushed over and both embraced Jess in a most loving hug. It felt good. He wished then that Molly had come along.

Jess motioned to a side room. After they closed the door, he filled Rob in on the unusual circumstances at the Fisher ranch. He nearly lost control in recounting the emotionally and physically draining experience. He also shared how he found Veda Mae in the closet with the 12-gauge shotgun. All of them burst into laughter, even as they acknowledged the seriousness of the situation. Recounting finding John was more difficult than he expected, but Rob needed to know what happened.

"Well, that is a sketch of the background, so let's go meet this incredible couple," Jess said.

When they got near the room, they could hear laughter, and it felt good. On entering, Veda Mae was wiping tears from her eyes, still chuckling. When they saw the trio, they invited them in with a warm welcome.

"I would like to talk first about a place for Veda Mae. Then I need to head back to Somewhere," Jess said. "We have a hayfield that needs to be tended, and I am sure it won't get done without help."

"That isn't a problem at all," Lottie said. "She will stay with us, and I can take her anywhere she needs to go. Or she can use one of our cars anytime. We want to get down to your country soon anyway, and as soon as John can travel, we can take care of two birds with one stone, as they say." Relief showed on Veda Mae's face, and John just nodded.

"I know we don't really know you at all yet," Rob said, "but that won't last for long. It is our privilege to be a help to people, and we get to know a lot of folks that way, so let's consider it settled."

"Then I want to get going. But I want to talk with Rob on our other problem for a few minutes," Jess said.

"Good, Let's just go out to your car, and Lottie and the Fishers can get acquainted. It is good to meet you, and I'll be back soon," Rob said as he and Jess left the room. Down the hall was an empty room, and Rob motioned that way. He closed the door and invited Jess to sit down.

"I don't know just where to start, but for one, the law firm is a legitimate outfit. It isn't clear why they are involved, but it seems that the Linderman estate had been involved in other matters and hired them before. At this point there doesn't seem to be anything sinister about their operation. Having this visitor is clearly puzzling, but nothing bad has happened up to this point. We need to keep our eyes and ears open though. And this mess with John Fisher is a real problem. You said that someone told you that the State Patrol was involved. How did they know?" Rob said.

"It was the next day, when I went over there to check on the livestock. Two guys drove up in a side-by-side. I kept the 12 gauge handy, and they respected that. They said they were State Patrol and showed what appeared to be authentic ID, but Sheriff Parks didn't seem to know anything about contacting the patrol either."

"I have connection, and we can check on that too. Sorry I can't give you any better report, but that is all I have found out so far. By the way, could we come down the end of next week to have a look around? I have a small camper that we will bring. We won't need lodging if we can park at you place. It doesn't look like John will be ready to go home for a few weeks at least."

"That would be great. Well I better get moving. It will be late enough when I get home. I can't tell you how much your help has given us hope, and your taking Veda Mae will be wonderful. She really needed to see John," Jess said as they shook hands and Jess turned to go.

CHAPTER 22

T he trip home was uneventful. About fifteen miles out of Meeteetse he saw something he had not seen before. It was getting dark, and there was a vehicle up one of the two-tracker roads at a cut that went over into a heavy forest. "Now why is someone up there, and why this late in the day? They aren't hunting; there aren't any seasons open now. They aren't going to go far even with that four-wheeler. No one uses that road unless they lost a cow or something over the hill," he said to himself. Curious!

Arriving home just at dark, Jess saw Terry coming up from the corral with the milk pail. He was thankful again that Terry had shown up when he did. He noticed some smoke coming from the chimney and assumed supper was almost ready. Then to his surprise, he saw the haystack and had to stop and just stare. It was amazing and gratifying at the same time.

As he got out of the Suburban in front of the house, from out of nowhere, a pair of arms encircled him and drew him into a passionate hug. Jess bent down and kissed the most beautiful woman in the world dressed in dirty jeans and with hay in her hair and a smile that couldn't be forgotten. This welcome home was worth all the hours away. The anguish of their situation melted into insignificance.

Terry stood off to the side and watched this display of true love. Again he longed for his family. It wasn't until Jess came and grabbed him in a bear hug and told him how glad he was to have him there that he knew he had a family.

As they sat down for supper, Jess again gave a lot longer blessing, thanking God for all the wonderful blessings of family, friends, and home.

"So what happened?" Molly asked impatiently.

"Well not much, but Rob and Lottie will have Veda Mae at their home until John can come home. John is quite banged up. He is in a recovery facility and will be there for a while. He told Rob all about his encounter, but he didn't say more than I knew already. I suspect he just didn't want anyone else to have the information that could be sensitive. Anyway, they all were just like old friends when I left. As for the visitor and the law firm, it seemed to Rob that it is a legitimate outfit. A few years ago the Linderman Ranch heirs had them do some kind of legal work for them, but nothing seemed out of place to him. So he advised that we just stay alert. He couldn't figure out what the visits were all about, but even that didn't seem as sinister as before. Rob and Lottie are coming down the end of next week and staying here. They have a camper and will park it here for their accommodations. I said we would be glad to have them. And that is about as much as I know now."

CHAPTER 23

Unknown to anyone in Wyoming, the Linderman heirs—three brothers and two sisters—were having a meeting at the home of the oldest, Otis Jr. They were discussing the future of the ranch since it had not been occupied for more than ten years after their father became ill and had to have twenty-four-hour care. They discovered that he had purchased more land, and the holdings increased to at least eighteen square miles. At least that was the latest estimate. They knew that was when he sold off the half-section plots to the folks now living near Somewhere. There were six owners, one for the town of Somewhere and a full section to the Moores and Fishers. But since there were no records, deed filings, or actual sale documents, no one really knew what happened. All they knew was who lived there now, thanks to the visits of the private detective they hired to visit each ranch without disclosing any hint as to why. The sisters, Millie and Alice, expressed that they wanted the ranch kept in the family if possible, but they and their families would not be able to consider living there. The three brothers—Otis, John, and Harry—were of the same mind; the land must be kept in the family.

Otis Jr. said he had wanted to move back to the home place, rebuilding all the facilities and making it a ranch again. He began to recount all the years growing up on the ranch and the visits when their father was still able to manage the financial issues of the spread. But he wasn't at all sure he was physically able to do so.

John had a thriving legal firm, so he could not see a way clear to live there. But he agreed with Otis Jr. about rebuilding and making it a working ranch again.

Harry was still single and not likely to marry. But he was involved in a very successful investment firm and a construction company, so he would not commit to living at the home place. He could see good investment potential and enthusiastically agreed with restoring the ranch to working status.

After settling the question of selling or restoring, John asked about the legal standing of the existing ranch. No one knew if there were any legal papers that described the ownership of the ranch or recorded deeds. So he put a note on his iPad to look into getting some information on ownership.

Harry brought up the visits they had initiated to each of the families that claimed to have dealt with Otis Sr. No one had bill of sale records or deeds, so it seemed they also had no legal claim to the land as it now existed.

"I believe that is where we have to start," Harry began. "We must get some kind of ownership established for the home ranch and an idea about where we stand with the small owners who claim to have bought their half-sections from Otis with a handshake and maybe some bank record of making payments. I don't question their integrity. It's just that we need to clear this up before we can make any kind of plans for the future of the Linderman Ranch, the BarJ."

Harry and John both lived near Cleveland and agreed to work together on the information they had. "It would be great if we had someone local who could help us with this. We don't know the sources. Nor do we know how the people in Wyoming think,"

John said. "By the way, has anyone been there recently?" He was met with blank stares.

No one had seen or even thought of the ranch for years. But the memories began to flood back of Christmas festivities, Thanksgiving dinners, and summer visits. Laughing about some of their antics brought a renewed interest in restoring the integrity of the Linderman Ranch. Otis summed it up: "The fact that Dad sold off those half-sections and the two complete sections at the south end of the ranch may have been his way of making it possible for him to ranch a little longer. So I think we have to set the record and the legal ownership straight so that we can have a clear path ahead. Besides, there is a lot of cash waiting to be claimed somewhere. The value of the land is probably almost more than we can even imagine."

"Which reminds me," Millie said, "I got a call just yesterday from a developer who wanted to know if we were interested in selling a portion of land for a luxury home development. He wanted room for ten to thirteen homes that would be secluded but accessible. They would cost in the range of $500,000 to $800,000 to build and sell for nearly twice that amount. I have his name written down somewhere. I can't remember where, but I'll find it and get it to John. If this were to happen, we could possibly finance the restoration of the ranch without even disturbing our own resources."

"Wow," exclaimed Alice. "We better get to work on this right away. I am still curious why the landowners near Somewhere didn't have deeds or some legal descriptions of their land."

"They probably didn't consider it important," John guessed. "They were used to doing business with a handshake, so they did it that way with Otis Sr. But you are right to be concerned. They probably have no legal claim to their property. We must make that right with them the best way we know how. It would only be the right thing for people who claim to follow God's way and claim Jesus as our Savior and Lord. We have a lot to think about. Let's get together in two weeks at Harry's place. With the size of his house, we could all stay a week and not see anyone else the whole time." Everyone laughed, but it was true. Harry had built a dream estate in the rural countryside west of Cleveland. It was beautiful. And he enthusiastically agreed with the plan.

"Two weeks it is," he exclaimed. "I will have the butler and maids get it all ready."

CHAPTER 24

Sunday dawned bright and cool. The hot summer days were always the best in the morning. Rob was up early, took his Bible and a note pad, and went out to his favorite bench to read a while, pray for the concerns that had piled up for him lately, and especially for John and Veda Mae for their comfort, healing, and a solution to their problem. It wasn't easy to concentrate, but this little hideaway helped. The quiet began to engulf him as he sat down and listened to the birds singing their song to God. The leaves rustled in the trees to keep time and provide needed background accompaniment. It was his and God's special rendezvous most mornings.

An hour later Rob was called from his peaceful retreat by sounds from the kitchen. Remembering they had a guest in their home, he reluctantly closed his prayer time with an additional plea for all the folks in Somewhere and for an answer to the danger they seemed to be in.

Nearing the back door, Rob could hear the chatter between Veda Mae and Lottie going a mile a minute. "It was right to bring Veda Mae home with us," he said to himself. And he agreed again that God had arranged this visit for a special purpose.

"Breakfast is nearly on the table, and if you don't want to be late for church, you better get to the table soon," Lottie instructed.

"Veda Mae wants to go with us, so we need to try to get a good seat nearer the front. So let's eat!"

On the way to church, they naturally talked about what a relationship with God meant to them. "I didn't grow up with church," Veda Mae explained, "but I have always wondered if it were true, that God really cares anything about us. When John was injured, I questioned it even more. I guess I want to know but am afraid to find out."

Pulling into the parking lot at the small church, they noticed an out-of-state license plate. Curiosity and caution made Rob write down the number and the kind of car, a late-model Mercedes Benz. "Not the kind of car you see around here very often," he said when he became aware of Veda Mae's questioning look. "Just curious."

Entering the small church, they were greeted by numerous friends and others. They introduced Veda Mae but were cautious about why she was visiting. One of the women mentioned that the women's room was just around the corner if Veda Mae wanted to go with her, and she did. It wasn't long before she was talking with two or three other women as they returned and entered the sanctuary. Seated about three rows from the front, they had a good view of the platform as the worship team assembled. They sang familiar hymns and finished off with a song the leader said he heard only a few weeks ago and felt it was just for him, so he wanted to share it because it might be just for those assembled. Veda Mae had tears in her eyes as the short chorus spoke of God's tender care and interest in our deepest longings. When the singing ended, the pastor prayed for the congregation and what he planned to share was what those there needed to hear.

The scripture passage surrounded the specific verse: "Casting all your care on Him, because He cares for you," from 1 Peter 5." The pastor said quietly, "God is the only One who can care for you because that 'you' includes all of us. We are not, as people, able to care for very many people or things, but God can and does care for everyone. Even those who turn against Him and do vile acts. There is no care that He does not know about or that He cannot provide resources either to solve the problem or give us the strength to endure them."

The rest of the sermon was lost to Veda Mae. She had never heard that God was anything but someone's idea of a "sugar daddy," as they said in Texas, where she grew up. This was new and aroused a longing in her that had not been there before. She wondered, *Could it mean that the trouble we are having on the ranch is part of God caring for them, and He sent Jess along just in time?* She didn't know the answer, but she would be asking some questions in the next few days.

As they left the church, Rob noticed a stranger among the congregation. He was dressed casually but obviously not cheaply. Rob went up to him, introduced himself, and asked where he was from.

"I'm from Cleveland, Ohio. I came out here to try to find out about the old Otis Linderman place and what the status is. I'm John Linderman, one of Otis's children. You wouldn't know of a competent local attorney whom I could engage to do some checking, probably sleuthing to get some answers. It appears that long ago nothing was done with more than a handshake in selling off part of the ranch, and legal descriptions and such just didn't matter much. Well now it does, and I mean to get the information I need to set the records and the ownership straight."

Wow, Rob thought. But he said, "I have done a lot of property work from my law office here in Cody, and it sounds like your problem is right down my alley. How long will you be here?"

"I want to leave by Tuesday since I have other places I need to go and to get home sometime next week," John replied. "I would like to talk to you more. Would you have time tomorrow morning?"

"I don't know of any reason why that wouldn't work just fine. But give me your number, and I will call you this afternoon after I have checked my calendar. I am curious why you came to church this morning."

"I wouldn't miss a worship time if there was any possible way to work it in. I have been a Christ follower for more than fifty years and don't expect to stop anytime soon." John laughed as he handed him his business card.

"Great. I'll call you this afternoon."

CHAPTER 25

Rob told Lottie about the visitor but carefully didn't mention his name or where he was from. "He may end up being a client, so it best you don't know more." He answered mysteriously.

Nothing more was said, but Rob was literally bubbling over inside. *Could this be the link we needed to solve all the land problems for the ranchers in Somewhere. How can it be that this stranger is a Linderman and from Cleveland if he is not a Wyoming Linderman heir.* His head was swirling and he barely kept it to himself. As an attorney he knew how the wrong impressions could be built from a little information, even if it is good information, so he decided to ask Mr. Linderman to do the same. Rob knew he had time in the morning, but it was good to be cautious and not rush into this. Besides, this afternoon gave him time to seek God for wisdom in the matter.

Monday morning Molly took Veda Mae to Riverside Recovery and Rob went to his office. It was not on the main street and this time Rob was glad it wasn't. An out-of-state license plate in a small town raises a lot of eyebrows. When he called John Linderman, he offered a 9:30 a.m. appointment. That was acceptable, and at 9:30 sharp, John Linderman enter the small law office. Rob's receptionist, secretary, janitor, nurse, or whatever else was needed, greeted this stranger with her cheerful, "Good morning. You must be Mr. Linderman. Rob is waiting for you, so please come back with me." John was impressed and told Rob that if they were in Cleveland he wouldn't have that receptionist very long because he would offer such a good deal she couldn't resist working for him. Both men laughed and it broke the formality.

Rob listened as John recounted the family meeting a few weeks back and the interest that all of them have in restoring the Linderman name and ranch to full working condition. He outlined the problems they felt needed to be researched and cleared up before anything could be done to begin restoration. Without warning, John went on to say, "There were some small ranchers who bought land from my father and have neither legal description nor any legal documentation for their land. He was certain they had all told the truth that they believed they owned it, but they wouldn't be able to prove it in any court of law. They are sitting ducks if someone got wind of their situations. They could be run off and lose everything they have worked for. I don't know what any of the places look like, so we hired a private detective from Casper to go to each of the ranches and ask about legal papers or documents. It is appalling what we found out. It is our, my brothers' and sisters', determined obligation and intention to set the record straight with these folks with proper surveys and legal deeds. We have been very prosperous, but if we use our wealth to hurt people we will be doing a disservice to them and to God, whom we all serve. So will you help us on this end? It is probably best that it be done quietly for the time being. But when it becomes public, we want it to be right legally, ethically and morally."

Rob couldn't believe his ears. *Here is the answer to so many questions and the solution to more than one of the problems we have struggled with for weeks.* His answer, however, was guarded. How could he be sure this man wasn't pulling a fast one too.

"What do you want out of this, and how can I be sure you are telling me the truth about your motive and your method?"

"The kind of question I would be pleased to answer, Rob. My brothers, sisters, and I are Linderman's children. All of us consider our lives belong to God through the Lord Jesus. Nothing we do can ever be seen as self-serving or crooked in any way. As I mentioned, we are all very wealthy, not bragging, but we have made the most of opportunities God has put in our paths. The family met a few weeks ago because we had heard rumors that there was illegal activity on our land, so we decided that something must be done to protect it. My brother Otis Jr. has often said he missed the place and has considered arranging his situations in the East to be able to move to the ranch, make it home, and raise his family on a working cattle ranch. But he is the oldest and knows it isn't likely he will be able to do so.

"We want someone who will shoot straight with us. We have too much at stake to get involved with someone who wants a cut of the pie or is just looking to get rich on us. I believe you may be that man, so I want your answer no later than Friday this week. I must leave here tomorrow in order to visit some of my other holdings. But if you are interested, I want references and a description of cases you have handled of similar nature and the outcome of those proceedings. It would be helpful if you had a judge who could vouch for you. The fact that we met at church makes me more confident that you could be our representative, but as I said, we want absolute integrity and honesty in this transaction."

Rob was overwhelmed. He sat silently for a few minutes on the outside. But on the inside, he was searching God's face for His approval. It wasn't long in coming.

"I am determined in all my cases to exhibit the highest ethical and moral attitudes as you have expressed. I have been approached by one of the landowners in Somewhere, about these very matters. I believe it is God's providence that we were to meet in the circumstances we did, and I have the sense that I am to proceed with this challenge. However, I want to consult legal counsel, my wife, before I give a definite answer." Both men laughed knowing the truth of Rob's comment.

"The references you mention will be no problem, and I will have a certified letter to your office no later than Friday this week and a phone confirmation before that. I appreciate the gravity of your situation. And I also feel the weight of responsibility to set this straight. Tentatively, I accept your offer. But before you leave, would you be offended if I were to pray for wisdom for both of us."

"Not at all," John Linderman said. He rose and offered his hand.

As they gripped each other's hand, Rob prayed, "God, You are the Maker and definer of all things. You heard our conversation, and You know our hearts. If we agree to help each other on this grave and potentially difficult matter and cannot have Your unqualified blessing, please give us insight to terminate our relationship. But Lord, we both believe that our meeting signals Your approval and Your smile on our endeavor, and because of this, we commit our ways into Your hand. Amen."

As their eyes met there were tears of joy for each of them. As they parted they promised prayer for wisdom for each other and to communicate again soon. With that John left the office, and the door shut.

"What was that all about?" Joyce asked.

"Well, I can't tell you just yet, but if this deal comes about, you will be busier than a one-armed paperhanger for a long time and will probably need extra help."

A gasp escaped his receptionist's lips. Joyce just stood there and stared for what seemed like hours. Then they both set to work getting as much of the current business done before the storm hit.

CHAPTER 26

J ess and Terry hauled hay all day on Thursday. The field was nearly empty, and the stack at home was almost beyond reach. They closed it in with the last load in the evening.

The horses and the cow really liked the new hay and ate well. They didn't get a lot so they could get adjusted to the new hay. Too much fresh feed would be hard on them since they had been in the corral for some weeks now.

After breakfast on Friday, Jess and Terry decided to go over to the Fisher place to check on the stock and just to look around. Molly wanted to go along, so all three squeezed into Terry's S10.

As they came around the last bend in the lane, they noticed some movement near the barn. Jess had kept the 12 gauge and made sure it was loaded each time they went to the ranch. All the stock was huddled against the poles as far from the movement as possible, and the horses were snorting their fear.

Coming closer they discovered the source of the trouble. A raccoon had invaded the water trough, fell in, and couldn't get out. It was making an awful scene trying to get out but to no avail. Relieved but cautious, Jess and Terry got a long pole and stuck it into the trough. The raccoon grabbed it and jumped free, beating a hasty retreat into the hills. They all laughed with relief that it wasn't worse.

Piling the feed bunks high with hay and making sure the water in both troughs was up to the top, they turned their attention to the barn. The cowpony was still there but restless. All the hay was gone and most of the water. But supplying the needed food and water didn't solve the nervous actions of the buckskin. Then Terry discovered a footprint in the soft dirt on the barn floor. It wasn't either of their prints. It had a strange toe mark, and the heel was partly missing, prompting a thorough search of each of the stalls and the loft.

"Who would be looking for something in here?" Jess asked to no one in particular. "I wonder if he or she is still here, but we don't know it yet. We had better look around here in the barn and also in the house. It wouldn't do to have a vagrant loose at the Fisher's who could cause trouble."

Just then they heard Molly scream. As they raced out to where she was, they saw her staring at the house and pointing, "I saw that curtain move," she yelled fearfully. "It moved, and there is no reason for it. It moved! It moved!"

"I believe you, Molly," Jess said more calmly than he felt. "You stay here behind the pickup. Terry, you come with me!" When they reached the side of the house, Jess whispered, "You slip up close to the front door. If someone is in there, they may come out the back way. I am going to the back and see if we can flush them out."

Running past the back corner, Jess saw the door was open and caught a glimpse of a girl running through the woods behind the house. "I see her, Jess yelled. "Come on, let's try to catch her."

They made a circling pattern into the trees and came together near the road. Jess hadn't spotted any tracks, so they felt sure she was still in the forest somewhere. As they moved their circle closer and began to go back toward the house, Terry shouted, "I spotted her! She is trying to get to the road."

Jess retreated just as the intruder came out of the trees by the road. He leveled the shotgun at her. "You had better stop running. This scatter gun can make life very miserable for you, so just stay where you are," he yelled.

Terry heard the yelling and came up behind the girl. He tackled her, and they both fell to the ground, twisting and turning in the mud. Terry hung on to the girl, who was desparately trying to escape. She quit fighting as Jess grabbed her by the wrist, lifting her to her feet, and freeing Terry.

"All right," he said in a stern voice, "you have some explaining to do. Who are you? Where do you come from, and why are you in the Fishers's house. How long have you been here?"

As Terry got to his feet, he remarked, "That footprint in the barn is from her left boot. Look at the toe, nearly worn through and twisted out. And the heel is broken. This is certainly our mystery guest."

"Let's go!" Jess commanded as he nearly dragged the young woman with him through the trees toward the pickup. "When we get to the house, we will get Molly to clean you up, and then we want some answers. Is that clear?"

The girl just nodded. Coming into the yard from around the house, Molly ran to meet them. White with fear, she saw the intruder and melted with compassion for the fearful look on her face.

"I was so worried when you said you spotted the intruder that he would be dangerous and you be hurt. But this changes everything. I don't understand."

"We don't either, but we are going to understand a lot more when this little woman spills the beans about trespassing, breaking and entering, stealing food or whatever, and why she is here!" Jess replied.

The young girl froze. She had not considered the charges that could be against her. Her eyes betrayed the fear, but her attitude remained. It had been a long time since she had left home and now felt this couldn't be any worse. Could it really be that she was in as much trouble as it seemed?

Molly came close and spoke softly to the girl. "Who are you?" There was no response. Molly tried again. "We don't really want to hurt you, but if you don't help us, we will have no choice but to contact the sheriff and press charges. You aren't exactly welcome here, and you don't have permission to be here."

Nothing seemed to work in getting answers. Jess suggested that Molly get the girl cleaned up and find some clothes that might fit a little bit. So they took her to the house through the back door. Jess posted himself in front of it and sent Terry to the front to guard that escape route. It was important to take care of the Fisher ranch as well as their own, and this must be dealt with.

Soon after Molly and the girl went toward the bedroom, Jess heard sobbing, and his heart broke. He nearly cried too. He had been harsh with the young woman, and perhaps it wasn't necessary. But it was a serious matter. He also knew that Molly could charm a rattlesnake, so he was confident she could break through the hard shell the girl had put up. Low voices began to replace the crying, and soon they emerged with the girl looking a little awkward in John's jeans rolled up at the bottom and one of Veda Mae's work shirts tucked in the top. The muddy boots were off but needed to be cleaned up so the girl could wear them again.

"This is Sarah," Molly introduced the girl to the others. "She is lost and doesn't know for sure how she got here except that she was pushed out of a car somewhere down the road. She found this house with the back door unlocked, so she slept here the last two days, ate everything in the cupboard, and didn't know what to do or where to go. Then we came along. Jess, we need to get her home and some food into her. Maybe I can find some old clothes that I could make fit a little better. We can't leave her here, and we don't have a way to contact the sheriff," Molly said.

"Then let's go. I'll drive. Terry, you sit in the back. Don't you try anything, young lady. I still have this shotgun, and you don't want to be on the business end of it anytime," Jess commanded.

Making sure Fisher's back door was secure, they left and went home, where Sarah would stay until they decided what to do with her.

After getting Sarah cleaned up and comfortable in the bedroom that Terry gave up to sleep on the back porch, Jess and Molly walked down to the corral. The stars were close enough to touch, and they felt a peace they hadn't felt for a long time. As they crawled into bed late that night, they couldn't sleep.

"It's a curious thing isn't it?" Molly mused. "We can't have any children of our own, and then Terry showed up in an unusual way. Now Sarah's appearance is a real mystery. I get the feeling we are supposed to be something for both of them, but I just can't understand how or why. We aren't their parents. Terry has become so near and dear to us and I expect that Sarah will too if she decides to still be here in the morning. What is going on, Jess?"

"I have been thinking about the same thing. It seems we have been given a job we haven't looked for and one that we don't know how to do. Do you suppose God is trying to get our attention by putting us in such unusual circumstances with the mysterious threat of the ranch ownership and the equally unexpected appearance of Terry, the fire in the barn and now Sarah? Oh, and remember that Rob and Lottie are coming down next week to try to get the lay of the land and begin to make sense of our troubling circumstances. Maybe they can help us see what is going on. Anyway, let's get some sleep. We need to finish that hay tomorrow if at all possible. And I just want you to know that you and Terry did an absolutely amazing job while I was gone, Thank you, and I love you."

Jess drew Molly close and they went to sleep, secure in each other's arms.

CHAPTER 27

S arah was still sleeping when Jess came back from milking the
cow. Terry was feeding and watering the horses and having
his good morning talk with Buck. So Jess and Molly were alone.
Molly started breakfast and Jess put dishes on the table, something
he never did before. Jess broke the silence first.

"It is the middle of August, and the days are going to get a
lot colder. We can't have Terry sleeping on the back porch much
longer. I have been wondering if we could afford to build the porch
in and make an additional room for our growing family," Jess said.
"We needed it twice this summer, and it looks like we might need
it this winter too."

"Our bank account is going down with all the travel and other
expenses, as well as hoping to build a new barn," Molly replied.
"But I don't see any way around it. We can't offer Sarah a place to
stay if we don't, and we can't have Terry out there much longer.
What we really need is a new house, isn't it?"

Terry came in to the rich smell of bacon and eggs and felt the
warmth of both the room and the people in it. He couldn't explain
his feeling at the moment, but he liked it just the same. This really
was his family. He would have never thought the work he did
would build such a bond, but it had.

"Well the chores are done," he said a little too loudly. "Maybe
we can get the rest of the hay in today."

No one answered. The awkward silence was broken as a sleepy Sarah quietly came into the kitchen. No one spoke. They all stood awkwardly, wondering what to do next. Molly finally broke the spell and warmly greeted Sarah, who looked quite well rested and also well dressed in some of Molly's clothes.

"Let's eat it before it gets cold." Molly said. Sitting down with a place already set for Sarah across from Terry, Jess bowed his head and gave his usual blessing, "God, we thank You for the food and rest. Amen. Well, let's eat."

Jess began laying out the day's work. "Terry and I are going to finish the haying today. We can get it all in and maybe get a small second cutting before the winter. What do you think, Terry, can we do it?"

"I don't know why not," Terry replied. "Molly and I got most of it the other day."

"I want to do some rearranging in the chicken bunkhouse," Molly offered as Terry and Jess laughed. "Would you like to help, Sarah?"

"I wouldn't know what to do. I've never done anything like that before," she replied.

"We'll figure it out together since I never tried to turn a cowboy bunkhouse into a chicken coop. Besides, those few chickens don't need the whole place to themselves. So what do you think, can we do it?" Molly asked.

Sarah shrugged and pushed her food around on her plate. Molly took that as a yes and hoped for the best.

After breakfast everyone headed outside in a different direction. Jess and Terry hooked up the S10 and headed for the field. Molly and Sarah went to the bunkhouse. Molly explained the chickens were in there in the first place as the barn had burned down in a lightning storm. Sarah went along but it was obvious her heart wasn't in it.

Opening the door, Molly exclaimed, "This place is a mess! Well first off, I suppose we better clean it out." The smell was overwhelming. As they began to work, Molly saw Sarah begin to catch on and see things to be done. It was exciting to see her seem to feel a little at home.

"It is so good to have someone around to talk to. When the guys are out in the field, I just talked to the chickens or the cow, but they didn't seem too interested in what I was saying. That must seem pretty strange. Most of our neighbors are a couple of miles away, except for Fishers, and they are busy too. So it is usually just me here."

Sarah looked up and just seemed to take in all Molly had said. Absently she said, "I feel like that sometimes. No one really cares what others think or say anyway, so what does it matter if you talk to the cow or the chickens?"

Molly's heart leaped just to hear Sarah talk. *This is going to work out somehow*, she thought. *It is a start.*

"I think we should put something up that would keep the chickens in just half of this room. We could use the bunkbeds for some lumber and build a wall between the windows," Molly suggested. "Let's go get some tools."

Getting out of that room and into the fresh air was a welcome relief. They looked in the Suburban and found a hammer, crowbar, and nails. Sarah didn't have a clue what each of those did but was willing to carry tools to the bunkhouse. The women spent the rest of the morning tearing down the bunks, and by noon they had a pile of boards. It was a dirty job, and both looked pretty worn-out. By late in the afternoon, Sarah was driving nails quite well and it looked like they might get the job done.

Jess and Terry had hauled three loads in by that time. As they came with the last load, they yelled that this was all, and they seemed happy to see the last load go on the stack.

"Get cleaned up for supper in about an hours," Molly called. "It's going to take about that long for Sarah and me to wash off the dust from that messy place. But we got a lot done."

Supper was ready about six, and everyone sat down to a meal of beef burgers and potatoes with some good fresh milk. Everyone ate all they could hold, which cleaned up most of the food Molly had prepared. It was good.

After the dishes were done, Jess and Terry went out to the corral and worked on light things until dark. Molly asked Sarah if she would like to walk up to the spring. Surprising she said she would. As they walked, Molly began to feel that Sarah was feeling more comfortable, even though it had only been two days since she arrived under unusual circumstances.

"Where are you from, Sarah?" Molly asked.

The silence was long, but Sarah finally said, "Nowhere in particular."

Molly chuckled. "Well at least now you're less than a mile to Somewhere," which brought a startled look from Sarah. Molly explained, "The town that is just down the road about a mile is called Somewhere, Wyoming. It really isn't much more than a general store, which seldom has anything anyone needs, and a few rundown vacant houses. But it is still called Somewhere."

Sarah looked up and a faint smile almost broke on her sullen face. It was a good sign to Molly. She was quiet the rest of the way up to the spring, and as they walked back down the hill, the sun began to set in a spectacular sunset that stopped them both in a clearing. They just watched for a long time.

"Are there lions or bears in the forest here?" Sarah asked with a shiver.

"Not that I know of, but there may be over to the west, in the national forest. I have never seen anything but deer or sometimes an elk around here."

Sarah seemed calmer, and they walked to the house in silence. Sarah went to her room, and Molly sat at the kitchen table, wondering about the special afternoon she had. Jess and Terry came in just at dark, and they sat quietly at the table too. It had been a good day. Maybe everything was going to be just fine.

The days went by with work on the chicken house and other ranch chores going smoothly. Not much conversation happened with Sarah, but little by little she seemed calmer and maybe even happier. It was good.

CHAPTER 28

Monday morning's overcast sky looked as though it could rain any minute. Jess and Terry rode out to check the cattle in the west pasture. They had a lunch in case it took longer than planned.

"What do you think of Sarah's story of being pushed out of a car along the rode from Meeteetse?" Terry asked Jess as they rode slowly toward the pasture.

"I don't know what to think," Jess replied. "It isn't likely that anyone would be going toward Somewhere unless they had a reason. But you never know about some of the things that happen these days."

Coming over the hill about that time they could see the small herd in the valley ahead. They rode on in silence and circled the cows to move them closer together so they could get a good count. The count turned out as it was supposed to, so they rode toward the hayfield.

"We are going to sell calves about the beginning of October. Then maybe we can see about adding another room on the house and the barn. It isn't likely we can do both, but we need some shelter for the horses and the milk cow during the winter. We keep the cattle in closer, too, so feeding isn't as much of a problem," Jess explained.

The conversation continued somewhat aimlessly, with both

men having thoughts of their own on the situation they now faced with Sarah. Should they notify the authorities about her break in and how she got there? It was all very puzzling.

"Terry, what are you going to do come winter? There won't be much work at the ranch, and I have been wondering if you had a mind to move on," Jess asked. "I wouldn't blame you, but when we sell the calves, Molly and I intend to give some of that income to you. You have earned it and more. We usually scrape by with what comes in, so you may feel like looking for something else."

Silence greeted Jess question. Terry didn't know how to respond. Pay or no pay, this had been the most rewarding and happiest few months of his life. He hadn't even considered leaving, but he wondered if Jess was trying to get him to go without telling him they couldn't keep him around anymore. He didn't know what to say so he didn't say anything.

Riding into the yard they saw a late-model pickup with a camper-trailer parked in front of the house. Jess didn't recognize it from anything he had seen around there. It brought new fears and raised real questions about what to do. After unsaddling the horses and putting the tack away in the newly created bunkhouse storeroom, the two of them walked slowly toward the house. As they got nearer, they heard voices, and they didn't sound angry or threatening. Suddenly Terry recognized the explosive laughter and yelled, "It's Rob!" Jess felt care and fear drain from him in an instant. They both picked up their steps to get to the house and join in.

Seeing Jess and Terry, Rob rushed over to greet the two friends. "We had the chance to leave a little early and hoped it would be okay to park here for a week or so. If it isn't too much trouble."

"Trouble? You would never be trouble to us. We want you to feel right at home as long as you can stay," Jess replied. "How long do you intend to stay?"

"We arranged for all our business to be taken care of for the next two weeks. We have a lot of paperwork that needs done, and doing it in the office sometimes suffers from too many interruptions. So we thought we would stay until a week from Thursday if that works for you."

"You bet it does," Jess replied. "We might even be able to put you to work and get those muscles tightened up again."

"Where would be the best place for us to park our trailer? We don't want to be in the way, but sleeping arrangements are easier if we can use the camper," Rob said. "It is all pretty much self-contained, so we don't need much except water to fill the tank."

"You are certainly right about sleeping arrangements. I guess you met Sarah," Jess said as they went out to locate the trailer. "We will tell you about that soon enough, but it has put a crimp in our space. Terry sleeps on the screened porch in the back, but that can't last much longer."

"We did see her and was introduced, but she went to her room right away. Lovely girl but obviously quite troubled about something. I was surprised she was here. I thought Terry was the only younger person with you."

"He was until we caught her in John Fisher's house. We couldn't just let her stay in the forest so we brought her here. It is a drain, but we really want to help Sarah. We can't have any children, so her coming seemed to be right somehow," Jess answered.

"Where did she come from?" Rob asked.

"She says some guy just pushed her out on the road a few miles away and left her. She found the Fisher's house, sort of broke in, but the back door wasn't locked. She ate everything she could find. When we went over there to check on the livestock, Molly saw a curtain move. We went to look, and Sarah bolted out the back door. Terry and I chased her, and Terry tackled her in a mud bog in the trees. Both of them were a real mess. We brought her home after that, and she has been here almost two weeks now. She is relaxing a little but not providing much information," Jess said. "Kind of a drain on the supplies, too, but we wouldn't want to do anything else either."

"You are remarkable folks," Rob said. "There aren't many who would keep her. They would give her to the sheriff as soon as they could. You have an opportunity to make a real difference for Sarah. Keep at it. And if there is anything we can do to help, let us know."

After parking the camper, they went back to the house and could smell supper on the stove. The warmth around the table was evident. Even Sarah smiled a little and seemed to feel included. It did Molly's heart good to see her still with them after the meal was over, and they just sat around the table and talked.

CHAPTER 29

Rob and Lottie were awake far into the night. They prayed and talked and prayed and talked about the circumstances Jess and Molly were facing. They knew that to try to give them anything could be an insult, but they couldn't just sit by and let the Martins struggle. It just wasn't in them to do things like that.

"We will just have to leave it in God's hands to lead us and supply what is needed for Jess and Molly," Lottie concluded. "They are such wonderful people. I wonder if they have any spiritual strength for the trial that is ahead of them."

"My guess is, not much," Rob answered. "Their generous spirits are certainly something God loves. We need the right kind of opportunity to encourage them to consider their personal connection to God's grace. It can't be pushed on them either. So just pray, Lottie. God will make a way." Rob rolled over, and they went to sleep.

The next morning, Rob asked Jess if he would show him around the area. He would like to meet the ranchers and formulate some kind of plan to fix the problem they all faced. He didn't let on that the fix would be as good as he had reason to believe, but it wouldn't hurt to have met the five ranchers.

Jess agreed, and they set out in Rob's pickup. Even though it was not a new pickup, it was nice to ride in. They went pretty much the same way the Martins had gone the time before they went to

Cody. First the McNernys and then the Youngs. Stopping at the Fishers they fed and watered the stock and checked the house and barn again. Then they stopped to see Ronnie and Laverne Moore.

At each place they arranged for them all to come to Jess and Molly's place on Friday afternoon for a cookout and a meeting about the ownership and disposition of each ranch. When they found out that Rob was an attorney Jess had contacted, they all enthusiastically agreed to be at the meeting.

Thursday, Terry and Jess went to Meeteetse to get some supplies. On the way Terry tentatively brought up the conversation about his leaving. "Once I had been here for about two weeks, I realized that this was home. I never enjoyed life and the purpose of work like I have here. It would be very hard for me to go away and not look back. So if it is all the same to you, I want to stay. I don't care if I ever get paid. You have given me so much more than anything money could buy, and I feel as though it may even be right if I paid for the privilege of staying. As for Sarah, she is a lot like me. She is lost and certainly not able to take care of herself. It won't be long, I think, until she feels the same as I do. So if you need me to leave, I will. But if I can stay I will be forever grateful." Terry sat quietly.

Jess couldn't take it. He couldn't see the road for the tears. He pulled over and stopped. The silence in the Suburban was broken only by blowing noses and sniffles.

"I couldn't ask for more," Jess answered softly. "I have worried you would leave but am more than happy you want to stay. I love you!"

No one had ever told Terry they loved him. It was more than he could take, and he broke down in tears. The men hugged there on the road to Somewhere and went on with joy in their hearts.

They went to the post office first and got what little mail was there. As they were about to leave, the sheriff came in. He stopped and just stared at Terry. He came over and asked his name.

Terry replied, "It's Terry Lund."

The sheriff, matter-of-factly said, "Then you will have to come with me. You are wanted on a runaway warrant from Ohio. So please don't make a scene. Just come quietly."

Jess had overheard part of the conversation and came over and asked what was going on. "This young man is wanted on a runaway warrant from Ohio. I must take him in until he can be shipped back there to stand charges of robbery and other minor offenses."

The color drained from Jess's face. He couldn't comprehend what was happening. He finally asked, "How long will it would be before he is sent away?"

"Well I have to send some information to the authorities and then find a way to get him there. But it will only be about a week."

"Well don't get in too big a hurry. I will be back this afternoon to pick him up and take him home. Don't worry, Terry. Rob didn't come down early for nothing. I just know it," Jess blurted out and then headed for the Suburban.

Supplies forgotten and speeds above what the old Suburban could really stand got him home in a short time.

After Jess left, the sheriff took Terry and put him in the Meeteetse jail. He called Cody and got the information he asked for on the case.

"I don't know what you did in Cleveland, but someone wants you to pay for it. I guess you just figured you could hide out up toward Somewhere. Justice will always prevail, even if it takes a long time. You should be ashamed of yourself."

Terry didn't know what to say. He hadn't stolen anything. He hadn't assaulted anyone. He just left. "Could you tell me who filed the charges against me?"

"I guess you have a right to know. It was a woman named Samantha Barlow," the sheriff replied.

"That's my sister. Her boyfriend's name is Barlow, and he never did like me. He probably couldn't find something, so he blamed me, which only makes sense. It was probably something he hadn't used in years but just discovered it was missing and thought he would get even with me for it. My mom may have even put him up to it," Terry said bitterly.

"Well that's a good story, but it doesn't change the warrant. So just cool your jets," Sheriff Parks replied, and all was silent.

The time went by slowly. Nearly four hours had passed before a vehicle drove up to the sheriff's office and jail. There were no windows, so Terry couldn't see that it was Rob's pickup, with him and Jess in it. When they came into the office, the sheriff looked up. Seeing Jess, he just laughed. "Is this a jailbreak?"

"No, but just the same it will empty your jail," Rob stated. "I have here a sworn court order signed by the judge in Cody releasing Terry into my custody. So let's get this little detail taken care of."

Immediately after looking at the document, the sheriff took his keys and opened the cell to let Terry out. He did not seem unhappy about it and changed his attitude toward Terry. The sheriff knew Robert Evans and didn't even question his honesty. Releasing Terry would be good because he wouldn't have to deal with all the paperwork involved in getting him back to Ohio. The charges would still be in force, but Rob could probably deal with them.

As they rode home in almost total silence, Jess suggested they stop at the Fisher's and check on the livestock. "I would like to see the place anyway," Rob said. "John has told me a lot about what happened—at least what he can remember—but seeing it firsthand could help make more sense about the situation and the outcome."

After feeding and watering the stock, they walked up the trail to where John was found. Rob remembered the description John had given him. He made some notes and observations. Then they left and went home.

Rob and Terry shared all the things that happened. Molly wanted so much to hug Terry but refrained with all the people looking on.

"So what is next for Terry?" Jess asked.

"I will contact the attorney in Ohio and make arrangements to drop the charges. I have a feeling that all this guy wants is money. But it might not be a bad thing if we could reestablish some contact with his mother, brother, and sister. But that will be up to Terry."

CHAPTER 30

All the neighbors came to the meeting on Friday. The yard was crowded with pickups. Jess had arranged for some plank tables to hold the food near the porch. People found places to spread out blankets or tarps to sit on. Jess got up when everyone was settled and gave a brief introduction of Robert Evans

"Rob has some important information regarding our land and the possibility we might have it taken from us. I am as anxious to hear what he has to say as you are. So let's get some food and renew friendships with all the neighbors. Even though we are so close together, we seldom see each other. Let's eat."

The line formed, and Rob stood to the side, meeting each family as they passed by. He had a way with people that built trust and confidence. The tension began to ease as the line came to an end, and Rob and Lottie came through to get a loaded plate. They found a seat with some of the people he sensed were less involved. The McNernys were the first they ate with, and it wasn't long until he had them laughing and sharing stories of their first years in Somewhere. For nearly an hour, Rob and Lottie moved through the group feeling the bonds among them and sensing the anxiety they all felt.

The sun was still high in the afternoon sky, so it was warm with a slight breeze. Comfortable surroundings made bad news everyone expected easier to accept. But today there would be no tears of fear or loss when Rob began his presentation.

"I came to know about the problem and the anxiety you are dealing with when Jess, Molly, and Terry came to Cody to try and find some documentation for their purchase. Their search didn't yield much, but Molly had a little accident, and Terry was left behind in the bank. I just can't stay away if I see someone who looks like they need help."

A loud, "Amen," came from Lottie. "He picks up strays faster than rustlers do!" Everyone laughed.

Rob continued. "Guilty as charged. But this time I found a problem I have had some experience with. It also made it possible for the Fishers to have good care when John was injured and a place for Veda Mae to be close by. Anyway, I found out about the mysterious black SUV that visited everyone." A murmur of fear rippled through the group. "It turns out there is nothing sinister about it. The owners, the heirs of the Linderman Ranch, wanted to find out if any of you had legal ownership since Otis usually did business with a handshake and often didn't follow up. I can't tell you what the plans are for the future, but it is the family's determined intention to make it right for all of you. They sent a private detective from Casper here to get information. I am involved, at least for now, because they got my name from our circuit court judge to help with the details and to work with all of you for your satisfaction. One note I am able to share with you is that there are five Linderman heirs. They all agree that they want good legal and ethical property rights put in each of your names, without your paying for the surveying or the hours it takes. Now that is about all I can tell you for now. Some things are still in the planning stages, but you may rest assured that you will not lose your land now. And when we are through, not in the future either because you will have legal documentation for every inch you own. Any questions?"

Dead silence surprised Rob. It was as if they had been stunned by an explosion and didn't have anything else to say. Finally the tension eased, and Ronnie Moore spoke up. "I for one have lost a lot of sleep over this. We worked hard and don't really have much, but we are making a good living. This lifts a heavy burden from us."

There was general agreement from everyone in the group. Paul Young stood up and thanked Rob for coming. "We had been praying for some kind of miracle when we felt threatened by that guy. I can't tell you how much this means to us and to everyone here. Thanks, Mr. Evans."

Cheers erupted. Rob blushed and accepted the thanks gracefully. After it calmed down, he shared that he would be here for a week and would be coming around to visit with everyone and get some idea of their spread. Rob also invited everyone back on Sunday morning, if it wasn't raining, for a time of worship and fellowship. "We really need to give thanks where thanks is due. Thank you for coming."

With that, people started talking. As it started to turn dark, they began to leave. It had been a good day. Trouble seemed to fade away some, and they left feeling better than when they came.

CHAPTER 31

J ess couldn't wait to get alone with Rob to find out how he had come to know what he shared with the ranchers. That didn't happen until the next morning as he sat in the corral milking the cow. Rob had already been up for a long time and had been walking around the homestead and out into the fields to get some feel for the kind of operation Jess was running. As he approached the corral, he heard the milk splashing into the bucket and found Jess doing his chores.

"How's the dairy man this morning?" Rob asked with a chuckle. "How many cows do you milk?"

"Only one," Jess answered. "That is enough for our needs and some for a calf when we have one. I wouldn't want more. I did want to ask you about the information you shared yesterday. How can you be sure that the Linderman family wants to do all the things you shared? It seems to me that the home ranch has been neglected so long that no one really cared. Why would they care what happened to the folks around Somewhere?"

"That may be more than I am willing or allowed to share," Rob replied. "I have talked with one of the family members about your situation. He assured me that there is more than meets the eye at this time happening to the Linderman spread, but there are some complicated legal and ethical hurdles to overcome—this being one of them before we can settle everything. The one thing that makes me confident about the solution is that the representative I talked to, or talked to me would be better, assured me of the family's desire to present a unified front, an ethical solution, a result that is God-honoring in final outcome.

"You see, Jess, it isn't enough for me to do a good job, just be legal, or make decisions that don't hurt others. I believe I am responsible to God for everything I do. A long time ago I came to the realization that a personal relationship with God is the only way a person can really sleep at night and face the quagmire of horror in the legal profession the next day with confidence. It was then that I made a decision. I decided that what God told us in the Bible—that Jesus came to forgive us and to give us His life, which is more abundant—is absolutely true and trustworthy. In my backyard, at that old bench in the garden, I got down on my knees and told God that I accepted His offer of eternal life and a full, rich life now by accepting that I was a sinner, unable to satisfy a Holy God. If Jesus was willing to die for me, I accepted His life, His will, and His way. Nothing I have ever encountered has been more rewarding. So relying on God's wisdom and constantly submitting to His way, I have been able to avoid a lot of bad situations. This is one of those times I believe we can put our confidence in the Linderman family as they expressed their desire to do things worthy of God's favor as well."

Jess finished milking. When he got up, his eyes were filled with tears, and his heart ached to know for himself the peace and trust that Rob had just described.

It wasn't lost on Rob either. He sensed Jess's tenderness regarding God's gift. "Would you want to tell God what is in your heart, Jess?" Rob asked tenderly.

"I'm not sure," Jess answered. "I don't know just what it would mean for my future. But I want to know the kind of peace you have. I feel as though I can't go on any longer on my own. So I just don't know what the next step really is."

When Jess set down the milk pail to close the gate, he was engulfed in the warmest hug as Rob threw his arms around him and told him how he had been praying for Jess to know God's forgiveness, presence, and power. "You can be sure that God is faithful to His promises. Maybe we can get some time alone this week to read what God says about it in the Bible!"

As they came into the kitchen, Molly looked up. A puzzled look came over her face as she saw Jess. She didn't understand what it was, but she sensed it was different. Something good and big was about to happen to Jess. She just knew it.

"Let's get up to the table, or it will go out to the cat we don't have before you get a chance," Molly ordered.

Rob ran out to the trailer, where Lottie was just about to come out. "I saw what was going on by the corral. Is it what I think it is?"

"Jess is very tender now, but he has to decide in his own time," Rob replied.

"Well I think it may be time for Molly to have a talk," Lottie said. "We will just have to trust that God is opening the gate."

"You better hurry up or we won't get breakfast. Race you to the house," Rob shouted, running away.

Lottie followed and caught up just as they came to the door. Panting they went in and were greeted by the delicious smells of a farm breakfast.

"Sit down," Molly ordered. Everyone sat: Jess, Terry, Sarah next, and Molly at the end, with Rob and Lottie filling the final two chairs. Jess bowed his head to give thanks but couldn't talk for the lump in his throat. Finally, he asked Rob to give thanks for the meal. Breakfast was exciting as they talked and ate.

"I'm going over to the Fisher's this morning. Anyone want to come along?" Rob announced. To his surprise, everyone wanted to go. So after breakfast was completed, they squeezed into the Suburban. Sarah ended up between Rob and Lottie. Terry jumped in behind the back seat on the floor, and they left. It was only a few minutes until they were parked in front of the house. Sarah was obviously troubled but tried not to show it. It was then that Lottie quietly reached over and touched her arm. Sarah looked up nervously, but when she saw the compassion in Lottie's face, she began to relax.

"Maybe you could show me around a little," Lottie said quietly when they got out. Sarah wasn't sure that was a good idea but agreed. Sarah had explored the barn and the corral before getting into the house and before she was caught a few weeks ago. As they walked away, Molly noticed how they were drawn to each other and was very happy. She hoped she could soon get beyond the thick shell Sarah had built around herself. She also wondered how that would even be possible.

Jess showed Rob all the outbuildings and remarked that it was a good thing the corral was as big as it is. It kept all the cattle and horses quite comfortably. But something was nagging at him all the time. Finally he told Rob, "I don't think there are as many cows in here today as before. I haven't been counting, but it just doesn't feel right."

As Jess and Rob talked about the ranch, Terry called from the trail leading up the valley, "Come look at this. I didn't notice this before, but here is fresh cow manure. And there is more up the trail. Something is happening to the stock. It looks like some have been let out and taken away."

Just then Terry noticed a boot print and put his beside it. It did not match. *What is going on* he wondered?

Jess put words to his deepest fear. "Someone is taking cows out of the corral and driving them up the trail into the hills a few at a time so we wouldn't notice. We had better notify the sheriff about this and post a guard twenty-four hours a day. This could be serious." They decided to go to Meeteetse after they got home and report what they had found.

Molly was waiting for them when they came back. but Lottie and Sarah had not returned. They all fanned out to look for them and found them sitting on the back porch. Sarah was crying, and Lottie was holding her in the warmest hug. Molly tentatively approached and sat next to Sarah, who grabbed her in a passionate hug and sobbed out her thanks for rescuing her from terrible fear and showing her the love she had never had before. It was hard to come there, but how wonderful it was to be wanted and not on the run anymore.

Molly couldn't hold it in anymore and cried as much as Sarah, assuring her that she could stay with them as long as she wanted. Rob, Jess, and Terry watched from a distance. Rob sent a silent thanks to God and a prayer for continued blessings on the Martins. This was more than anyone had expected. but it was exceptionally wonderful. God looked down and smiled.

Pulling into the yard, Rob offered to take his pickup into town and report the possibility of rustling at the Fisher's. He could file an official complaint on Jess's behalf, which would have the strength of an attorney too. He also decided he would call the judge in Cody and see if he had heard of any activity in the area. As soon as they arrived home, the men left on their way to Meeteetse. Terry had wanted to go along as well, even though he would have to face the sheriff who arrested him a week ago. He believed that it would be a sign he didn't feel guilty over what he had done and show the sheriff that he expected to be cleared of any charges. Rob was proud of this young man's courage.

Jess had a troubling thought. *Have any of my cows been rustled?* He decided that when they got back, they would go out to the pasture and count the herd. He was so quiet the rest of the way to town that Rob asked if he were feeling alright.

"I'm fine. I just thought that if John Fisher's cattle are disappearing, maybe I ought to check mine to see if they are all there. When we get back I want to go looking around."

"Good idea. No need to shut the door after the cows get out," Rob replied.

CHAPTER 32

When Jess and Terry returned from checking the cattle, they seemed in a better mood. Molly greeted them as they rode into the yard. "Well are they all there?"

"It looks like we still have all the cows we started with, but it was a little hard to get an accurate calf count. Those young steers are all over the place, so we may have counted some more than once. All in all, it looks like nothing has disturbed our herd. But it also looks like the hay is nearly ready to cut again, and there is some fence that needs to be fixed. So I guess the next few days we will be out in the pasture. Did Rob and Lottie go visiting?" Jess asked.

"Yes. They left right after you rode out. I gave them general directions, and they thought they could find the neighbors from there. I just know they are going to like everyone they meet. We have such good neighbors and friends," Molly said. "They also said they were going to go into Meeteetse to call and check on John and Veda Mae. It will be good to hear how they are getting along. I imagine John is anxious to get back home as soon as possible."

"We will be cutting hay all day tomorrow, so they will have plenty of time to get their work done," Jess replied.

"You do remember that this is Friday, don't you? Rob said he wanted the neighbors to come for an outdoor church service on Sunday."

"You're right," Jess said. "Taking off Sunday will be well worth the time spent. The hay will just have to wait."

"I hope John doesn't take it too hard when he finds out some of his cattle are gone," Jess said softly. "It could be quite a shock to tell him all the stuff going on around here. How are they going to get here?"

"They will drive Lottie's little car. And when Rob goes home, one will drive it home while the other drives the camper. I guess they are planning to go home Thursday."

When Rob and Lottie weren't home by suppertime, Jess got a little worried. "Hope they didn't run into some trouble," he said at supper. "The stuff going on around the area is not especially comforting."

About that time they saw the lights of the pickup turn into the drive. The report from Rob said they had visited with two of the other ranchers, and it was very helpful. Their time in Meeteetse was also productive. Besides calling John, they were able to get more information on the warrant on Terry. It seems that he had been right; was his sister who filed the complaint. But her boyfriend was the one that pushed for his return in custody. The officials in Cleveland didn't know just what Terry was charged with, and they labeled his future brother-in-law as a real troublemaker. They had found Terry's mother and talked with her, which was revealing when she showed real concern for his location and his condition.

"I talked to her, assured her that Terry had grown up and was very reliable and could be trusted to do the right things. He is a hard worker and a real help to you folks," Rob shared. "I think she was nearly in tears and hoped she could see him sometime soon. No word on his little brother, and she said she would try to get the charges dropped that set this whole thing in motion. She couldn't promise, but it sounded hopeful."

"Supper in forty-five minutes," Lottie called from the camper.

"It's on us tonight, so come on over. Let me do the work for a change."

Chores done and livestock taken care of, everyone met in the camper. It was bigger than it looked from the outside, and they gathered around the table. Rob gave a blessing, and Lottie served a delicious stew and homemade bread. For dessert she had some fresh rhubarb pie from rhubarb grown in her garden. It was a wonderful meal and everyone had a wonderful time. Sarah came alive and was such fun. Nothing could take away the feeling of peace and that everything was good as they wandered across the yard after supper, watching the sunset that was spectacular.

"Can't beat God's special gift, can you?" Molly said quietly. "We have had such a great day, and this week has brought some really good things our way." She turned to hug Jess, gathered Terry and Sarah into their arms, and felt the closeness that was growing. It was a good day!

CHAPTER 33

Sunday dawned with clouds on the horizon. It didn't look like rain, but you often can't tell in the mountains. Rob had prepared to share a special idea that had been rolling around in his mind most of the week. He hoped it wouldn't rain and cause the others to stay away. But he could only trust God had a special time for all of them in store.

By 9:00 the sky was overcast, and the wind had come up. Ronnie Moore drove into the yard and jumped out of his pickup. He ran up to the house and knocked on the door as if it were an emergency. Jess went to the door. "Hi, Ronnie. What's up?"

"Well I saw the clouds last evening and just knew it was going to rain this morning. So I cleaned out the middle of the barn and want all of you to come there for our first official church time. Bring some chairs if you can. I can't wait to tell everyone else. See you there."

With that he was in the truck, tearing down the drive and turned toward the McNernys and Youngs. Jess just stood with his mouth open. He couldn't believe his ears. When he shared what had happened, everyone was excited. They gathered some chairs, a bench out of the feed room from the old bunkhouse, and some blankets. Jess ran over and told the Evans what was happening. Then they got ready to leave for church.

Everyone put on clean clothes and clean boots. They didn't have Bibles, but they figured no one else would either. They heard Rob and

Lottie come out of the camper, and they all headed for the Moore's barn for the first official church service in Somewhere. Who would have thought it would stir such interest? Who would have guessed it would be Ronnie Moore to make sure it happened? Even Ike Sellers from the General Store came when he heard about the time and place. This was something new, and no one wanted to be left out. No one questioned the place, the time, or the surroundings as they came together that special Sunday morning. Just as they got seated, the rain started and pelted the barn with torrents of water. Now everyone was praising Lonnie for thinking about the possibility of rain.

Rob had copied a couple of old hymns to sing. Surprisingly, most of the folks knew both of them. So they sang. They bowed in prayer. They listened carefully to what Rob had prepared. It wasn't a long sermon, but the message it held was just right for the folks of Somewhere.

"All of us are somewhere in our search for the meaning of our lives. We are all looking for something or someone that will help us find that meaning and fulfillment in living. There are many who offer a shiny promise of a glorious future with all the stuff you could ever want. Others try to fool us by telling us that it is only by hard work and a lot of determination that we can get all the stuff we want and that is all there is to have. Both of these ideas hold something of the truth in them. The future does often promise a better situation than we are usually in. It is always possible that things can go better than they are. We had a taste of this in the news I was able to bring about the mysterious visitor asking about your ownership. The other choice we can make is the one that only looks bright and shiny. Someone gets us to believe that the offer he has is so good that only a few will get it, and you can get in on the ground floor by signing up today. Don't wait; this offer may not be there tomorrow! And so we sign up only to realize we have lost so much—or sometimes everything—for an empty promise.

"Jesus told a story about the farmer who had great crops perhaps for some years. So he decided that working was just not for him. He built bigger barns and put his grain in storage. He saved it up in such a way that it gave him confidence in his ability and his shrewdness. One evening I can imagine him saying to his wife, 'We have it made. We have enough and more to just eat, drink, and be merry the rest of our lives. I am such an important, ingenious provider that there is nothing we can't do.' He didn't reckon with the fact of mortality. God decreed that very night he would die. The question he hadn't considered was, 'Who will get all that I have done then.' It is important to plant for the future as well as provide for the present. God calls this arrogant man a FOOL in capital letters. Remember that to have abundant living, our need to provide the material stuff isn't nearly as important as it is to be focused on the spiritual. Man does not live by bread alone, Jesus warned. Our connection with God is even more important. Look for the abundant life. Not life filled only with a bunch of stuff, money, fame, or possessions. I recommend Jesus become your most important pursuit, your family next, and it will keep perspective on your prosperity. Everything else is relative.

"Let's sing the last song on the sheet, 'My Jesus I Love Thee.' If you wish to talk more about your relationship to God or your ranch, corner me here this afternoon, and we can work something out for a time to get serious about it.

"Right now, I think we are all very hungry. The smells we caught when people were bringing in all those covered dishes gave me hope there would be something really special at dinner. So come and get it. Mrs. Moore, tell us how this is going to work."

After a prayer of thanksgiving and instructions on the serving, everyone filled plates and cups and sat wherever they could find a place, visiting and just enjoying each other.

CHAPTER 34

Terry sat by himself while others were getting their food. He was considering the priorities he had chosen for his life and the surprising satisfaction he found in what he had always scoffed at, work and family. He wondered if what he had heard in Sunday school back in Ohio had any practical value. Now it looked as though one of the valued people in his life, Rob, said it was the most important thing. How was he to react to all of this? Was it really true that what was said about Jesus really meant something after all? He just didn't know and felt uneasy in asking. But he didn't have to ponder long. Rob slipped, almost unnoticed, on to the other end of the bale. When Terry looked up, Rob asked if he wanted to talk.

"I could see the wheels turning for you and the puzzled expression. So if you want to talk, I'm available," Rob said quietly.

"I do have some questions, but I'm not sure I know how to ask them," Terry replied. "This might take some time, but ..."

"Let's go into that last stall back there. We might have a better chance of privacy than here in the middle of lunch," Rob suggested.

Both men slipped unnoticed into the stall and found another bale of straw to sit on. They sat quietly as Terry tried to get up the nerve to admit his questions, which seemed rather trivial. Rob was patient. He knew how hard it was to find out you don't have the answers you want and are embarrassed to admit it.

Terry began tentatively. "Rob, if Jesus is so important to us, why does He seem so unnecessary in life? I don't understand what it means to know Him in any practical way. I have always thought I didn't need another confusing thing in my life. I haven't done bad for myself without Jesus, but your statement—that it is perspective we need, and it comes by putting Jesus first in our lives—is new to me. So how does that work?"

"Well for one thing, none of us is perfect. Our messed-up lives contribute to the problem. Can you think of a situation where something is totally wrong but appears exciting? Do we do it? How do we decide? We have to have some fixed standard to be able to see the wrong, what is covered up by the exciting wrapping. God's moral law is the only fixed and settled standard we have for discerning moral issues. If we don't accept that, we get tangled up in contradiction and guilt. So what is your moral standard for choosing your actions?"

"Well I came here because I didn't want to keep feeling bad where I was. I didn't like the things my sister was doing, and I felt put on by my mom's continual nagging. So I left. I didn't really consider if it was right or wrong. I wouldn't have known how to do that anyway. I hated work and assumed that not having any would be great. But being with Jess and Molly, I found out that work has meaning to it, and I am happier that I have ever been. But I am not sure just how to say it. Something still seems to be missing."

"Probably that missing piece is spiritual, something that can't be explained by what we can feel, touch or taste. And explaining what is missing will need some time to figure out, so we can talk again if you like," Rob offered. "This is a serious choice that must not be made lightly."

Terry was grateful to Rob for not pushing him and felt as though it wouldn't have much meaning or staying power. He needed to think about what it all meant to enter into a relationship with God through Jesus. He knew that it would be a lifetime choice either way, and he wanted to be sure of his desire before he made a decision. He could see the consequences of rejecting God's offer, but did he want, or have the will to accept God's offer for a lifetime? Only Terry could decide. And Rob silently prayed he would make the right choice.

The rain stopped, and the doors of the barn were opened. The cool fresh air was great. Everyone stood around talking softly. No one seemed to be in any hurry to leave. It had been a good Sunday morning.

Sally Young timidly asked, "Is there any reason we can't meet like this more often? We could sing some of the songs and read a part of the Bible each Sunday, even if Rob isn't here to help us. Or maybe there is someone who would be willing to come out to Somewhere each week and help us. I think we should try."

Sally's comment was met with a rousing affirmation. Rob felt his heart would burst with joy. Maybe this was the one reason he had come there that would make all the difference in this small community.

"Smoke!" someone yelled. "It's coming from the direction of Somewhere. We better get there and help if we can!"

All peace was shattered. Men jumped into their vehicles and tore out the drive toward Somewhere. The women were left to clean up and prepare for whatever they could do to help later. Fortunately some of the pickups were left, so they would have transportation home.

Rounding the bend into Somewhere, Ronnie saw the source of the smoke. It was one of the abandoned houses across from the General Store. Luckily there were no other buildings close by, but the tall grass was also beginning to burn and spreading fast. Some of the men grabbed shovels, raced past the perimeter of the fire, and began making a break in the dry grass. It was enough, and when the fire reached the dry ground they had uncovered, it began to die out. The old house was nearly completely burned, and it, too, was smoldering its last.

Somewhere sits on a rise that gave a beautiful view of the valley out toward Meeteetse and across the Fisher and Moore ranches. As the men were wiping sweat from their foreheads, someone called, "What do you suppose all that dust is all about?"

All eyes turned to look, but Jess knew. "It is a bunch of cattle being moved fast, and I am sure I know where they came from. John Fisher has had a few cows missing each week from the corral at the homeplace. Terry and I have been feeding and watering them, but each day there are just a few more gone. I think this fire is a distraction so that the rustlers can move the rest of the herd without us noticing it."

"Well we can't let that happen!" Ronnie said. "I'll hightail it to Meeteetse for the sheriff. I think the rest of us should get our guns and horses, and ride out there and find out what is going on. We could all be targets since it is so remote out here, and there is no phone service."

"That's a good idea. But let me do the run to Meeteetse," Rob offered. "You guys know the country better than I do and could do more here. I'll not only get the sheriff but notify the State Patrol as well. We better get going if we hope to do any good either way." Everyone checked that the fire was out and headed home for horses and guns.

Jess and Terry drove into the yard just as someone ran out from behind the haystack. "Get the horses saddled while I get my guns and you find out who that is making a getaway," Jess ordered.

Both jumped from the Suburban running in different directions. Terry approached the corral quietly and led both horses out, tying them to the corral poles. While getting the saddles from the grain room and bringing them outside, he saw the runner again. This time he noticed the bright red bandana around his neck. Saddling Buck first and slipping the bridle on, he vaulted into the saddle and raced after the runner. It wasn't long before he found him running down the road and easily caught him. Jumping off as Buck slid to a stop, he surprised the fugitive, making him trip. Terry was on him in a flash. Using a short rope, he tied his hands and legs to a fence post. Terry left him there without a word and rode quickly back to the yard. Jess was saddling his horse, wondering where Terry had gone.

As Terry rode up, Jess handed him a belt and gun to strap on. Terry didn't know what to do, "I never shot a gun before," he said quietly.

"Well you are going to learn how quick. Where did you go just now?" Jess asked.

Terry explained, and they both hurried to the immobile fugitive. He was shouting and trying to get untied. The tying wasn't very good, but it was enough to keep him there.

"Just who are you, and why are you on my place?" Jess yelled in the young man's face.

"I ain't tellin'," he answered.

"Fine. You can tell it to the judge because that's where you will end up," Jess warned him. He tied the boy more securely with some leather thongs to the post and motioned to Terry that they needed to go.

Coming to the Fisher gate, neither knew just what to do. To ride into the yard could be their last ride, so they circled behind the house and came up behind the barn. Jess slipped into the barn and heard the restless cowpony in the stall. He spoke softly, and the horse quieted when he heard the familiar voice. "Thankfully they didn't take you," he said to the pony. "But there aren't any cows left out there."

Jess decided to ride John's horse. He reasoned it was more

surefooted than Babe, and could probably hold up longer if needed. He put his horse in the barn with water and feed, took his rifle and rope from the saddle, and went back out, mounted, and motioned to go around the rest of the barn before riding into the yard.

No cows were left in the corral. The gate was open, which meant they had taken two other horses with them.

As the others came riding down the lane into the yard, Jess explained, "They took everything but John's best saddle horse that was in the barn. Probably around fifty head of cattle, and two saddle horses. My guess is they went up that trail. How far I don't know, nor where they would take them after that. It shouldn't be hard to follow their trail. We caught a guy fooling around at our place when we drove in. Terry tied him to the fence so we could pick him up later."

Everyone laughed. One of them said, "We saw the kid trying to get away. But we checked the ties and knew he couldn't without help, so we just kept on coming." It was a good laugh, but it made everything just that much more serious.

Rob stopped at Moore's to share the situation with the women. "I suggest that if you can figure out a way to get home, you do so. If you have a gun, get it out and be prepared to use it. I'm going for the sheriff and hope to be back later this evening. Lottie, you stay in the house with Molly and Sarah. No need to be separated if not necessary. I better be going!"

CHAPTER 35

Turning onto the country road, Rob set a pace he had never expected possible on country gravel roads. Fortunately it was well maintained and he covered the twenty-eight miles to Meeteetse faster than he expected. Sliding to a stop at the sheriff's office, he noticed a note on the door: "Closed. Emergency. See General Store."

Rob went to the store. But it was Sunday evening, and it was also closed. "I wonder if there is a church in town," he said absently. Just then he heard the bell and quickly drove to the little church. A number of people were just entering. He slid to a stop, making some look his way. "Is the sheriff in there?" he called. Someone yelled back, "I think so."

Rob ran ahead of the folks. Entering the sanctuary, he called out, "Is the sheriff here? We have an emergency!"

"I'm the sheriff," a man right next to him answered. "Oh, it's you again. What is it this time?"

"I'm sorry we met under difficult conditions the last time, but this may involve a much bigger problem that can't be stopped if we can't get help from you. Can we go outside and let me fill you in," Rob said softly.

As the story unfolded, the sheriff became all business. "Let me get some deputies, and I'll call in the state troopers before we leave. They have some air power that might help spot this operation. Now tell me just where this is taking place."

"It is on the John Fisher ranch, about a mile from Somewhere. He was the one rescued by the Forest Service and is still in Cody with his wife, so no one is living at the house now. Jess Martin and Terry Lund, the kid you apprehended before, have been taking care of the stock while they are gone. Jess was suspicious that some cows were being taken from the corral. But now they are all gone, and the trail leads up the same trail John Fisher was found on earlier. All five ranchers are up there now, intending to follow the rustler, if that's what they are, but would like official help with the plan."

"Well, let's get going. You get back up there. See if you can get them to wait until I get there. We can certainly use them, but we need a plan on how. Just get going. I will be there ASAP."

"Thanks, Sheriff! Those wonderful folks won't forget it either," Rob replied.

"My wife will have our church folks praying for them within the hour. You wait and see," the Sheriff said. "They won't miss a time until the mystery is settled, and the crooks brought to their undesirable end."

Jumping in his pickup and heading toward the road to Somewhere, Rob sent up a prayer of gratitude for what he had just heard and a prayer for protection on the way back as well as for the ranchers and their wives.

As Rob passed the Moore's he noticed no vehicles in the yard. "Good," he said to himself. Going toward Jess's place, he saw the fugitive still tied to the post. Stopping, he went over to him. "How did you get tied to that post and why?"

" I ain't talking," he said.

"Fine. I'll just leave you here for the sheriff when he comes by." The young man's eyes widened, but he didn't say anything as Rob left.

Turning into the Martin drive, everything was dark. There was a dim light in the house, but it was eerie and mysterious. He parked near the house and got out.

"You ain't goin' any farther. Just reach for the stars if you value your life," Molly yelled from the shadow.

"Molly, it's me, Rob. I just got back from seeing the sheriff. He is on the way."

"What is the name of the girl we have living here?" Molly asked. "I don't trust you any farther than I can see you."

"Sarah," Rob said calmly. With that Molly ran and threw her arms around Rob, sobbing out the fear she had held in all afternoon.

"It's okay now." Rob comforted her. "Is everyone else in the house?"

"Yes, come on in," Molly said, wiping tears.

Lottie ran to Rob and hugged him. "We were so worried about everyone. What is going on? Who did this? Why?" The questions just kept coming. Out of the corner of his eye he saw Sarah, slightly hidden, just watching. When Lottie finally began to catch her breath, she sat down, and Rob slowly moved toward Sarah.

"How are you doing with all this turmoil?" he asked. "You must feel like you are forgotten, but that is not the case."

Rob could see the tears glistening in the lamplight. He opened his arms, and she flew into them and sobbed out her anxious thoughts. No one spoke as Sarah felt the loving care from everyone in the room. Molly just couldn't stay away and came close and enclosed Sarah in her embrace too. They all just stood there and cried for a long time. Lottie began to sing, "Jesus loves me, for the Bible tells me so," and, "My Lord knows the way through the wilderness. All we have to do is follow …" Her sweet voice began to soothe the jangled nerves and calm the fear that had engulfed them. Silently they sat around the table. Molly put on some coffee and set out some bread and jam. It was good, and they felt a peace settle over everyone.

CHAPTER 36

The ranchers decided they would go by twos up the trail. Two would follow the trail, two would try to cross the creek and circle to the south. The others would go up the trail to the end of the fence and circle around to the north.

None of them had been on the Fisher land. John Fisher had bought a full section in his initial deal so it was a large area to cover.

A square mile can provide a lot of hiding places. They decided that if anyone found something, he would ride back down the trail nearer the house and fire two shots into the air. Everyone would return and decide what to do from there.

Meanwhile Sheriff Parks was gathering a few trusted deputies from other small towns. Seven men who knew the area had arrived and were given what little was known of the problem near Somewhere.

With horses and four-wheelers, they would be able to cover a lot of territory. What they didn't know was where the Somewhere posse would be. They just had to get there and find out. Although it was nearly dark, they were confident they could accomplish something tonight.

Approaching the Fisher ranch, they spotted the boy tied to the fence post. Stopping, they untied and put him into the squad car. "Now who are you, and why are you tied to this post? Who did it and where did you come from?" the sheriff asked. "We knew about you being here, but no one knows why. So start talking loud and clear before we tie you up again."

"My name is Jerry. I was with the bunch that intended to take the cattle. I came from Colorado, but the leader of this outfit took me down around Powell. I found out about the Fisher deal and wanted out, but they said I knew too much to let me go. So they sent me to steal a horse to ride, and I got caught by that kid at the next place up the road. His dad or boss or something tied me the way you found me. I know where the camp is but not how to get there from here. We always came in off the highway south of Meeteetse, and I suppose that is where they are taking the herd now. They always work at night. I don't know the boss of the outfit. I don't know the names of any of the others. I just thought it was kind of exciting, and I went along for the ride. I didn't do anything wrong. I—"

"Well that settles it," the sheriff interrupted. "You aren't leaving either because you know too much. Let's get going. We can't wait too long. One of you take this kid, go south on the 120, and get him to tell you where they go in. Radio us ASAP when you have any reliable info. The rest of us will try to catch up with the posse. I just hope we aren't too late to help. God knows this could be a dangerous situation. So let's just pray we can take this bunch by surprise and save a life or two."

The deputy left with the captive in his car. The remaining four turned in at the Fisher ranch, unloaded their horses, and using a spotlight, headed up the trail that had the recent prints of a number of horses. It wasn't far before they noticed some had turned off, crossed the creek, and headed into the trees on the south side of the meadow. Others went on across the meadow and followed a well-marked trail into the forest. Moving as quietly as possible and as fast as that allowed, the sheriff followed the the trail. They hoped to catch up with the ranchers where the trail climbed a steep ridge following the line of the mountain.

Calling for a halt, Sheriff Parks signaled silence, as much as was possible. They all strained to hear any sounds above the forest sounds of wind and night birds. A shot was heard from a long way off, seemingly from the other side of the point they were rounding.

Hurrying on, they found a fork in the trail. The left fork showed that cattle had recently been on it, and not just one or two. Proceeding silently and with caution, the light of the moon was just enough to see without using the spotlight.

Another shot was fired about thirty minutes later. The posse stopped to listen. Then one of the deputies spotted a light from a vehicle at the bottom of the ravine they were following. It wasn't moving, but there was a lot of activity around it. The posse moved on around the side of the mountain, coming to a fork that dropped off toward the valley below.

"I wish I knew where that other group is and where the ranchers are," Sheriff Parks whispered. "We don't want to get them or us caught in a cross fire. Jim, you ride around this mountain on the upper trail a few hundred yard while we just wait here. If the others came from the other side, they could be close to where we are now. If we are together, it may be easier to take these crooks by surprise. We'll wait here for you to come back. Take this light, and use it when you need to. So get going. We will wait for fifteen minutes."

Not five minutes had passed before they heard horses coming back around the mountain. Jim rode up with three ranchers following him and flashed the light on the ground.

"Good," Sheriff Parks said. "Now let's decide what to do from here. I am pretty sure they don't know we are here, so surprise is on our side. They may be nearly ready to leave, so time is running out. Does anyone know the lay of this valley and how we get down from here without going right into them?"

"I was here once before with John," Paul spoke up. "I think that just below us is a trail leading off to the east. It drops into the valley below, where the truck is now. I can't remember if there is another opening farther up, but I don't think so. The next intersection should be no more than fifty to sixty yards ahead."

"Good. Lead on," Sheriff Parks said.

Slowly the men eased ahead and down. The trail leading to the bottom was just where Paul thought it was. They all stopped. They could hear the rustlers chasing cows into the truck. There was enough noise, so they didn't worry about being heard. But how was the truck to get out of the canyon? Were they headed down or up? How many rustlers were there, and were there some standing guard away from the truck who could sound an alarm? Or worse, shoot some of the posse?

"Sure wish we knew how many there are," Sheriff Parks whispered.

"I would be willing to slip down on foot to get some idea," Ronnie Moore offered. "It might take a while if I do it quietly. I could be back in twenty minutes, I think. And meanwhile you could delay any escape down the valley."

"Let's do it," the sheriff agreed. "We will get a little closer to the bottom and set up a blockade there. Get going. The rest of us will be down farther."

Tying his horse securely, Ronnie went on foot. It was about two hundred yards to the truck, but he kept high on the ridge before dropping down. As he got closer, he heard a dog bark.

This could be a problem, he thought. But as he listened, he realized the dog was barking at the cattle. Slowly he made his way down closer. Soon the forms of three men and the dog came into view. There was a fire burning pretty hot and the smell of singed hair, so he knew they had already altered some brands. Watching a few minutes longer, he heard one of them call that there were only five more to load and then they could get out of here.

"None too soon," an older man replied. "I don't like the quietness. No night birds calling. Nothing moving. Let's get it done."

Ronnie had heard enough. He went straight up the mountain to put as much distance between him and the rustlers as possible. Coming to the trail, he ran with his flashlight covered to put light only on the trail. He found his horse and vaulted into the saddle. He was with the rest in about five minutes. Hurriedly he shared what he heard. "I think that the two-track road leads down the valley since that is the direction the truck is faced, and behind them is a sharp rise."

The sheriff sent two of the men farther down to cross to the other side, and go up into the trees. They would have a good view of the trail. The other five were stationed about twenty yards above the valley floor, along the south side of the valley above and below where the trail entered.

"I will make the first move," Sheriff Parks ordered. "I will be near the road, hidden from view, and will call out for them to surrender. Hopefully they won't be too gun happy, but if they are, those behind them offer a warning shot in the trees near them. If that doesn't stop them, you two on the other side offer a shot in front of them. This should suggest they are surrounded. If they answer, I will order them to get into the headlights and lie face down on the ground. The rest of you, with me, will then approach and make the arrests. How many did you see?" he asked Ronnie.

"I think five in all, but there could have been another in the truck. So not more than six."

"All right. Pray this works without any of us or them gettin' hurt," Sheriff Parks said. The sheriff took off his hat and offered a short prayer for safety and success.

141

Each of the men got into their positions and waited for the truck to come down the valley. They could hear the rustlers yelling and pushing the cattle on board. Finally all was quiet, and a mount-up command was given. The truck's diesel engine made a lot of noise as it moved slowly down the two-track road. There were two men in the cab as they came into view. One was walking ahead with his rifle and there were three following, armed as well.

The sheriff yelled out, "Stop the truck! Get into the headlights and lie down on the ground. This is the county sheriff, and you are all under arrest!"

A shot was fired from behind the truck in the direction of the voice, but the sheriff had dropped to the ground, so he wasn't hit. A volley from the near-side posse sent two men hurrying toward the lights with weapons held high. The truck ground to a halt but was still running. A shot from the far side of the valley made the remaining three, two from the cab and the other from the back, come into the lights, weapons held high. They dropped their weapons, and dropped to the ground as ordered. The sheriff and the remaining men hurried down, tying the rustlers' hands behind them and picking up the guns.

The two from the other side of the valley came into the light leading their horses. Just then they heard ATVs coming down the road. As they rounded the bend, the sheriff signaled them in close. All four of the riders showed relief. It was the Powell sheriff. As they came to a stop, the sheriff lowered his weapon with a sigh.

Jim NcNerny crawled up on the truck and counted the cows in the truck. He yelled back down that there were only fifteen head in there. "I wonder where the rest of them are. There were probably at least fifty head in that corral. So this is only part of the cows and probably only part of the crooks."

With that, the ATVs roared into life and headed up the road to see if they could find the rest of the cows. They saw a few here and there along the hillside. Not stopping to count, they hurried back and shared the find with the others.

"They're probably all here somewhere," Jim offered. "They probably do this all the time. They bring a bunch in, let them graze, and ship a few out. Then they come back in a few days for more. Or they have another crew who comes in for the rest of them. I say we go on and drive out with this load, like nothing happened, and see what we find on the other end."

"There is very little sign of anyone having been up here for a while" one of the officers said. "I thought you said that one of the deputies had a kid with him who would tell where they come in from the 120. Where are they?"

"I don't know," Sheriff Parks answered. "They should have found the place before now. Maybe the kid didn't recognize it in the dark. Let's move on down slowly and see what happens. You men on horseback, see if you can circle up the hill. Stay out of sight as much as possible, but keep us in sight. We may need your persuasion again if we run into trouble down the road. Let's get these crooks loaded and get moving."

Pushing the cuffed men ahead of them, they put them in the crew cab and started moving slowly down the road. It was so crowded that the deputy driving had trouble getting around the corner, but he was satisfied that they wouldn't be causing much trouble either as tight as they were packed in the crew cab.

A rider was in front of and one beside the truck with their rifles at ready. When the road started to level off, the scout motioned to stop and turn off the lights. All was quiet, but as they listened, they could hear cattle and voices somewhere ahead. The smell of singed hair was heavy on the evening breeze.

Sheriff Parks got down behind the truck and opened his radio. "Do you hear me?" he asked quietly.

"I do, but we have a situation here. There are about thirty cows in a pole corral here and some fifteen men. They are doing some 'running' on the brands, so there is a lot of noise, but I don't think we can take them. We have five deputies with us. Where are you, and how many do you have?"

"I'd say we are about a hundred yards up the trail. I have five ranchers and four deputies, all armed. Can we get somewhere to see the lay of the situation without revealing we are here?" Sheriff Parks responded.

"We are on the south side. I think I see where the road comes out along the creek and around the low rise to the east of you. If you could get some of your men up on the mountain to the north of this bowl, we could have them surrounded at least. I better get quiet now."

Sheriff Parks drew what he thought was a rough diagram in the dust to where everything was ahead of them. "This two-tracker comes out just around that rise ahead on the east side. The other deputies are on the south, near the clearing. He was sure that if we could get around to the north, here, we could have them surrounded and not be too exposed. What do you think, Jess?"

"I haven't been here before, but from the way other valleys lay in this area, that makes sense. I just wonder if they have any sentries looking for movement. It isn't going to be easy in the dark, but it could be done. And I don't see any other choice. They will be expecting the truck soon, and that would give cover until you are quite close. I say let's go for it," Jess replied.

Having the plan, they split up and began moving slowly up the mountain on the north to be able to get around without being detected. Terry went with Jess. "I'm scared," he said shakily. "I don't know if I could shoot one of them even, if I were in danger. I just never thought of this being a life-or-death choice. I am not sure I would want to die either."

"This isn't my idea of a Sunday picnic either," Jess said. "But we can't let John and Veda Mae down now. I am sure Rob, Lottie, Molly, and Sarah are praying for us right now, as well as folks in Meeteetse and up and down the valley. Death isn't my idea of a good deal; I'm not sure I would be ready for that either. But we can't let these crooks get away if we can stop them. So let's go and do our best."

Climbing high on the mountain they could see the fire and the men from behind a row of serviceberry bushes. Only six or seven men could be seen around the camp. There might be more, but the way the first six had operated, neither Jess nor Terry believed that would be the case. They thought they were safe, yelling, laughing, and joking about how much they would get from this load. What they didn't reckon with was that such talk only made the posse more determined to take them all alive and see that justice was done.

CHAPTER 37

A pickup drove into the Martin yard. Rob blew out the lamp and motioned for Molly to get the shotgun. He drew his pistol, and they slipped out the back way, splitting up and coming around the house.

"Who are you, and what do you want?" Molly barked. "I want to see you in the lights with your hands empty and held high!"

"Molly, it's Sally and Leona. We couldn't stand it any longer and decided to come down here. We're scared!"

Rob came out from the other side of the house, pistol at the ready, and instructed the two women to head for the front door. As they obeyed, he jerked open the back door of the car. When he found no one there, he breathed a sigh of relief. "All clear, Molly. There is a bunch of food in here, so I'll bring that in. Help the ladies relax."

When Rob entered with the box of food, Sally thanked him. "I'm glad you're not taking any chances." She started to tell her story of loneliness and fear being alone at home. It hadn't been long until Leona drove up, "She was treated with the business end of a shotgun, too, until I could be sure who she was."

"But where is LaVerne?" Sarah asked. A blank stare showed on every face. They hadn't thought of her. One began to cry; others had tears to wipe away.

"I'm going down to Moore's to get her," Rob said decisively.

"She must be beside herself with fear. Do any of you have your weapons with you?" All of them did. They quickly got them out of their cars, went back into the house and pulled the curtains nearly shut.

Rob drove into the yard at Lonnie Moore's house blowing the horn. He wasn't about to go in and face a frightened frontier woman with a shotgun again. It was too close with Molly, and he had enough for his money. Just as he drove up to the house, he saw the lamp go out. He knew then that LaVerne was ready for anything. Leaning out the window of the pickup, he yelled, "LaVerne, it is me, Rob. All the other women are up at Molly's, and we were worried about you."

A voice off to the side surprised him. "I know how to use this 12 gauge, can take a sage grouse in flight, and I ain't about to trust anyone any farther than I can see them. So get out slowly, move around in front of the truck in the light so's I can see ya. I'll decide who you are!"

Rob left the motor running, and the dome light came on when he opened the door. He lifted his hands and moved around in front of the headlight, got down on his knees, held his hands high, and waited.

He didn't have to wait long. LaVerne rushed to him and hugged him tighter than Molly had. She sobbed out her fear and uncertainty. After what seemed like a long time, she said sobbing, "I have some leftover food from dinner. Let's get that and some other things. I guess you came to take me up to Martin's?"

"You're absolutely right. Don't forget the shotgun and some extra shells. Can I help?" Rob followed her into the house, moved three or four boxes to the pickup, looked around as LaVerne made sure the doors were locked, and they pulled out of the drive toward the Martin ranch.

They were met by the same warning and the same lethal

weapon as Rob had been earlier. "They're not taking any chances, are they?" LaVerne asked.

"Did you?" Rob laughed.

"Get out, come into the light, and state your name," Molly commanded.

Doing as they were instructed, each said their name with a little snicker that did not set well with Molly. "So you think this is funny. Well let me tell you—". Rob cut her off, telling her that that was exactly the greeting he had at the Moore ranch not thirty minutes ago. And that he was proud of her and all the rest for being extra cautious.

Carrying in the food boxes was met with a friendship that none of them had experienced in all the time they had been in Somewhere. The bond of love and protection grew and included everyone from the oldest to the youngest. A new time had begun that they didn't know how to react to. After the food was put away, they just sat around silently, feeling their fears and their anxieties. The load was heavy, but they were determined to carry it.

Lottie broke the silence. "I think we should pray together, maybe sing a familiar song, recognize that God is here with us and that we can trust Him to give us strength to carry this heavy load. I am an outsider here, but after the last few days, I feel like I belong here. You are so loving and including. Rob and I are strangers but you have opened you hearts and your homes to us freely. We both feel the burden of this night on your shoulders. Let us help carry it. So let's pray."

"I wouldn't know what to say," Molly admitted.

"Well then," Rob offered, "let's just talk to each other and let God hear how afraid we are and how much we want this all to end. I think that is what prayer should be anyway. A conversation where God is included. So I will start. I am really worried about our menfolk and what they are getting into. It just feels really bad."

"I know. We can't talk to them. I'm so afraid," Molly said.

"I know Sheriff Parks, and he doesn't take foolish chances. So if they are together, it would help me feel better to know it," LaVerne said.

"The darkness is scary for me," Sally shared.

"Not being able to talk to them is so hard. We don't go anywhere alone much and to be in this situation is very difficult," Leona confessed and then sobbed.

"I'm so glad Rob is here," Sally said. All the others agreed and began to tell Rob and Lottie what their coming had meant. But nothing like it meant now.

And on they talked until Rob broke in. "You know, God has been listening and I think He is smiling at us right now. Maybe you can feel the peace He has spread around the room. You see, we make such a fuss over praying that we don't find the true presence of His peace because we are doing all the talking, and most of the time, it doesn't amount to all that much either. So now let's just talk about the peace we are feeling with God in the room with us."

"I feel so much better," Sarah said timidly. "I didn't know He even cared but I can feel Him here, making me relax. Maybe I shouldn't be talking, but I couldn't keep still any longer. He just kept saying, 'Tell them, tell them.' So I did."

A chorus of affirmation greeted Sarah. Many of the others shared how much better they felt, even though their fear for the men was still on their minds.

The conversation with God went on into the night. Peace settled over all of them and they began to yawn. Trying to make sleeping arrangements became a game they all enjoyed. Rob and Lottie brought pillows and pads from the camper and most everyone had a little softer spot to rest. Some slept. Some just kept on praying. Some worried. But all of them felt God's presence like they never had before.

Rob whispered in Lottie's ear, "Isn't that the best prayer meeting you have ever attended?" All he heard was a grunt and soft steady breathing. "Good night, Lottie." Rob added, "And God, take care of our men out there in harm's way." With that he, too, slept soundly in an uncomfortable position.

CHAPTER 38

It was nearly 2:00 in the morning. The sheriff knew they would have to make a move soon as it would be much harder when it was light. He climbed the rise between him and the rustlers. Getting a good look, it appeared there were eight men, all armed, working the cattle. He had most of the area surrounded and could call them in at any time. But he wasn't sure if they could subdue all of them at once.

Just then he heard the growl of a heavy truck coming up the road. The cattle truck with a large trailer came into view. There were only two men in the front seat, but their coming complicated the plan, and where they parked the truck complicated it even more. It cut off five of his men who were across the dry creek bed from seeing everyone in the camp. Giving it serious thought, the sheriff finally concluded that the semi actually could be helpful. It would make a great jail for the time being. Once inside and the gate latched, there was no way out but plenty air and light.

Giving the signal, Sheriff Parks raised up so he could see the camp in front of him. His men had gone up to the corner and were ready. He assumed those on the north hillside were in place, so he yelled, "This is Sheriff Parks. You are surrounded and will not be allowed to leave. Lay down your weapons. Get facedown on the ground. And do not move!"

Fear and panic seized the rustlers. They didn't know what

to do. They looked for the boss, but he was tied and gagged in the truck one of the ranchers was driving. One of them reached for his gun, and a shot rang out from the cover of the trees on the north side of the clearing. Others began to run for the truck for protection, but a shot bit the dirt in front of them, and they stopped, dropped their weapons, and threw themselves on the ground.

The ranchers and deputies on the south side had moved up to the truck and were in position to start cuffing the rustlers on the ground. Two of them set to the task. One of them found a feed bucket and began collecting the pistols in it. No one moved.

Just as they thought they had captured everyone, a man emerged from the back of the truck and fired toward one of the Meeteetse deputies. The bullet grazed his shoulder. He screamed in pain and fear. A shot rang out from the hillside, hitting the truck above the outlaw. He ducked and turned toward the sound, giving Lonnie time to tackle him from behind. He threw the rustler to the ground, sending his revolver sliding toward the fire.

All fifteen rustlers had been cuffed, put inside the stock trailer, and its gate close on their escape. One of the men started to say, "I wasn't …" but was cut off and shoved inside.

Someone asked if they should get the others out of the other truck and put them in the stock trailer. "By all means. Let's have a big family reunion before we get them to the jail in Cody," replied the sheriff. "Ronnie, you and Paul do the honors of escorting our 'guests' to their quarters." Everyone laughed. Except the rustlers of course.

It was decided that they would try to turn the semi around and head for town. By this time, all the ranchers and deputies had come down off the mountain into the light of the fire. They were an impressive bunch of determined ranchers. No one harassed the detainees, but it was clear to all that there was little love lost on their being there.

"We want a lawyer," one of the prisoners said.

"You will have your say soon enough. So just keep it to yourself," a deputy responded. "I don't think a judge will have much trouble getting what you need, knowing that you are entitled to counsel. But for now, button it up!"

"Let's get this rig turned around. Anyone here know how to drive this rig?" someone asked.

"Ronnie was an over-the-road driver before he got married," Paul said. "He may be looking over the place now to see how he would do it."

Sure enough, Lonnie came into the firelight and told the sheriff that he thought the big rig could be driven up enough to back it into the clearing and be headed down the road.

So the only problem they had now was what to do with all the cattle. Unnoticed, Jess and Terry were already setting up a rope corral to keep the herd together for the night. Some of the men volunteered to stay with the herd, and others would return in the morning to trail them back to the Fisher place. So it was decided and arranged.

Ronnie fired up the "jail" and pulled ahead so he could back into the clearing. As skillfully as threading a needle, he turned the truck around and was ready to head for Meeteetse. A sheriff from Powell agreed to escort him into town and maybe all the way to Cody. The prisoners were not happy, but they didn't have much say in the decision either.

Pulling onto the two-tracker, Ronnie eased the semi toward the highway. The trooper followed with lights flashing. The lights of a truck lit up the road ahead. It was coming from the highway into the operation. Sheriff Parks took two men and moved into the shadows in order to stop it. Caution was unnecessary since it was the deputy with the "fence post fugitive," who had just found the right fork to get to the site. Everyone breathed a sigh of relief. The deputy in the patrol car rolled down the window and yelled, "Is this the rustler truck? This kid kept giving me bad information, so I didn't show up. But I still have him in the car."

"It sure is," Ronnie answered. "But you don't have the kid anymore unless you can catch him running toward the hills!" Startled, the deputy turned to see the fugitive get to the fence and then get caught on the barbed wire. It wasn't much of chase to grab him and take him back to the police cruiser.

"Guess I will just have to put him in the cage this time," he yelled at Ronnie with a laugh. And so the young kid found himself in a secure cage on his way to jail this time.

The drive into Meeteetse was uneventful. The state trooper from Cody was at the jail to greet them. After looking at the prisoners and calling his superior, they decided that taking them to Cody would be best. "I'll bring you back," he told Ronnie. "They will probably want the truck for evidence anyway. So let's get moving, or we will be up all night."

With lights flashing and the occasional sound of the siren, they drove to Cody and pulled into the prison yard. The guards were waiting, ready to take the suspects into their special care. They also wanted to impound the semi, so Ronnie and the deputy took their belongs and returned to Somewhere in the patrol car.

CHAPTER 39

Sheriff Parks and the posse rounded up as many of the cows and calves as they could find in the dark. They finished putting up the corral of sorts and decided who would stay the night to watch the herd. The rustlers' other truck was driven up to the pen for the guard to use for shelter and warmth. After all the excitement, everyone was exhausted and just wanted to go home. Jess and Terry volunteered to stay with the herd, and the rest were loaded into patrol cars and taken the long way back to Somewhere.

As the night wore on, both men felt the fatigue and agreed to take shifts to sleep a little and watch through the night. Finally, as the sun began climbing into the clear blue sky, a pickup drove up toward the truck. "Brought you some breakfast," the state trooper said. "All the folks in Somewhere were at your house all night, so they didn't get a really good sleep either. But they said it was worth it to hear that everyone was safe, and the herd was recovered."

"Thanks for the food and the report," Jess said wearily. "We will be glad to get this over with too. I think there are a few strays up on the hill, but most of them are here. Did the crooks get delivered?"

"They are safe and unhappily sleeping in the prison at Cody prison. The semi is impounded, and as soon as we can, they want this rig too. We don't know if there are others involved, but it looks like there are, all working the same kind of scam as these guys were. This truck may have been ID'd at sale barns, etc., so we want to go over it pretty thoroughly. By this time next week, we should have a much better idea how it all fits together. You didn't have any other visitors during the night, did you?"

The question gave Jess chills. "None that we saw," he answered. "We took turns staying awake to watch for anything else but didn't see anything. They may have been suspicious at the number of tracks turning in here. That kid we caught couldn't see where it was right away either."

"Well, we are going to stake out this area for a few days," the officer shared. "With an operation as big as this, there may be more involved that we haven't seen. By the way, a number of men will be coming this morning to trail the herd back to the Fisher place. Then you can go home too. Bet you're not sad to hear that."

"Not at all," both men replied at once.

About 9:30, a pickup came up the road. Jess didn't recognize it and brought his gun up to ready. It turned out it was Molly with one of the troopers. A sigh of relief escaped him, and Jess nearly cried.

Jumping out of the truck, both men were rushed by a grateful and relieved wife and friend. They held a group hug for some time, until they thought maybe it would be best to get going back home. The deputy had brought his pickup so he could send them on their way, and he would take the truck in to Cody as evidence. He also took pictures of everything around and went up the canyon where the truck was first spotted. When he finished, he handed Jess the key and said he would get his truck sometime next week, and not to worry about using it all they wanted. The trip home was one of the best times the three of them could remember. The relief and the comfort of being together was the perfect end to a very trying and dangerous event.

When Terry asked about Sarah, Molly shot a quick glance

to the back seat. She felt like she was seeing something that had never been there before. Terry was concerned about someone else, genuinely interested in another person's well-being.

"Sarah has really become a beautiful young lady in just a day. I don't know what I would have done without her, and she was able to give so much encouragement to others. She is just a different person. Everyone just loves her so much. When we were so worried that you and all the others were in a dangerous situation, she just came alive and encouraged everyone with her peace. Rob and Lottie spent some time with her late yesterday afternoon, and since that, it is amazing who Sarah has become." Molly said, tears in her eyes.

Driving into the Martin driveway, Jess couldn't keep the tears from flowing freely. All the neighbors were there and mobbed the three of them. Rob and Lottie stood a little to the side and watched in amazement. The day was complete. The mission accomplished, nothing could make the relief and joy fade. It was a good day.

CHAPTER 40

Late the next morning, a strange vehicle turned in at the Martin's gate and came up the drive. Rob was the first to recognize Otis Linderman driving the late-model SUV. A flood of relief swept over him, but also made him wonder, *Why is he here now, and what is he going to tell all these people?* It wasn't until he got out of the SUV and opened the back door that Otis Linderman's mission was beginning to take shape. John and Veda Mae got out of the back seat.

A cheer of relief and joy swept over those assembled. Questions and love flowed equally. This homecoming was more than anyone had even imagined. All the fear and anguish of the last few days were swept away. John looked well and strong. He walked up to Rob with strength and resolve. They hugged over and over, until John finally called for attention.

"I want to thank you for the generous gift of your friendship. Veda Mae and I can't begin to imagine being able to endure all that has happened without your help. These weeks in the hospital were not easy and not without great anxiety. But knowing what you all were doing here made it bearable. Veda Mae told me about your special care, Jess, Molly, and Terry. How do we thank you? Saying, 'Thank you, doesn't seem like enough!"

While this homecoming was happening, Rob was behind the SUV, talking with Otis Linderman. "I thought you were coming next week. What happened, and how did you find out about John and Veda Mae?"

"It is rather complicated, but I found out about the Fishers at your house since Veda Mae was staying there. In the course of time, we decided to come down here. As for coming now, I was in Cheyenne for some other business and had time after that, so I decided to rent this outfit and come up to Cody to see you. This is better than I could have imagined. To see the care these folks have for each other is refreshing to say the least. I want to talk to them some on the plans. But that can wait."

John saw Sarah standing next to Molly and asked Jess who she was. "Well it's a long story, and some of it involves you too. Let's just say for now that she was a stray and has come to be a trusted member of our family, unofficially that is. Nevertheless, we don't know what we would do if she were to leave. Both Sarah now and Terry are so much a part of us that it is as if they really belong to us. Molly and me couldn't be happier that they are here. Sarah did give us some anxious moments earlier on, that is before we caught her. I'll tell you later what all happened, but we caught her at your place. Well let's join the crowd. Other people want to talk to you too."

As they moved toward the crowd, Veda Mae joined the two men. Just outside the circle, Sarah came up to them, and with tears in her eyes, began to tell her story. It was a gruesome tale of being mistreated and alone. Of fear and having to be strong. When she came to the part about being in their house, she broke down and cried. Not wanting others to be alarmed, both Fishers moved beside her.

"I knew it was wrong to go into other people's houses, but I didn't have anywhere to go. I watched the place for a day, and no one came or went, so that night I slipped in. I ate everything I could find—crackers, bread, anything. I slept on the couch; it was so soft compared to the ground I had slept on the last few days, and I slept way past sunup. I heard the Martins's truck drive in. I didn't know what to do. Molly was helping with the chores, but she turned and looked at the house just as I pulled back the curtain. I knew she had seen it, but I waited. When no one came for a while, I thought they wouldn't come looking. Then I heard someone at the front door. It was Molly. I panicked and ran out the back, where Jess and Terry were waiting. Terry finally tackled me in a muddy spot and took me back to the house. Molly cleaned me up and took some of your clothes. Then we came here. I was so afraid they would just turn me over to the police. I didn't know what they did to someone who broke into a house, but it must be awful. I was surprised. All of them, even Terry, treated me like I had been there all the time. It was the most wonderful feeling I have ever had. Someone wanted me! Every day has been better. I am so sorry I broke into your house! I will work for you to pay what I owe for food and clothes. Whatever you say. Just don't send me to the authorities. Please forgive me."

Veda Mae was sobbing openly, and everyone else in that small group had wet eyes. Veda Mae engulfed Sarah in her arms. "You are forgiven. Nothing more is necessary. I am sure what you did in the house was not that terrible, and if it were, you would still be forgiven. We are so blessed to have these people taking care of us, we wouldn't think of not seeing that you are safe here in Somewhere too."

By this time, all the others had drifted around the six friends. There was not a dry eye in the group. Hugs were lavished on Sarah and Molly too. It was a special time.

Otis Linderman looked on as he stood to the side. His heart was full. He knew that these were people worthy of knowing what he wanted to do. "Could we all gather in a shady spot? I would like to tell you who I am and why I am here," he called out.

So they went to the cool back porch. Some sat on the floor, some sat on Terry's bed, and others stood around the edges of the group. This stranger had their complete attention. What was so important? He looked very rich, so how could he ever relate to these ranchers, rich in love for each other and struggling to make a living in the harsh Wyoming rangeland?

"My name is Otis Linderman. I came here because my father, Otis Linderman Sr., owned the BarJ Ranch that you all bought you piece of land from. My family, there are five of us left, wants to restore the ranch, and one of my brothers wants to make it into a first-class cattle ranch again. We found out that all of you are lacking legal documents for your land, and we want to set that straight. All of us Lindermans have become very wealthy. We started much the same way you did, with little or nothing, but God has blessed us with great careers and marvelous incomes. I say this to put your mind at ease. We don't want your land. In fact, we want to make sure you have what you paid for. And we are sure you actually paid for it. So here is the plan.

"First, we intend to employ a certified surveyor to reestablish the boundaries of the Linderman ranch, about eighteen sections, and the portions each of you purchased.

"Second, when the survey is complete, we will provide each of you with a certified description of your property and a deed that identifies you as the owners.

"Third, our interest is in providing the best possible circumstances for each family. Seeing you today makes me—and it will make my family—even more determined to make your futures as secure as we can regarding the land.

"Fourth, and this is most important, I can see you calculating how much this will cost you out of what you don't have. The Linderman family intends to do this for you absolutely free of cost. You will have the expense of filing the proper papers when it is finished, but that should be it.

"Fifth, we live in Ohio. So our representative here in Wyoming you have already met. Rob Evans, a wonderful godly man we have been privileged to meet, will be our personal representative. I don't know how we could have found anyone more qualified or highly spoken of by everyone we have asked. So that is the plan. It may take a long time to get it done. Are there any questions?"

Dead silence met Otis Linderman. No one said a word. No one moved. A few sobs were heard, but no one questioned what he had said.

"We met Rob when we first went to Cody to find out if we had any kind of documentation for our land," Jess began. "I had no idea this was in the works."

"It wasn't then," Otis said.

"Anyway, the kindness he showed us and the concern he expressed were things that could not be questioned," Jess continued. "Then when John had to be taken to Cody, we contacted him again, and his genuine concern and generosity were very generous. I wouldn't want anyone else representing us in this matter. We will get a fair deal with Rob on the job."

"Thank you, Jess," Rob said. "I want you to know a little of why I became so involved here. Many years ago, Lottie and I were down and out. It was then that I began thinking seriously about my understanding of God. I had always believed He was but was also far-off. As I studied and got in contact with others who had personal acquaintances with God's presence in them, we came to embrace His offer of a life worth living. When John Linderman, Otis Jr.'s brother, and I met him at church one Sunday, I found out he, too, was a follower of Jesus Christ and was to be trusted. Many conversations since have confirmed that he is motivated by his love of God and his absolute determination to live that out in his business dealings. Later, meeting Otis was just as comforting, and it is my privilege to represent the Linderman family in this most important business. If you have any questions or doubts, I will be glad to visit with you.

"As you all know, most of our men are out trailing the Fisher herd back to the ranch. They should be getting in sometime this afternoon. I am so amazed at the selflessness I have seen among everyone here. God is pleased, I am sure. I have only one more request of Mr. Linderman. I believe we need a meeting place in Somewhere so we could have a place for church services, and all the community could use it. What do you say, Otis?"

"That is a marvelous idea," Otis responded. Everyone cheered for the first time that afternoon.

"You said trailing the Fisher herd back to the ranch? What do you mean?" John asked.

"Well, it's a long story for another time, Jess said. "But in a nutshell, your entire herd was stolen two day ago. All of us, and the Meeteetse sheriff, located the rustlers, and they are in jail. Your herd, hopefully all of it, is on its way home as we speak."

John stood there dazed. He just couldn't imagine something like that could happen, but he also had an encounter with the rustlers, which he had never shared before.

CHAPTER 41

The rest of the afternoon was spent in setting food out for a well-deserved and happy feast of thanksgiving. They could see the dust of the herd coming into the Fisher yard, and everyone was beginning to relax. After the men got the cows in the corral, they watered and fed the horses and the cows. It was a good day. Jess's horses were with the herd, and they were quickly caught and led out. The horse in the barn was let out into corral. As the men saw John and Veda Mae and heard the news from Otis, they just couldn't believe that it was so. But they, too, were thankful.

As they enjoyed the feast, Paul Young brought up a forgotten subject. "When are we going to rebuild Jess's barn?"

No one spoke. After an awkward silence, Jess explained that he couldn't afford to do it until the calves were sold, and maybe that wouldn't be enough. So he had decided to build a lean-to on the old bunkhouse for the horses and the cow. The rest of the cattle would have to shelter in the hayfield for the winter. He had a more urgent need, a place for Terry to sleep during the winter since he couldn't stay on the back porch much longer now that they had two young people in the family.

Everyone cheered for this unexpected blessing. Terry and Sarah glanced nervously at each other and at Molly, not able to say anything, but with true gratitude in their hearts. Molly moved between the two most unlikely members of their family. She slipped her arm around them both and drew them close.

"You don't know how much you are needed and wanted. Someday we will tell you our story, and you will understand how very much you have each brought to us in such an unusual way," she whispered. Tears flowed freely down her cheeks and began to glisten in both young people's eyes. It was truly a marvelous event on a great day for the Somewhere community.

CHAPTER 42

S tanding off to the side, two men and a few women were conversing in low tones. No one noticed they were not in the group, but it didn't seem to bother them or anyone else.

"I think it could be done," one of the men agreed. "It wouldn't be fancy, but it would be sturdy, and it is needed."

"The Evans would not hold back all they have for any of the rest of us, so why not us for them," the older woman offered.

"Let's just keep this under our hats until we can talk privately with each of the other ranchers, maybe even Rob or Mr. Linderman. But let's not let it get out," the older man suggested.

"We better break it up and get back, or someone will get suspicious," one of the women suggested. Moving back into the crowd, each conspirator breathed a sigh of relief in spite of the excitement they could barely contain.

Sunday dawned bright and clear. Ronnie was up early, arranging bales and tables in the barn for the second church service in Somewhere. No one was more excited than he was, though he couldn't quite figure out just what it was that made him think about life in a different way. He had always been very self-sufficient and never needed anyone else. Then he met LaVerne at a country barn dance in Powell. Nothing would do but to have her as his wife. Two years later they were married, and Ronnie decided to buy this little ranch from the BarJ. Otis Linderman Sr. had made an offer that couldn't be resisted. But it wasn't LaVerne's idea of, "happily ever after." Now nothing could take her or them away from the hard work, isolation, and the satisfaction they found in western Wyoming.

About 10:30, people began to arrive. The Young's were first. They were the farthest away, but they were always first. Two more families, husbands and wives, the McNernys and the Fishers, were next. The Martins came in last, followed by ribbing from the others since they lived closest and were last to arrive.

"But we have more bodies to get ready than any of the rest of you do," Molly argued. No one objected.

The friendly teasing came to an end when John Fisher stood. No one knew what he had to say, but he had made it clear he wanted to share something very special with all his precious friends that Sunday morning.

"It seems like you never really begin to appreciate all the special possessions and people in your life until you come to a crisis of some kind. All of you know of our rustling episode because all of you were part of saving our ranch. But there's something you don't know.

"When I went out that morning to check on the cows and get ready to trail them to pasture, I never thought I would encounter any problems. I saddled my horse and began trailing my little herd up the canyon. It wasn't until I saw three strangers riding toward me that I had any idea that trouble was brewing. The first one told me to get off my horse. I did as I was told, but that wasn't enough. He hit me on the side of the head with his gun. I staggered toward the creek, trying to get away. Following me, this man pushed me into the water and beat me and kicked me hard. Then said he hoped the crows would find me before anyone else did. Everything went black. I don't remember anything that happened after that until I woke up in the hospital in Cody. I understand that Jess came over for something, saw the cows gone and the gate open, my horse just standing by the barn with a saddle on, and that frightened him a lot. He took the horse and rode up the trail, finding most of the cows in the hayfield. He rounded them up and started them down toward the corral. They knew where to go and went easily, but he didn't follow because he saw my bandana in a bush. When he went down toward the creek, he found me half in the water. I don't know how Ronnie got involved, but the chopper crew told me that he came to Meeteetse to report the problem. They came and flew me to Cody."

Veda Mae sobbed silently as John continued. "It wasn't until Jess told how he found her in the closet with the 12 gauge that she was able to talk again and how she was able stay in Cody to be with me. If it weren't for Jess, Molly, and Terry, I may not have made it.

"But what I really want to share with you is an experience that could only have come out of tragedy. Veda Mae and I are very self-sufficient. We did it ourselves, everything. We didn't need help from anyone. But God had a different idea. Jess put us in touch with a man who knows hard knocks, but he also knows where to get the strength to go on. You have all met him, Rob Evans. Rob and Lottie were my family for two weeks. Lottie took Veda Mae into their house to stay as long as was needed. Such kindness comes natural to the Evans. But as Rob told me, it wasn't always that way. Living on the edge of ruin as an attorney, he began to ask what was worth living for. He fought with his wife, hated his neighbors, and gave everyone trouble all the time. After a particularly difficult court battle, a wise judge demanded to see him in his office on Monday. Rob went expecting some kind of reprimand. What he got was advice that changed his life and his outlook. The judge asked, 'Rob, when are you going to quit fighting God and serving the devil? Every case you represent is just an opportunity to spray the court with your hatred and your fear.' Rob had no answer. The judge was right. Rob didn't think anyone had noticed and thought, since he nearly always won his cases, it made him popular. But that question hit him like getting kicked by a mule. Rob told me he couldn't breathe; it was as though all his breath was gone. Yes, the judge was right. Rob was angry with the whole world. So what did this judge have in mind that would make a difference? He painted a picture of the Supreme Judge, sitting in judgment of the world, and how He found no one who was without fault. He demonstrated His anger by sentencing the defendant in each case, which is each of us, to punishment worse than just death—to be cast into hell. Then he stood. The courtroom became deathly silent. No judge had ever done this before. He took off His judge's robe, walked to the front of the bench, grabbed the despicable criminal in His arms, and declared, 'I will take the penalty for this man's crimes. I will suffer his death. I will set him free and give him eternal life with Me.' Rob sat sobbing out his fear and his failure. The judge came beside him and told him the One who took the sinner's place was Jesus, and that he, too, could find the forgiveness and take away the penalty of death by accepting the sacrifice Jesus made for him on the cross.

"I didn't know it, but I was sobbing at the end of the story too. Rob shared with me how I, too, could be the criminal that God, the judge, could forgive and take away my penalty. That morning in the Cody hospital, I told God I wanted that kind of forgiveness and the life He offered. Veda Mae realized she, too, needed that kind of life and freedom from fear. So I just want to tell you that you can also find freedom from the kind of fear that you have living without God. You can have His life and purpose too."

No one moved. Someone began to sing, "What a Friend We Have in Jesus." The friendship brought many conversations about needing God's arms around them too. Something unexpected and great was happening in Somewhere.

CHAPTER 43

The next morning was no different than any other. Jess and his growing family ate breakfast about the same time as usual. The morning chores needed to be completed. But this was to be one of the most terrifying and transforming days in the Martin family.

Jess finished milking the cow and went to the bunkhouse storeroom to get some grain for the horses and feed for the chickens. As he started to open the door, he found it stuck. It had never been hard to open before. As he pushed it open, he detected a sound above the door he had never heard before. Fear leaped into his heart, and he backed away as quickly as could. He sat down on an old bucket ten yards from the storeroom to recover from the fear. Of what he didn't know, but it gripped him as nothing ever had. He couldn't seem to calm down, so he sat still, waiting but not knowing what he was waiting for.

It seemed that he had been there for hours before his senses and his breathing returned to normal, He thought about what happened. As he contemplated it, Jess noticed a wire hanging down from the middle of the door. A single wire. Jess tried to remember if there had ever been any kind of wire in the bunkhouse, but none came to mind.

Jess cautiously crept up to the door to see what kind of wire it was. Years ago he had worked for a road construction company, and they had used wire like this for their explosive detonators. But there had been two wires twisted together. This wire hung from the corner of the door frame. Cautiously looking inside, Jess saw the wire, one strand from the top of the door hanging down the middle of the door, and the other one going down to the bottom of the wall. He followed them around the side of the small shed and found where the two wires went out the back of the shed's wall through a tiny hole, probably made by a jackknife. Slowly he moved toward the door and out of the bunkhouse storeroom. Once outside, he sat again to catch his breath and try to guess what he would find at the other end of those suspicious wires. Going around the side of the bunkhouse, he carefully peeked toward the back wall. There he saw some fresh digging and dirt piled on something in the hole he felt had to be part of the mystery. Looking closer, he made out the word "dynamite" on the top of the box. His knees nearly buckled. A cold sweat came on his forehead, and he nearly lost his balance. Jess couldn't imagine what was going on. *Why would someone try to hurt anyone here in this remote area? What does it all mean? Who is responsible for it, and why us?*

Terry came up from watering and feeding the horses and saw Jess down on his knees. Running to him, he asked what happened. Jess couldn't talk. Fear and anger mixed his emotions into a boiling caldron. Terry knelt and asked again what was wrong. Jess feebly pointed and muttered a warning not to go near the bunkhouse.

White as a sheet, Jess stumbled toward the house with Terry holding him up. Molly came out with fear in her eyes and wanted to help. Both now were waved away as Jess sat on the porch step. He finally told them what he had seen and instructed Terry to get to town and report to the sheriff as quickly as he could.

Terry ran for the S10. He had filled it with gasoline last night, expecting to start haying again today. But when he turned the switch, the gauge registered empty. Not sure what to do, he hesitated for just a moment. Racing toward the corral, he whistled for Buck. The horse was waiting at the gate when he got there. He grabbed a bridle, slipped it on, and grabbing the horse's mane, he vaulted onto his back. Buck was in full gallop by the time they reached the main road. Knowing that it was less than a mile to Moore's, he pulled Buck to a ground-eating lope.

Just as he passed the Fisher ranch, John was driving out the gate. Seeing Terry race by, he turned and followed.

As Terry rode into Ronnie Moore's yard, Ronnie was coming up from the barn with a bucket of milk. He stopped short, sat the pail down, and ran toward Terry. Terry blurted out what had happened and that he needed to go to Meeteetse for the sheriff, but someone had stolen the gasoline from his pickup. John Fisher drove in right behind Terry. Stopping by the panting horse, he heard what Terry related.

Ronnie didn't hesitate. "Get in my pickup. We are going to town." John joined them, and they raced toward town with all the skill Ronnie had gained driving stock cars. On the way, Terry told them what Jess had found and how he found it. Both neighbors were white with fear after hearing the situation.

Sliding to a stop outside the sheriff's office, they all jumped out and stormed the office. Sheriff Park was doing bookwork at the desk and looked up, startled. Listening to the story, he grabbed a rifle, strapped on his revolver, and went to the radio, putting out a call for the help of a munition expert. Giving directions and location took only a few minutes. Then the sheriff motioned for them all to get going. He had not said more than five words to the three men since they entered the office, but they had not been wasted when he put out the call for help.

"Let's get out there as soon as we can. I hope Jess doesn't try something foolish in the meantime. This could be a disaster," Sheriff Parks barked.

If Terry thought they had come to town fast, it wasn't anything like the speed they took going home. Stopping at Ronnie's for John's truck, Ronnie went on to the Martin's along with Terry, on Buck. The sheriff was already talking to Jess, Molly, and Sarah when he arrived, and the faint sound of a helicopter could be heard coming their way. As Terry rode into the yard, the chopper was landing in the yard. Two men were being briefed on the situation as they pulled on protective clothing. Taking a tool kit, they cautiously approached the bunkhouse storeroom. Moving around to the back, they probed for dynamite with long poles. When they finally discovered the box and pulled the top off, it revealed a half-full case of dynamite, enough to level the tool shed, the bunkhouse and probably damage the house too. Disarming the detonators, the men began to look for clues, fingerprints, footprints, and so on. After taking pictures and carefully removing the wire and the switch, they loaded the dynamite into the helicopter and lifted off, saying they would get back to them as soon as they knew something.

Seeing the chopper disappear left the group in silence. Nothing seemed right to say. Finally, Sheriff Parks suggested that they go into the house and ask God to reveal what was going on and what they should do about it.

Arnie Parks was not only sheriff, he was also a leader in the community church in Meeteetse. He knew a thing or two about hard times and prayer. So as hard as he seemed on the outside, he gathered the few there in Jess and Molly's little house, reached out his arms as wide as he could, and showered a prayer of praise and petition on them. When he closed, Sheriff Parks assured them that he would be praying for them as well as all the others in the

Meeteetse Community Church. With that, he said he had to get back home and left.

No one moved. No one talked. But no one doubted that something good would come from this frightening circumstance and from the disturbing events of the summer. The question— What is going on and why here?—loomed large and foreboding.

CHAPTER 44

———✺———

September in Somewhere Valley started with a beautiful fall day. The chill of shorter days was in the air, and excitement was about to begin. Harry Linderman turned in at the BarJ gate. He hoped he could get the road done and the equipment moved so it wouldn't get too much attention at the beginning of his great adventure.

A large flatbed truck with an enormous bulldozer pulled off Highway 120 shortly after dawn. The driver stopped his rig, got out, and stretched. It wasn't long until two late-model diesel pickups pulled in behind the truck.

"I see you made it and turned at the right place. It is hard to tell where this road is anymore, but that won't take long to remedy," Harry Linderman said. "Jim is the best cat skinner in the country, and he makes every move count. We should have a decent road into the home place by evening."

"When is the lumber coming in?" the truck driver asked.

"It should be here by Wednesday and the building crew won't be far behind. By this time next week the Linderman BarJ will begin to look like a real cattle ranch. I have a cattle buyer working in Kansas City, picking out some choice critters to get started. It feels good!"

The "cat skinner" skillfully unloaded the D9 and began cutting the top of the two-track rutted trail that one time saw numerous cattle trucks, buyers, and family members going in and out of the BarJ Ranch. Each foot gave Harry a thrill that he could hardly contain. By noon, the road began to take shape about halfway to the house site. They were out of sight from the highway by then. The semi had left, and both pickups were hidden from view of Highway 120.

Harry had gone into Cody and bought enough food, especially hamburgers, to feed an army, and that is about what it took to satisfy the two men as they ate lunch on a log in a beautiful aspen grove. The smells and the birds made both smile and enjoy the quiet that much more.

Silence was shattered as the D9 came to life again and began the final push toward the ranch site. As the trail opened into a broad valley, they could see the decaying ranch buildings and corrals. The excitement of being this close was enough to spur them on until nearly dark to complete the rough road up to the old ranch house. Tomorrow Jim would go back over the whole driveway, and by tomorrow night, it would be nearly as smooth as Highway 120.

Pitching the wall tent and setting up simple housekeeping didn't take long. A fire was built from broken fence rails just outside the entrance of the tent. Cots and sleeping bags made it feel a little like a home away from home. Not really, but neither man complained. A meal of roast beef stew made the quiet evening complete. Harry brought out a pan of cinnamon rolls for an unexpected dessert.

"My sister made these for us just before I left Cleveland. I wasn't sure they would make it here in good shape, but it looks like she was right again," Harry explained.

Life was good. The men rolled into bed, turned off the lantern, and slept soundly. The sun peaked over the ridge and warmed the tent as both woke to the sound of a lonely coyote welcoming the dawn and birds singing on the tent. Breakfast was some bacon and eggs over the campfire. Coffee washed it all down, and they went to work.

Having cut out the basic road, Jim went about making it drivable. He pushed fresh soil up one side all the way to the highway. Then he did the same on the other side back to the ranch house. Having a good supply of soft dirt to work with, he began to spread and pack it into a masterpiece of highway restoration. When it came time to turn in, Jim was about fifty yards from the tent. It was too dark to see well, so he walked down to the tent, where Harry was cooking up some might good-smelling food.

"I went out and got a couple of sage grouse for supper tonight. I think we will enjoy having to live off the land and be able to see how God supplies our needs," Harry announced. "This place has been abandoned so long that there are lots of good eating within easy walking distance. I don't want to take anything we can't use, and there may be laws prohibiting hunting now, so we need to be careful. But making our dinner tonight will be from God's abundant flock on the thousand hills. Let's give thanks and eat. I am hungry and tired, and I can't imagine you aren't." After having all they could eat, the men slipped into their sleeping bags and were sound asleep before the fire had completely died out.

CHAPTER 45

Terry was jolted out of his sleep but couldn't tell what it was that woke him up. The sun had not shown over the ridge. In September it was coming up later, so he decided to get up anyway. It was much colder on the screen porch this morning, which made him wonder about his sleeping quarters for the winter months.

As he left the porch to do the morning chores, he looked toward the mountain that rose from the back of the haystack. It was covered with pine and aspen but had interesting clearings. He had seen deer quite often and began looking for some this morning.

Movement caught his eye, and he concentrated on one of the clearings high on the hillside. It wasn't a deer that emerged but a rider on a large black horse with a packhorse on a lead rope. The rider stopped, lifted his binoculars, and looked toward the ranch buildings. Terry stayed in the shadow and watched as the man scanned the entire yard. Apparently he didn't find what he was looking for and moved on, entering a thick growth of bushes and evergreen trees. Terry watched him emerge and disappear into the forest over the far ridge. Now he wasn't sure what to do. *Should I tell Jess?* He thought it best not to let any of the others know about this stranger, but it was troubling with the recent events strong in his memory.

Life went on as usual on the Martin spread. Chores to do,

horses to feed, and always eggs to collect. Jess came out just as Terry was finishing the milking and announced that this morning they would round up the herd and bring them in to a closer pasture so that winter feeding wouldn't be a problem. Terry looked forward to a long day riding Buck. He hadn't been on a horse for more than a month since the rustler incident. So herding cattle seemed to be the right thing to be doing.

Riding out Jess asked, "What do you suppose will happen next? We have had such an unusual summer that it will seem rather dull if something doesn't happen soon. We could have two more months until snow, or it could snow any time now. By the way, how are you doing on the porch? I bet it was pretty cool this morning?"

"I wasn't very ready to get out of a warm bed, but I survived the shock. It is pretty cold out there these mornings," Terry replied, wondering if there was some announcement coming. Jess didn't reply and was quiet for a long time.

As they came over the last hill, they could see the herd scattered along the hillside. Jess went one way and sent Terry around the north side, near the fence. The cows did not notice either rider until they started to close in on them from both sides. Moving slowly, Jess and Terry funneled the herd toward the ranch buildings. They were fat, and the yearlings looked much bigger than before. Good grass and fresh water made growing an easy job for this bunch.

Looking away toward the north fence, Terry spotted the black horse and rider at the edge of a clearing on the west side of a steep mountain. The rider was doing something on the ground with a funny-looking pole that had a large pancake on the top. Terry didn't know it, but the tool was a GPS surveying tool that gave the surveyor his exact location and established a point of reference for his next location. He whistled for Jess and waved him over. They both watched the surveyor for some time, not knowing just what he was doing. It seemed kind of sinister to them, but nothing gave them cause to stay any longer.

"What do you suppose he is doing over there?" Terry asked.

"I'm not sure, but it is over on the Linderman spread, so they must know he is out there," Jess replied. "I wonder if someone is at the home place yet."

The last of the herd was disappearing over the rise, as the men galloped to catch up. Everything was going as planned. Both broke into a laugh and moved apart to keep it that way. Getting the herd into the smaller pasture, which had good grass, was no problem. Closing the gate behind the last calf, both riders sat watching the young calves checking out the new pasture. They seemed satisfied it was okay.

CHAPTER 46

That afternoon, Jess suggested they drive over to the Linderman ranch and see what was going on. "We may not be able to get in there. The last time I looked, the road in wasn't fit for man nor beast. I'm not sure either of our outfits could be driven on it," Jess said.

"Let's take the S10 since it has four-wheel drive," Terry suggested. "We may be able to get close enough to see what it looks like at least."

As they approached the gate, Jess saw the new road, smooth and widened. He couldn't believe what he was seeing. Turning in, Terry slowed to test what he expected to be a rough, rutted two-tracker. As they progressed, it obviously wasn't that anymore, and it hadn't been this way very long. Rounding the last bend, the ranch buildings came into sight. The tent and the D9 Cat were obvious. No one seemed to be around as they drove up to the tent.

Harry heard them drive up and came out of the tent. "Welcome to the BarJ," he shouted and grinned. "Come on in and sit a spell." Getting out of the pickup, Terry and Jess couldn't figure out just what was going on.

Jess spoke first. "I'm Jess Martin from just down the road, and this is Terry. We just came over to see what the place looked like, but we maybe shouldn't have."

"Nonsense." Harry laughed. "I'm Harry Linderman. I hope

to be able to live here and get this place humming again. We just got the road fixed up, and the trucks with the house and the construction crew should be showing up any time. Welcome."

From there, the questions flowed fast and freely. Jess tentatively brought up the stranger on the mountain across from his pasture. "We saw a man on a black horse and a packhorse out on your land over by our pasture. He was acting kind of strange. He had some kind of contraption we didn't recognize. Thought you should know about it if he is not supposed to be there."

Harry laughed again. "That is probably Ike Sanders. He is the surveyor we hired to get some specific information on our land and yours."

"I saw him up on the mountain early this morning, looking over our place with binoculars," Terry said. "I didn't say anything about it since he rode on and seemed to be going somewhere else."

"Well he will probably be around for a couple of months. He is using a newer method of locating exact points, a satellite receiver and marking the locations on the ground. When he gets through, we will all know exactly what the boundaries of all our land really are. Pretty amazing."

"I guess we had better be getting home. Are you going to have enough people to do all the work you want to accomplish?" Jess asked.

"Probably. But if you are asking about some part-time work, we may be interested. It is going to be a big job putting this mess back together and making it look like a ranch again. Do you have a phone?"

"No one around Somewhere does," Jess said and laughed. "But if you go toward Somewhere, we are about a mile from the General Store on the right-hand side."

"Let's keep in touch," Harry offered, shaking hands with both men.

Driving home, Jess began to think out loud. "If I could work over here a few hours a week, we just may be able to get that barn built and the porch enclosed."

"Suppose both of us did?" Terry added. "It just may be a good thing." Neither said anything else the rest of the way home, but both were pretty much thinking the same thing about the possibility of extra income.

CHAPTER 47

Molly was watching out the window as they drove into the yard. She ran out to ask where they had gone. As the story unfolded, Molly was more and more excited. "I have wondered all along just how real all this Linderman talk was. I couldn't believe that a rich person from Ohio would even consider moving to Wyoming, especially this far out of town. It didn't make sense, but now …"

"I know just how you feel," Jess replied. "I couldn't figure it out either. Having Otis Linderman show up helped, but it isn't something that happens every day. So maybe it is true, and all the promises he made will be kept. By the way, how would you like to be able to build a barn and enclose the screen porch?"

"I would love that. But it just can't happen," Molly said firmly.

"Well maybe it can. We went over to the BarJ this afternoon, and they have a new road, are beginning to tear down all the old corrals, and are expecting the house to arrive on trucks any day now. And they offered us jobs if we want them. It could help financially and just might make it possible to get those things built. I think it could be a start," Jess said.

"Don't count you chickens," Molly said. Everyone laughed, but all of them hoped it was so.

"By the way, where is Sarah?" Jess asked.

"She walked over to Fisher's this afternoon to see Veda Mae.

184

They have a good friendship going and I am glad for her. She has grown up so much the last few weeks. I don't know what we would do without her now," Molly answered.

As they spoke, the Fishers drove into the yard. Sarah jumped out of the back seat and ran to Molly, throwing her arms around her, nearly choking Molly.

"I'm glad to see you too," Molly said.

Veda Mae came close and shared the scare they had when a strange car came into the Fisher yard that afternoon. Sarah said it looked like the men who had kidnapped her and threw her out on the road months ago. John had gone out with the shotgun and asked what they wanted. There was a heated discussion, and the men said they had seen Sarah—they said Sally—walking down this driveway earlier, so they knew she was there and would be back to get her. It was made clear they weren't welcome and had better not show up again."

"But I am sure they will try something," Veda Mae said. "They were pretty bad-looking customers and acted like they meant business. We came over to see if it would be all right with you to contact Rob and see if he could take Sarah to live with them for a while, until this is settled."

Shock registered on Molly, Jess, and Terry as they listened to this bizarre story. Jess recovered enough to say what he felt.

"Sarah, we love you like our own child. I wouldn't want anything to happen to you and would defend you with all I have. If you would go to Cody with Rob, we would think it best for now. What do you want to do?"

"I'm not sure. I am afraid. They hurt me a lot when I was with them. I don't want to leave my family, uh, any of you, but I don't want you in danger. I would go if you think it is best but …"

"Did you get license number and make of car?" Jess asked John.

"Yes. I have it right here."

"Would they recognize your truck?" Jess asked.

" I suppose so. It was in the yard."

"Then I suggest we send Terry to Meeteetse to see Sheriff Parks. Call Rob and meet him, or go all the way to Cody if necessary. I have Rob's phone number and the sheriff could call him. Or Sarah could ride with the sheriff to Cody if he thinks that would be safer," Jess suggested.

"I would be glad to do it," Terry said. "But what if they recognize my pickup?"

"That is a chance we have to take," Jess said. "Let's get going. Sarah, get your clothes. Terry, gas up the S10, and I will get the phone number."

CHAPTER 48

The trip into Meeteetse was uneventful. The sheriff was just leaving his office when they arrived. Terry shared the problem, and the sheriff got a funny look on his face. "I just got an APB on two men in a late-model car wanted on serious drug charges in another state, and the authorities thought they might be around here. What do you know about them, Sarah?" Sheriff Parks asked.

"I'm not sure what they did, but they always had a lot of cash. They could be the type to do that."

"Then I think I will get my personal car and take you to Cody myself, Sarah. You can come along if you want to, Terry. Let's get your truck out of sight and get moving."

The drive to Cody was fast. Just after leaving Meeteetse, Sarah called out, "That car that just passed, I think it is them. It looks like the same car they had when they got rid of me. I'm not real sure, but it looks like it."

"I'm glad you aren't driving in your S10, Terry. They may have recognized that too. I'm calling the Highway Patrol and have them watch out for that car. I believe I remember the plate."

Sheriff Parks picked up the mike and keyed in the code for the Highway Patrol. "Mike, here," a voice answered.

"Where are you now?"

"Just leaving Meeteetse, going south," Mike answered.

"Turn around and head north. We passed a late-model Ford, license 6-1397 WY. Arrest and detain. We think we may have a drug bust in the making. You may want to get backup, but I need to be in Cody this evening. Be back ASAP. Over and out."

The speed increased to nearly ninety, and the miles sped by. It wasn't long until they were in Cody. The sheriff knew just where to go. Stopping at the Evan's house, he quickly explained and left Sarah and Terry standing there with their mouths open.

"Let's get you settled and something to eat," Lottie said. "You must be worn out and worried. We'll pray that everything works out just right. Come on in."

In the confusion, Sarah had forgotten all about her clothes in the pickup. Terry had only the clothes he was wearing too. When they looked at each other, they knew just what the other was thinking and laughed. It was the first time they were able to relax since this morning.

"Now tell me what happened," Rob Evans said as they sat around the supper table.

Sarah shared her story from the beginning. How she went to visit Veda Mae and about the men showing up. Terry told them that he was chosen to get her to the sheriff and the trip to Cody, seeing the car, and why the sheriff needed to get back so fast. "I just hope they get them," Terry said. "We don't need another disaster in our family." He hadn't realized what he said until it came out, and it surprised him. Yes, they really were a family and he knew it now more than ever.

CHAPTER 49

Sheriff Parks didn't waste time on the return trip down Highway 189. He had his flashers blinking and hoped that he would be able to get to the place of arrest to help with putting these crooks away permanently. He didn't know why, but he felt that it was a part of his family being threatened, and he didn't like it.

Twenty mile out of Cody, Sheriff Parks saw two state trooper squad cars and another black car crosswise in the road. His heart was in his throat as he pulled up and stopped. One of the troopers noticed him and warily approached.

"There is no need for you to stop, sir," the patrolman said tersely. "We have everything under control and don't want to involve anyone else in this affair."

"I realize that. I am Sheriff Parks out of Meeteetse and called in the HP while on another call. Is Patrolman Jones on this call?"

"Yes he is, but you cannot approach him now. He is searching the car. We suspect a drug or other stolen items situation and do not want to contaminate the evidence," the patrolman replied. "The driver and passenger are in the squad car cage to prevent flight."

"Jim, take a look at this," the other patrolman called. As he looked up, he saw Sheriff Parks and invited him to see what he had uncovered too. "This will put these guys away for a long time. In addition to any other charges, we can probably connect them to the rustling op too. Here is a running iron if I ever saw one, and this bag of powder was probably used to melt ice. So let's call in the Feds and wrap this up."

"Thanks, Arny, for the tip," the patrolman said.

"I think I may have a material witness who has some history with these crooks. Let me know what the DA says, and we will see if the info could be of any help. I don't want to let this out if it isn't any good, but this person was also involuntarily involved with them some time ago," Sheriff Parks offered. "It helps to know these men are not on the prowl anymore. I am sure it will help the emotional well-being of my acquaintance and friends too. Keep in touch."

When Sheriff Parks went back to his car, he turned around toward Cody once more. It was late, and he decided to find a room and wait until morning to pick up Terry and Sarah.

After showering and relaxing a bit, the sheriff slid off the side of his bed and poured out his prayer of thanks to God for keeping Sarah safe in this situation. He was especially careful to remember Jess and Molly, who were no doubt beside themselves with worry. "Now, dear God, please bring justice to the folks in Somewhere. They have suffered so much this last year. Bring some good news to them that can begin to move their hearts to become vitally connected to you by your grace and mercy. Amen."

The sheriff slipped back in bed. He reached for the phone and called his wife to let her know that all was well, and he would be home in the morning. "Please pray for all the folks in Somewhere for a spiritual breakthrough and the peace they all long for. I love you. Bye."

CHAPTER 50

Arriving at Rob Evan's home in the morning was not as dramatic as yesterday. Rob greeted Sheriff Parks and invited him in. Lottie offered some coffee.

"That would be welcome," Arny answered. He shared a little of what happened and knew that Rob and Lottie would be careful with the information. "By the way, where are Sarah and Terry?"

"They took a walk down the street and should be back soon. They needed some time to get some things figured out they said. They are sure good kids. I think Jess and Molly couldn't have done better choosing a family if they had tried. God really knows what He is doing, doesn't He?" Lottie said.

"We'd better get back soon. Jess will be beside himself by now, and they have no phone to let them know what has happened. I guess it will remove all that when we get there," Sheriff Parks said.

As if on cue, Sarah and Terry opened the door. Seeing Sheriff Parks seemed to lift a load off their thinking. Sheriff Parks explained why he was there again.

"We better get going, or your folks will think I abducted you two." Sheriff Parks laughed.

Pulling into the Martin ranch late that afternoon, both Jess and Molly came out to see why the sheriff was coming to see them. As they approached, Terry pulled in behind the sheriff with the

S10. A sigh of relief escaped from Molly as everyone got out of the vehicles.

"Sorry we were so long in getting back, but it is a long story and not without extra drama," Sheriff Parks said. He told the whole story of starting to Cody and encountering the car that Sarah identified as having been seen at the Fishers's the day before. Molly was visibly shaken hearing of the capture of the criminals and how close they all came to another tragedy in Somewhere.

"We have been beside ourselves with fear the last couple of days. We couldn't understand why Terry hadn't come home after taking Sarah to Meeteetse, but it is so good to see all you again," Molly said nearly in tears.

"I'm sorry it turned out this way," Sheriff Parks replied. "There was no way to contact you. We really need to find out what the county can do to help get some kind of phone service up here. With all the problems you have had, we may have been able to solve some of them if we had known about them sooner."

"That would be good," Jess replied. "But it won't happen tomorrow, so we just need to make the best of it for now. We are just so relieved to see both the kids back with us."

Being called "the kids" brought tears to Sarah's eyes, and she noticed Terry was close. It was good to have a family. It was so strange to know that someone cared enough to worry about either of them. Sarah determined right then to make sure she lived up to the trust that Jess and Molly showered on them both.

"By the way," Sheriff Parks asked, "have you had anymore Sunday meetings since Rob left? I have been wondering if we couldn't get someone to come up here and begin to help out in getting a regular meeting started. I would suppose it wouldn't be like a regular church in town, but getting together and sharing God's Word and each other's burdens is what a church should be. Have you thought about it?"

Silence met the sheriff's question. It hadn't come up, and no one knew how it could happen. Arny Parks took that as a positive sign. "Well before I leave the valley today, I am going to visit all five ranches and invite everyone to get together again at the Moore's barn. I think Ronnie will be up for that, but just in case, I will go there first and clear with him. Are you folks in?"

"You bet," Jess nearly shouted. Everyone nodded.

The sheriff turned and left without more conversation but with a light heart and a prayer of thanks on his lips as he drove out of the ranch.

Ronnie and LaVerne were thrilled with the idea. There was no question they would be ready by next week for everyone to gather at their barn. The last two meetings were such an inspiration and encouragement, they couldn't see any reason not to do it regularly.

CHAPTER 51

Sheriff Parks drove home singing all the way. He called Beulah on the car phone and told her all about the last couple of days. He apologized for not letting her know before.

"I know how you get involved and don't think about anything but the problems in front of you. I worried some, but mostly I prayed for you that all would be well. I just heard on the radio that you were right about the drug bust on 120. They said it was a break in a long-standing investigation over near Powell. It looks like this incident did more good then we could have done on our own."

"That is good news, but I have even better news. We are going to have regular Sunday meetings in Somewhere beginning this week. What do you think of that?" Sheriff Parks shared.

"That is the best news of all," Beulah said.

The rest of the drive home was without incident, and Arny Parks looked forward to a day of rest at home. *Law keeping can just wait,* he thought.

When he arrived at home, Sheriff Parks asked his wife if she would like to take a ride up toward the BarJ Ranch. Packing a lunch, they left home and turned south toward Somewhere. Coming to the Linderman gate, they saw a semi loaded with lumber. Two more followed them through the gate. Sandwiched between the trucks in the caravan, they made their way down the newly constructed road toward the home place. As the ranch came into view, they saw Harry and the D9 Cat smoothing out the place where the corrals had been. They were amazed at the transformation from the last time they had seen the ranch nearly two years ago.

"I'd say they were serious about what they said they were going to do," Beulah said. "I can see the old place coming back to life. Can't you, Arny?"

"I sure can. Let's see who is here and get acquainted. This is marvelous and will be a real good thing for our neighborhood. It is exciting!"

Pulling up to the tent headquarters, Harry came out. "Come on in! You must be some of our neighbors, and you are welcome. Just let me direct the truck where they need to unload, and we can sit and have a cup of camp coffee—you know, more grounds than flavor." Laughing all the way out to the trucks, Beulah and Arny felt right at home. As they walked around the old house, it brought back memories of parties and community gatherings when they were a lot younger.

"It will be good to see this restored," Arny said.

"I'm Harry Linderman." Harry introduced himself and offered his hand when he returned. "We had another visitor a week or so ago, Jess something and his son. They were curious as you must be. And now you are seeing the real stuff getting ready to begin. The building crew should be here tomorrow, and the house construction will begin in earnest. We hope to have a Christmas celebration here this year, and it will top anything we have had for a long time. The whole family is planning to be here, and all the neighbors will be invited. I can't wait. I am rather excited about the whole thing!"

"I can see that," Beulah answered with a laugh. "We are the Parks, Arny and Beulah. My husband is the sheriff. I try to keep him out of trouble. It is a big job, but I love it. It is so good to see the ranch being restored. God must have a plan for the community if He sees fit to let this happen. We are excited too."

"Come in and sit a spell," Harry said with a flourish. "It ain't much, but the coffee is hot." The rest of the afternoon went by fast, and Beulah's lunch was much appreciated.

"We better be getting home," Arny said. "I have some catching up to do. Thanks, Harry, for your hospitality. We are excited to have you here." Driving home both Arny and Beulah quietly enjoyed what they had seen and heard. It was a bright spot in an otherwise troubling week.

CHAPTER 52

Jess stepped out of the Suburban in front of the supermarket in Meeteetse. A stranger approached him and held out his hand. He really wasn't a stranger as Harry greeted Jess by name and refreshed his memory of an enjoyable visit a couple of weeks ago.

"Sorry I didn't recognize you at first," Jess said enthusiastically. "We need to have you over for some of Molly's cookin' and get acquainted better."

"I would like that very much. The crew at the ranch would probably like a rest from my pushing to get things done. And I would like to talk to you about maybe buying some of your yearlings," Harry replied. "I think I could get our herd started with a few young cows from the ranches around here. They wouldn't need to get used to the altitude, and from what I hear, they bring top dollar at sale barns in the area. What ya say about that?"

"I am sure we could make a deal, and we are about ship anyway. Why not come over tomorrow, Saturday, and let's talk about it. I wouldn't be surprised if you could also scare up a few cows from other herds. I know most of ranchers sell off some of the older cows each year, which doesn't mean they are old, but need to be rotated to keep the herd fresh."

"I am bringing in a couple of good bulls from Kansas, which would also provide just what we need. So let's get together Saturday afternoon. My crew will want a couple of nights in Cody to sleep on a bed and get some dirt washed off. I'll see you around four then?" Harry replied.

Jess could hardly wait to tell Molly. This would work out great for all the ranchers. It was better than he could have expected since that was exactly why he came to town, to make arrangements.

"Molly, "Jess called as he burst into the kitchen, "you won't believe what just happened. I can hardly believe it myself."

Molly met him with skeptical eyes. With all the problems they had this past summer, she was fearful to ask what the news was this time.

"You won't believe what just happened!" Jess yelled again.

"Well what kind of problem do we have this time?" Molly asked.

"Not a problem, truly a miracle," Jess replied, eyes brimming with tears of excitement. "I met Harry Linderman at the General Store. He wants to buy some of our yearlings and probably some from the other ranchers up here. He is coming over tomorrow afternoon to see if we can make a deal. And he will ship the rest. What do you think of that?"

Molly stared in unbelief. She didn't know what to make of this news. For once this fall there was good news. Now she hesitated, uncertain. So much had happened, yet she, too, had heard what Rob and Mr. Linderman had said that afternoon in the summer. Timidly she turned away from Jess to clear her thoughts. When she felt his arms around her and his face next to hers, she sobbed out what had so long been bottled up inside.

"I know I should be happy, and I am for you and us. But so much has happened that is beyond my ability to cope and I don't know what to say. I am happy that Mr. Linderman wants to buy our stock. I am happy he may be able to help all our neighbors. But most of all, I am just tired and feeling out of hope. If it weren't for you and Terry and Sarah, I would have nothing!"

Turning in Jess's arms, Molly planted the biggest kiss on his surprised face and whispered, "I love you. You can't even know how much. I know how hard you work for me and now for Sarah and Terry, but I love you more than anything good that might happen to us, now or forever."

"Then let's tell the kids," Jess said, a puzzled look on his face. "'Tell the kids' has a nice ring to it, doesn't it? We are a family, and we could not have planned it any better than God did!"

CHAPTER 53

Saturday dawned bright and clear. Fall days had a different feel, and everybody at the ranch felt it. It was cooler, and the sun didn't come up as earlier. With the miking done, chickens fed, and horses coming up for their ration of grain—which was almost gone—Jess, Sarah, and Terry headed to the house and breakfast.

"We are just about out of some things from the store, so breakfast will be a little short this morning. Hope you don't mind. But there is something we need to talk about," Molly said and turned away. Jess kept his head down so no one could see his smile.

"Molly's right. All our resources are running on less than a quarter tank. If we aren't able to sell our yearlings, we may have to leave the ranch and find work somewhere else."

Sarah and Terry looked up, startled. "What does that mean?" Sarah asked tentatively. "I don't really belong here, so I could leave, and there would be more for the rest of you."

"If you leave, I will go with you, wherever that happens to be," Terry said. "It wouldn't be right for me to stay either. I have been given more than I can expect for a lot longer than you."

It was all Molly could do to keep from crying and laughing at the same time. She didn't realize how much they were all tied together, and from such different times and places. She burst into laughter, making Terry and Sarah feel very much ashamed. "I could no more let you to go than I could Jess. We love you too much, and to have been given this great gift has been one of the most precious gifts. You cannot leave under any circumstances! Tell them, Jess."

It took a while for Jess to regain his own control. But when he looked up, with tears running down his face, he told them what happened yesterday morning. He could barely contain his excitement about the possibilities it presented. Maybe even a new barn, maybe even a chicken coop, maybe even … well, he didn't know what else could be mentioned. But the news made the short rations taste better than any breakfast they had for a long time.

As they finished breakfast, they heard a pickup in the yard. It was Jim McNerny. Jess greeted him from the door and invited him in for coffee.

Jim was very quiet, not like he usually was. Closing the door, he took a seat at the table and shared his experience. "I just saw a strange guy, like a mountain man, on a big black horse with a pack mule behind him riding over close to my west fence. I don't like it, not at all. I yelled at him, but he wouldn't answer. So I came here to see if you would go with me to find out what he is doing near our property, and I suppose on Linderman land," Jim related with a worried look.

"I think I saw the same man about a week ago on the mountain to the north of us," Terry related. "Then Jess and I saw him again out on west pasture about two miles north on the side of a hill with some kind of stick with a bowl on top of it."

Before he could continue, Jim broke in. "That's the guy, all right. Can't be anything good about his being around here with so many strange things happening this summer. We got to run him off before he steals some of our cattle."

Hiding a chuckle, Terry told Jim what he needed to know and how they found out. You could see the relief register on Jim's face.

"But what if it isn't the same guy," he asked. "He looks kind of shady to me. I hope you are right, but …"

"Why don't you drive over the BarJ Ranch and see what is going on over there? Ask for Harry, and he can tell you all you need to know. I have a feeling he will want to buy your yearlings. He offered to buy some of ours and to ship them if he could have some young stock. I think he will pay top dollar too," Terry suggested.

"I will just do that. I need to go to town, so it wouldn't be out of the way. Leona wants to go too. I just hope I can get through on that road 'cause it ain't much to look at."

"You won't have any trouble. It is a smooth as 120 now," Terry shared.

About twenty minutes after Jim left, they saw him and Leona go by, headed toward town. Everyone breathed a sigh of relief at what could have been more trouble.

"Hope he doesn't miss Harry," Jess said.

CHAPTER 54

Harry Linderman showed up about 2:30. They talked awhile and then took his pickup and drove out to the winter pasture.

"Those are good-looking yearlings," Harry said. "How many do you have in there?"

"I think about forty," Jess replied.

"I'll take them all. Are they branded?" Harry asked.

"Yes, so we will have to through the brand inspector in Meeteetse. But that isn't a problem. He is easy to get along with, and it won't take long to check them and make the sale," Jess replied.

"Oh, I don't want to buy them. Just thought I'd take them off your hands as a matter of convenience," Harry replied with a straight face.

The silence was deafening. "That is what you wanted, wasn't it, Jess?" Harry asked quietly. But he couldn't contain himself and burst out laughing. "I wouldn't think of stealing these good-looking yearlings. It was fun to see your face though! When do you think it would be good time to ship? Do you think any of the other ranchers would want to go together on shipping?"

"I'm sure they would. Did Jim NcNerny come by to see you this morning?"

Sarah finished her chores as she thought about what had

happened to her in Somewhere. Remembering all the terrifying and uncertain days brought tears to her eyes. But this was a good day, filled with a good event for a change. What a day to be included in a family for the first time in her life. She wasn't sure who to thank or how to do it.

CHAPTER 55

Saturday dawned bright and cold. An east wind made morning chores hard at the Martin ranch, but Terry felt warm and secure behind the milk cow. He finished the milking and was about to feed the horses that had come up for their daily ration when Sarah came up behind him.

"Nice, isn't it?" she said quietly.

Startled, Terry turned around, nearly knocking over the milk pail. He caught it just in time not to lose more than a splash.

"I didn't hear you come up. But it is nice. I can't think of anyplace I would rather be than right here. Just look at that sky and the color of those little clouds. I suppose it won't be long before we see a change in the weather, but to hear the birds, see the sky, and just soak it all in, it can't get better. So what got you up so early?"

"I couldn't sleep anymore, and I wanted to talk to you alone. We don't get that chance much. But I was wondering if you feel the same as I do about Jess and Molly. I don't remember my mom ever teaching me anything or even speaking a civil word to me. And I know they aren't my parents, but I got to wondering if you felt the same way," Sarah suggested shyly.

"You bet I do," Terry replied. "I have a sister, I guess back in Ohio, but she's nothing like you. She never helps with anything, just complains. My little brother is the same way. My dad was gone most of my life, and Mom worked so many hours a day I didn't really know either of them well. I wandered into Somewhere in my S10, stopped at the General Store, and Jess was the first person to talk to me. They offered an overnight in the old bunkhouse, and I have been here ever since. It is really home for me."

"Do you think there is something we can do for them to show our appreciation?" Sarah asked.

"I don't know what it would be, but it is a good idea," Terry agreed.

"I have a little money, about $3 I hid in my dress when I was pushed out on the road. It isn't much but ..." Her voice trailed off.

"I have a little left from before too. Not much, maybe $10 that I didn't have to spend on a room that night. I intended to steal gas the next day and be long gone. So that is a little. We could go to Meeteetse in my pickup and see what we could find at the General Store. But it won't be enough, will it?" Terry wondered.

"Let's try it. Right after breakfast, before we get involved in something. Let's just leave and not say anything about it."

Picking up the milk bucket and heading to the house, they made conspiratorial plans for their secret mission. As they came into the house, breakfast was just getting started, and Sarah pitched in while Terry took care of the milk. By that time, Jess was up and ready to eat. They didn't notice anything wrong until Molly said the prayer. Jess didn't eat much and just held his head.

"I have this terrible headache, and I feel like I am burning up," Jess complained.

"I think we better try to get the doctor to come out here and see what is wrong," Molly said. "Terry, can you go to Meeteetse after we eat and see what can be done? I can take care of things here until you get back."

"Sarah and I can do that right after breakfast," Terry said.

Curiosity captured Jess. He looked up quickly, which wasn't a good idea, and stared at Terry. Terry didn't act as though he saw it but felt embarrassed just the same.

It was decided. Sarah and Terry were on the road to Meeteetse within the hour. Out on the road, both of them looked at each other. Laughter burst out and lasted for a long time.

"They don't know how easy that was, do they?" Terry asked. "I bet us doing something together never entered their minds. But I for one am glad to be going. I don't know if there is a doctor in town, but someone must take care of stuff like that with a school and sports and stuff. I guess we just have to ask the sheriff. He would know."

"Good idea," Sarah replied. "He will know, or he will do it himself. I like him."

Terry wasn't so sure about the liking, but he had become better acquainted, and after Rob had taken his side in the arrest, Sheriff Parks had become a friend of sorts. Anyway, it was decided they would go there first.

Parking by the sheriff's office, they noticed no car there. Sarah and Terry walked over to the General Store and asked where the sheriff could be found. The clerk didn't know but made a call and told them he would be there in a few minutes.

"I guess it's time to shop then," Sarah said. "Maybe we can at least get an idea and decide later. What should we look for?

"I have no idea. You go that way, and I will go the other. Meet you back there by that water cooler," Terry suggested.

In a short time, they had walked around the entire store.

"Find anything?" Sarah asked.

"Not really. Neat stuff, but nothing clicks with me," Terry replied. "Oh, there's Sheriff Parks stopping outside."

Leaving the store, they met the sheriff as he got out of the patrol car. "You youngsters are kind of early to be in town, aren't you? I bet you skipped out on the chores," Sheriff Parks said with a laugh.

"No. Sorry, we aren't guilty. Jess got up this morning quite sick. Molly was worried about him, so she sent us to get a doctor. We didn't know who that would be, but we know you. So ..."

"Well, ain't no doc here. Most cases of anything serious go to Cody. Often get advice from my wife if needed. How long did you say he was sick?"

"We didn't say," Sarah replied. "We just found out this morning, but he doesn't look good to me."

"Let's go see Beulah. She can ask some questions and make a better decision. Just follow me," Sheriff Parks said as he got in his patrol car.

On the way to his house, Sarah and Terry tried to think of what to buy but nothing seemed quite right. They decided to wait until they heard what Buelah thought and then go back and look again.

As they pulled up in front of the house, Buelah was coming out the door. She waited for them all and invited them in. Seating them in the living room, she went to the kitchen and returned with coffee and cinnamon rolls piled high on a tray.

"Just make yourself at home. You came in kind of early, and growing kids need to eat more often." Buelah chuckled. "Now tell me about Jess. We have come to appreciate all of you, especially Jess and Molly, so much out there."

"Well I got up and went out to do the milking and other chores, but usually Jess is already out. I didn't think much about it until we came in, and he wasn't up yet. Just as we were about to eat, he came to the table. He didn't say anything but just held his head in his hands. He looked up once, and he seemed in real pain. It isn't like him. He is so strong!" Terry explained.

"Did he eat of drink anything?" Beulah asked.

"No, nothing. Just sat there," Terry answered.

"Did he, was he okay when he came to the table?"

"I didn't notice anything wrong. Did you Sarah?" She shook her head.

"Has he been sick the last few days at all?"

"Didn't look like it," Sarah said.

"I think we should take a run out there right away." Beulah turned to Sheriff Parks. "He is never sick, and this doesn't sound good. I don't know what is wrong. We can use the patrol radio to get some doctor advice."

"Good idea," Sheriff Parks replied. "I will go down to the office and arrange for backup while I am gone. You gather up what you need and meet me there."

It was decided that Beulah would ride to the station with Terry and Sarah, if they all could get into the front seat. It was a challenge. Beulah said, "I can drive a stick shift just fine, if you don't mind, Terry. And you could get in the back for this little bit. Okay?"

"Great," Terry said, relieved. They made the switch and arrived at the office shortly.

Sheriff Parks met them and put Beulah's supplies in the patrol car. As Terry was getting back to the driver's seat, he came up and shared what she said. "If it is all right with you, I think we better get there as fast as we can. This doesn't sound good. That okay with you?"

Terry nodded. He didn't know what to say and felt helpless. Sarah gasped at the response but couldn't say anything either. They just sat there, trying to get their feelings straight as the sheriff left the parking lot in a hurry.

"I don't know what to do," Terry said dully. "What if ..." But he couldn't continue as a sob caught in his throat. "I wonder if the pastor at the church would get his folks to pray for us? I think it is worth a try. What do you think?" Sarah just nodded, looking at Terry through tear-filled eyes.

Terry ran into the store and asked the clerk where the pastor lived. She gave a knowing look at Sarah in the pickup, which made Terry angry.

"This is an emergency! Our friend out in Somewhere is ill, and we don't know what is wrong! We need …" He couldn't continue for the sob that wanted to escape.

"I'll call him right away," the clerk said. "He is a very kind man." As she dialed, she turned her back toward Terry to hide her embarrassed face.

"Pastor will be here shortly," the clerk said. "He remembers you from the rustling thing out there and how the church prayed for you. We all were so thankful when we heard that everything worked out quite well. Can we pray for you again? Who is sick? I'll get all our folks praying right away."

Overwhelmed, Terry said quietly, "It is our boss. Well no, but the people who took us in, Molly and Jess, are just like Mom and Dad to both of us. We couldn't bear having anything happen to them. Thanks, and sorry for—"

"Here's the pastor now," she interrupted.

Looking out he saw a giant of a man going to the S10. Sarah got out and was smothered in his arms. It was obvious she was sobbing and telling Pastor Mylon Hastings what was going on. Terry went out and got the same big hug. The three of them stood there as Pastor Hastings prayer for Jess could have been heard all over town. And so it was as phones began to ring, and the call to prayer was relayed to every member, who called another, and all prayed for God's timely attention and intervention for Jess Martin and for his wife, Molly, out in Somewhere, Wyoming. They all remembered the rustling incident and felt like they were a part of their family.

CHAPTER 56

On the way home, Sarah suggested they stop and let the Fishers know what was going on. Veda Mae was glad to hear the news but troubled by the symptoms.

"It's hard to tell what is going around these days," she said. "It could be nothing, but it could be serious. Be sure to keep us updated on the situation, and let us help if we can."

"We will, and it has been so good to see you again. It seems like the days go by without ever visiting our nearest neighbors," Sarah said.

As they were leaving, John ran out and flagged them down. "I heard that Linderman is interested in purchasing our yearlings and shipping the rest for us at a good price. Do you know anything about that, Terry?"

"I sure do. Harry Linderman was at our place last week and looked over our yearlings. He was very excited about buying some of them to help him get his herd started. He is supposed to come back next week and get together with all the ranchers to see what can be worked out on purchases and shipping the rest of our stock where we can get the best prices. I think it will work out great for everyone. He has trucks I guess of his own or knows who does. I will make sure Harry Linderman visits with you about it."

With that, the kids drove home silently. When they pulled into the yard, Sheriff Parks was in his car, talking on the radio. He saw them and motioned them over, holding up his hand to wait as he finished his conversation. "Just get here as soon as possible!" they heard him say. Fear leaped into their faces as they waited eagerly to talk with the sheriff.

Putting down the mic and coming out, Arny Parks took off his sheriff manner and went into friend and comforter mode. Sarah and Terry waited, fearing the worst.

"Jess is not responding to anything we can do for him," Sheriff Parks said softly. "We have called the ambulance to take him to Cody Hospital for diagnosis and treatment. It just isn't something we have seen around here, and we don't know what to do for him. The doctor in Cody isn't sure either, so they have sent out the air ambulance to pick him up. It should be here any time now. Let's pray for him together right now. Jess is a strong man and to have this happen isn't ordinary. Lord, God, we pray for our dear friend Jess." Arny couldn't go on. A sob escaped before he could control it, frightening Terry and Sarah even more. They heard the chopper in the distance and looking up, they saw it circle the ranch and settle in the yard.

EMTs jumped from the copter and with a stretcher, followed Sheriff Parks into the house. "Are you the Martin kids?" the pilot asked.

"Well, it's kind of complicated, but I guess we are as close as they're going to get. And we think of them as our mom and dad," Terry answered.

"Do you think they will be okay?" Sarah asked.

"We are going to do our best to see to it," the pilot replied. "These EMTs are top drawer, and the hospital is just as good. If Mr. Martin can be cured, they will do it."

The EMTs came out the door carrying the stretcher, with Molly following closely behind. She ran out to Sarah and Terry, who were standing off to the side, and drew them into a desperate embrace.

"I am going with Jess. Can you take care of the place for a couple of days? I know, it's not what I want either. But they think I should be with him."

"You go," Terry ordered. "And don't you even think about us here. We can get help if we need it, but I don't see why we can't take care of everything."

Sheriff Parks had heard the conversation and said softly, "And if they can't, I—we—will stay here with them. But these are amazing young people. I say you should keep them. They aren't made like this anymore. Just you get Jess well, and don't worry about anything here!"

Molly was helped into the Life-Flight chopper as it started to warm up. As it lifted, Sarah melted into Terry's arms and sobbed. Beulah Parks put her arms around both of them and assured the two teens of their love and concern.

When the chopper could no longer be seen or heard, Sheriff Parks said he needed to get back to town. He and Beulah got into the car and opened the windows. "Now you get to us as quick as you can if you need something," the sheriff said. He started to say something else, but instead closed the window, backed around, and drove out the gate, turning on the road toward Meeteetse.

CHAPTER 57

S arah and Terry walked toward the house. They sat on the step, almost afraid to say anything. Terry was trying to decide what to do first and how everything was going to work as they became ranchers on their own. The first thing they must do was to go to the Fishers and tell them what had happened. Then he wasn't sure what was next.

The sun was slipping behind the mountain, causing the evening chill to let them know they couldn't sit here forever. So they drove silently over to the Fisher ranch and shared what they knew and what had happened.

Veda Mae was adamant that John must go to town and call Rob to let him know of the events out here. "Rob and Lottie will be such a comfort and help. They would be so disappointed to find out we didn't tell them or ask for help," she said. "Besides, they are almost family for both our families, so you have to go now!"

John smiled, knowing he wanted to go as much as Veda Mae demanded, so he agreed as long as the kids would stay for supper while he was gone. He felt that everyone in the valley should know what happened, too, so he planned to tell them before going to town.

Every rancher was glad they were included but terribly troubled for Jess Martin. It brought up another subject at the first stop at the General Store in Somewhere. Ike was just closing up. John shared the news and then told him they would have a meeting at his place tomorrow evening to talk about the plan to rebuild Jess's barn. Ike agreed enthusiastically and assured John he would be there.

Next was McNerny's. They were just as concerned and enthusiastic about the barn, as were the Young's and the Moore's.

Having spread the news, John hightailed it to Meeteetse. The General Store was just about to close, but when they saw him drive up, they motioned him in. He was about to put his coins in the pay phone when the owner came up and asked where he was calling. As John shared the news yet one more time, the owner offered his private phone at no charge, and John called Rob Evans in Cody.

Rob was troubled to hear the news but glad John had called. "We will go to the hospital right now and try to make contact." John also told Rob about the barn project the ranchers had cooked up. Rob insisted that he be allowed to get involved. He had a good friend who built barns for a living. They were simple, sturdy, and cost-saving. "Would you like me to contact him for you?" Rob asked.

"Please do. We hadn't gotten that far, so we hadn't even thought of materials. That will make this go well. We would like to have it done before Jess comes home, so we don't have a lot of time. Thanks again for your special friendship." John hung up the phone and turned to go.

"All of you Somewhere folks do a lot of trading here in Meeteetse, and I can't see why we don't let the folks here know about this project. They may just be interested in helping too," the store owner said.

"That is very generous of you. Well I better be getting home." John turned to leave.

As John got in his pickup, someone parked next to him. Jumping out of the driver's door, the man ran up to John's truck. "I'm Pastor Mylon Hastings here at the Meeteetse Community

Church. How is the rancher who is ill? We talked to his kids when they called the sheriff. The whole church has been praying for him."

John was overwhelmed. He briefly shared the events and the not-so-satisfying status of the story so far. The pastor assured him of the continued care of his congregation. "We mean to be caring for our neighbors around here. Not many ranches left, but people live there just the same. God bless you."

John turned into the lane at his ranch late that evening. The S10 was still in the yard, and as he entered the door, he was greeted by sighs of relief. Everyone feared something bad had happened to keep him from getting home earlier. As he shared the whole story, Sarah began to cry again. Asking what the problem was, she replied, "I feel so cared for by all that is being done for my family. It is so wonderful I just can't help it."

Driving home that night was filled with joy and fear for Terry and Sarah. They made plans on who should sleep where and who would take care of which chores. They were the ones they always did, but it seemed like they needed to be organized.

Seeing the dark house brought the fear back some, but getting the lamp lit and a fire started made it feel like home again. Sarah fixed the bed in Jess and Molly's room for her, and Terry moved back to his old room in the lean-to. He brought in the few things he had on the back porch, and they were ready for a night alone.

Terry found the shotgun. He had learned how to load it from Jess, so he kept it in his room and made sure he could easily find it in the dark. With that, the two strangers who had become friends and now seemed like a sister and brother went to bed, hoping to sleep. But sleep came slowly, and the night sounds kept them both awake long into the night.

When Terry woke, he saw the sun was already high in the sky. Jumping into his clothes, he rushed out with the milk pail.

He found the cow right where she always was in the corral. As he was milking, the horses came in for their treat and water. Even being late, everything was coming together just fine. Terry noticed the cow wasn't giving much milk. He was troubled about it and decided to ask John when he came over what was wrong.

After he finished, he put the horses in the corral. They didn't seem to like it, but Terry wanted to ride out and check on the cows today and didn't want to have to find his horse. He gave them some new hay, and they munched contentedly, as did the cow. Terry felt good. He knew this could work. He thought of Sarah in the house fixing breakfast, and that felt right to him too. There was just something he didn't quite understand about his feelings when he thought of Sarah these days. It was different, and it felt good.

Putting the milk in the well house, he headed to the house, hoping breakfast was about ready. He was hungry. As he opened the door, a strange smell came to him. He hadn't smelled it before and asked what it was.

"I burned the eggs and had to start over," Sarah told him. "I needed some lard in the pan first and then the eggs. But they are about ready now, so get washed up. Want some coffee?"

Drying his hands and face, he mumbled he did, and Sarah put a cup on the table. It looked good, and bacon and eggs looked just like old times. As the two sat across from each other, they didn't know how to give thanks for the food. So Sarah just said, "Dear God, thanks for the food. Amen."

And they ate. It was not nearly as tasty as Molly's cooking, but not so bad for their first try alone. Terry smiled at Sarah and said it was good. She smiled back and said, "Thanks," even though she knew it wasn't. They both laughed. Love covers a whole lot of mistakes.

CHAPTER 58

The days wore on, and the worry increased on Martin Ranch. Two tired novice "ranchers" kept plodding through the days. It seemed much longer than five days since the chopper had lifted off, but they counted them again at supper. Monday, Tuesday, Wednesday, Thursday, Friday. And now it was Saturday, day 6. Keeping busy had helped, but the sadness was creeping in fast. No word made waiting painful.

About 2:00 p.m., Terry was filling the S10 with gas. He heard a pickup coming up the road and recognized Harry Linderman driving. It turned in at their gate, and just after that, Paul and Sally Young turned in too. Not five minutes passed before John and Veda Mae Fisher and Ronnie and LaVerne Moore followed by Jim and Leona McNerny. Last was Ike from the General Store stopped in the yard.

Men got out of their rigs and took out shovels, rolls of twine, a long level, and various stakes and hammers. Terry watched but couldn't say a word. What was going on? What are these neighbors about to do to him or to this ranch?

Terry approached Harry Linderman and bluntly asked, "What do you guys think you're doing here anyway? You can't just—"

"Well," Harry said, cutting Terry off, "we have a plan, and we intend to carry it out right here in this yard of one of our dearest neighbors and friends. Every one of us have 'conspired,' if you want to call it that, to replace a burned barn. I understand it has been much too long coming, but now we have the manpower and the tools, and we are going to do just that! If you don't like that, then just stand aside and stay out of the way," Harry said sternly. But he couldn't keep a straight face for long and burst out laughing, along with all the others, at the blank look on Terry's face. "Do you have any objection?"

Terry didn't know what to say, but he was catching on real fast that there would be a barn on this place again if these folks had anything to do with it. "I suppose. Of course it will be all right!"

"Great," John Fisher said. "Now where was Jess planning on rebuilding if he ever could?"

Terry pointed out the level area where the old barn had stood, next to the haystack. He mentioned that Jess wanted to make it a little larger and include a chicken coop too.

That is how it started. The men measured and drove stakes. They strung twine from each of the stakes, and the layout of the barn began to take shape. It was marvelous and exciting to every man and woman there. Terry just couldn't hold back the tears and finally retreated behind the bunkhouse and cried. He didn't want anyone to see him, especially all those out there working. What would he tell Jess when he saw him?

"Where is Terry?" someone yelled.

"He's around somewhere," a reply came.

Terry went around the other side of the bunkhouse and showed up again. John Fisher came up beside him and asked him to walk up to the house with him. They sat on the steps, and John couldn't help but give Terry a little hug.

"Now there is one thing you have to understand about this barn. The entire barn is on a truck headed this way. It should be here early next week. We have been planning this for months, but when Harry came along, he had connections and the means to get the barn here. Jess and Molly don't know nothin' about this. We had been trying to think of a way to get them gone for a couple of weeks. I'm sorry it was such a tragic situation that did it, but the barn will be complete in about four days after it gets here. We have the blueprints, and that is what we are doing now, laying out the floor plan and putting in holes for the poles that support it. Jess and Molly must not know anything, so don't tell them about this. Okay?"

Terry was stunned. This was just the best thing that had happened since he could remember. He didn't know what to say even if he could have said it. He sat still, looking at John for some time. Finally, he responded. "I don't know what to say. I have never seen anything like this happen to anyone in all my experience. You don't have to worry that I will say anything. I can't even if I wanted to, which I do. I want to know how Jess is and all that, too, but, I just don't know what to say."

"You are a special man, Terry. The day you showed up at the store in Somewhere was a blessing to everyone in the valley. Jess and Molly just happened to be the lucky family to get you. Thank you for staying and taking on this heavy load these days. If you need help, just ask. I don't think I could do what you are doing."

Just then Sally Young came out of the house with a big pitcher of lemonade. "Come and get it or miss out," she called. She didn't have to say it twice. Everyone came like flies to honey and enjoyed a few minutes rest.

Meanwhile, Veda Mae and Sarah were walking up the path to the spring behind the house. Veda Mae was saying the same things to her that John had shared with Terry.

"It must have been very difficult for you these few days. Being thrust into a place of responsibility in a strange set of circumstances is not an easy time. When John was hurt, I didn't know what I would do if he didn't survive. You must feel much the same way now. So I want to encourage you to use all your strength and all your God-given understanding to make this a real growing time. The men are going to replace Jess's barn, hopefully before he gets to come home. They are doing it because Jess is always one to be at the front to help, even at the expense of his own responsibility. And Molly can't be outgiven. She gives more than any of us women in Somewhere Valley have even thought of giving. And you, Sarah, are a lot like her. You came here with nothing, even less than nothing. But you have provided more than you can imagine to Molly. You probably don't know it, but the Martins cannot have children. Your coming has completed a family for them that could not have been done any other way. God has a marvelous future for you, Sarah. Just put all your trust in Him. Come to Him by believing that He really does love you and has provided a way for that love to be shown to others. If I had found you in my house, I would have just as quickly wanted to keep you as Molly did. You are becoming a beautiful young lady that God has placed here to help Jess and Molly feel God's blessing as they give their blessing to you. God will give you strength to make it happen."

Sarah's tears flowed freely as Veda Mae engulfed her in a special hug. She knew then, as she had hoped but feared it wasn't, that this was where God brought her to learn about Him and to bless Molly and Jess. And there was Terry too.

Nearing the house on the way back, the two women heard a tremendous cheer. Coming into the yard they saw the first of the corner posts being set for the barn. Everyone cheered. A new day had begun for Jess and Molly Martin.

CHAPTER 59

Lottie Evans stood outside the hospital room where Molly kept watch over Jess. Her heart ached. Praying didn't seem effective. Loving them both didn't help. Lottie looked at her watch for the hundredth time that afternoon. The doctor had said he expected a change in Jess, or they would have to Life-Flight" him to Denver or Billings for more intense treatment than he couldn't provide in Cody. Lottie asked God again to intervene. She had done so for two weeks now, but nothing seemed to move Jess toward recovery. No one really knew what caused the pain or the coma. Every day seemed to mock them and make them doubt that anything could be done. But Lottie and dozens of others she had enlisted around Cody did not give up. "God will come through," she had said over and over. But this test was more than she had ever had.

Wednesday morning dawned dark and overcast, rainy and cold. It fit Rob's mood at the office. His secretary knew of the heavy personal and spiritual burden he was carrying, and she had shouldered part of that burden, along with nearly one hundred others in Cody for Jess Martin's complete recovery.

Rob picked up the call and answered as calmly as he could, "Yes, this is Rob Evans. What is it that I can do for you?"

"Well for one thing, you can tell me what is going on in Somewhere. I haven't heard from Harry in three weeks. I know he is busy, but we have some decisions to make, and he better let me know what is happening," John Linderman thundered.

"John, it is good to hear your voice, but I can't really tell you what is happening there either. Those folks have suffered these past six months as you know, and two weeks ago, Jess Martin came down with a mysterious head pain and has been in a coma since he had to come here by Life-Flight two weeks ago. I can't get anything done for concern. I pray, but I don't feel God cares. I know He hears and does care, but the feeling isn't there. So I can't help you with the BarJ problems this morning. But it is good to hear your voice, brother."

"Well, I'll be," John replied. "I had the feeling something bad was going on and just had to find out. I thought it was Harry I should be worried about. We have a family dinner tomorrow evening to talk about Somewhere, and we will do much more than talk. God has listened to us pray and answered many of those prayers for fifty years. There ain't any reason why He should stop now!"

"I do have some papers being sent to you by registered mail. They have some preliminary descriptions of each of the ranch properties and the discrepancies. Please look them over and let me know what you think the best solution is. No real problem, but some of the fence lines are off as much as a quarter mile. Let me know ASAP and in the meantime, be praying for Jess and Molly. Love you, brother. Goodbye."

Hanging up the phone, Rob fell on his knees and poured our his thanks to God for the special friend he and all the Somewhere ranchers had in John Linderman. Rob knew he needed to go to Somewhere. His heart ached for the ranchers, but he wanted more than anything to take them some good news. and so far, there wasn't any. Rob knew nothing of the barn project being started, which would have thrilled him. But would Jess ever be able to enjoy it, even if he could go home soon?

Molly Martin sat by Jess's bed nearly twenty-four hours a day. She occasionally walked the hall awhile but couldn't tear herself away for long. It was an amazing sight to her though. There were some small sunrooms along the hallway. In each were five or six chairs, and she saw people in those rooms every day. One day she wandered in and took a seat. As she sat there, she realized the women were praying for someone. Molly had seen groups like this in all the other rooms, but she didn't know what they were doing. Exhausted with worry and fear, she closed her eyes to rest and heard one of the women pray for Jess Martin. She couldn't believe her ears. They didn't know Jess Martin. Why did they care?

When there was a break in the prayers, she timidly asked why they were praying for her husband. No one answered quickly, but one of the women came over and knelt in front of her. She explained how Lottie had enlisted them to pray, how they had prayed for many others in the past and how honored they all felt that Molly would stop in this circle. Tears flowed freely from all the women as they folded Molly in their care and love. She had never known anything like it but it felt good as the women began to pray again.

Dear God, Molly prayed silently, *I don't know what this all means, but I want to know You in such a way that I, too, can feel You so near that I can bring to You my hurts and blessings. There isn't anything else like this personal contact with You, and I want to be a part of it. How do I, how can I, what does it mean, who will help me?*

Molly slipped out while the others were praying. Lottie was waiting for her just outside the door. Molly embraced her fervently. "Lottie, I want to be like those ladies. I want to be so much a friend of God that I can talk to Him like they do and have the kind of special place in my life for Him to give me the peace and strength these ladies seem to have. I am a strong frontier woman, but I don't know anything about the kind of strength they seem to have, especially the personal, intimate friendship with God." The tears flowed freely for both of the dear friends. Their friendship had been birthed out of hardship, and their ties were becoming stronger.

"Let's go to the chapel where we can talk," Lottie suggested quietly. Along the way they met other teams coming to pray and Lottie introduced Molly. It was so overwhelming Molly was speechless. Going into the chapel, they went to a small office to one side and closed the door.

Lottie asked, "What would it take for you to believe that God is real, that He cares about you and that He wants to be personally involved with your life in every place not just in special situations?"

"I don't really know," Molly answered. "He always seems so far away, except the night of the rustlers when we prayed with you and Rob. I felt I wanted that then. I didn't know what it was, but I knew something was happening. Then today as I listened to the women praying for a stranger as though they knew who they were praying for and the God they were praying to. I need—I want—that kind of presence with me."

"God is real. He is not merely a presence but a personal, eternal, loving being. He wants you more than you want Him. You can be a part of His family and His purpose just by asking Him to take you in, by deciding to trust Him to be true to His Word. All who come to Him, Jesus promised, will be accepted into His family and we can have that by telling Him you want His change and His life. The biggest problem God has is that He is holy, and we are sinful. So Jesus died on the cross to pay the penalty for all sinners. Just ask Him to come, to shower you with forgiveness and assure Him you want to come to Him."

"God, this seems strange to talk to You, but I need Your

forgiveness. I want to be a part of Your family, to truly be able to talk to You and have You with me. Thank You for Lottie. That's all."

The chapel door opened, and the head nurse stepped in. "Mrs. Martin, you need to come with me right away!" Fear clutched Molly's whole being. *What is going on? Is Jess worse? Is he going to die? What is going on? Dear God. I can't take much more.*

Jess's room was filled with doctors all talking at once. "Doctor, this is Mrs. Martin," the nurse said.

"I cannot explain what has happened," Dr. Roberts related. "But in the last five minutes we have seen increased heart rate to nearly normal. His blood pressure and skin color have dramatically changed toward normal. We are sure that Mr. Martin can hear us and understand us. He doesn't seem to have regained full consciousness but has made significant change in that direction. Would you like to talk to him?"

"Oh, yes, I would," Molly said in a kind of daze. Most of the professionals left the room, leaving Lottie, the head nurse, and the doctor with her. Molly came close to the bed and could see the changes that had taken place. She touched Jess's hand and felt it move. Grasping his hand, she could feel how warm it felt and how the small movements kept happening.

"I love you, Jess Martin," Molly said softly. "God loves you. Terry and Sarah love you. I miss you and pray that you can come home with me." A slight movement in his hand signaled he had heard.

"God, thank You!" Molly sobbed.

That night Molly slept soundly on the cot in Jess's room for the first real sleep she had for at least ten days. In the days that followed, progress was obvious. But Jess was still not fully awake. He opened his eyes sometimes but didn't seem to see anything. Molly was so excited at this much change.

When Rob and Lottie came in one evening, Rob shared that he had been to Somewhere, and Terry and Sarah were taking care of everything quite well. The neighbors were helping, but for the most part, they did it themselves. "You have some mighty fine young people there. I think you should keep them," Rob said.

"We had already decided we loved them too much to let them go," Molly replied.

"They send their love too," Rob answered. "They wanted you not to worry about them. They are getting along fine and will have everything in good shape when you get home. I think they are doing a good job. All the other folks in the valley hope you get back soon."

"I would like that too," Molly replied. "I hope they are getting enough to eat. I don't know if either of them have ever cooked for themselves. But I suppose they will have to learn if they don't want to get too hungry."

Lottie laughed, making Jess move on his bed. Everyone kept watching Jess. He moaned and moved his hand toward his face. Molly quickly went to his side. She took his hand and Jess relaxed in her grip.

"Jess, can you hear me?" she asked tentatively. Jess's grip tightened with assurance he had heard for sure. Perhaps he had heard all about Terry and Sarah too. All in all, this was a red-letter day in Jess's recovery.

"Dear God," Rob prayed spontaneously, "we want to thank You for this sign that You are restoring Jess to health. Let him know that You are here with him and that You are giving him life and healing. We are so thankful for Your special gift of blessings. Keep us in Your love, Amen."

Jess rested quietly and the friends slipped into the hall, where Molly broke down in sobs of joy and relief. Lottie held her for some time, rejoicing with her as all three again gave thanks to God for His gift of life. The ladies from one of the prayer groups were just coming out and saw Lottie and Molly. "Is there any change?" they asked hopefully.

"There is remarkable change. I think Jess hears Molly especially and others and is responding. He is very weak, but it looks like he is going to be all right," Lottie shared.

CHAPTER 60

The barn on the Martin homestead was beginning to look like a barn. The men from the BarJ came one day and set up all the framework for the walls and lifted the rafters onto the walls. It was amazing how much was done in just one week. The other ranchers came when they had time. The project was well on its way to completion.

Terry saddled Buck and rode out to check on the cattle. As best as he could see and count, they were all there yet and growing faster than he thought they would. It felt good to be giving his time and effort to doing a good job and contributing to his family. There it was again, the family. It made him wonder about his real family back in Ohio. What was his mother doing, and did his younger brother have sense enough to stay out of trouble? Did his sister really get married or were they just living together? He wasn't sure that was a good idea anymore, but he didn't know exactly when he changed his thinking about such things. Terry wondered if he would ever see them again and what that would be like.

Little did Terry know Otis Linderman had found his mother and that she had been a financial officer for a law firm in Cleveland. He had been thinking about how to keep the financial records at the BarJ in good order and started to wonder if Mrs. Lund would be a good choice for that job.

"I'm going to have to see what God thinks of trying to get this family back together again. It is a big risk, but it could be worth it if it works out right," Otis thought aloud. "Just have to move forward and see what happens."

When Ronnie, John and Jim came the next day to work on the barn, they couldn't believe how far the construction had come. They crawled up on the roof to put up the sheeting and roofing. Some of the BarJ men were building the stalls and tack rooms inside. It wouldn't be long until the horses and the cow would again have a roof over their heads.

Terry could barely contain himself as he came in for dinner. "Have you looked at the barn today?" he asked Sarah. "I can hardly believe it has happened in less than a week. This is a real miracle. Jess and Molly will not believe their eyes!"

"I was watching the men from the BarJ and was thinking they aren't ranch hands. Those guys are real carpenters," Sarah said. "They know just what to do and when to do it. I am as amazed at it as you are. Well I have some dinner ready, so let's eat before it gets cold."

As they sat across from each other at the table, it felt right for Terry to suggest they give thanks for the food. He began to pray, "God, we thank You for the food and for all the help the ranchers have been on the barn. Take care of Jess and Molly. Amen."

Looking up, he saw tears in Sarah's eyes. "God felt so close just then, didn't He?" she asked. "Does He hear us like—"

Terry interrupted her. "I'm not really sure how that works, but it felt right to say that to Him. I felt that God was near too. I don't know much about what that means, but I will take all He wants to give."

The two novice ranchers ate in silence. When they finished, Terry looked up to see Sarah just watching him. A strange feeling came over him. One he had not had before. He saw a different person in Sarah than he had ever seen, and it felt good. Both young people stared at each other for what seemed a long time. Something passed between them, and from that day on they never felt the same about each other.

"That was a good dinner," Terry said. "You could get to be a good cook." After he said it, he was embarrassed and turned to leave. But not before Sarah paid him a compliment of her own.

"And you are looking more like a true rancher every day. And I like it," she said shyly.

Walking on air would be no exaggeration for either of the young ranchers for the whole afternoon. Their work took on new purpose and their futures looked brighter than they had in a long time. It didn't matter if it weren't here with the Martins. They just knew they had grown up a little more and both of them felt the future might hold something good, no matter what path they were to take.

And God smiled!

CHAPTER 61

All that was left to complete the barn was a coat of bright red barn paint. Everyone in the valley showed up to get that job done. Every man and woman found a bucket and a brush and gave all they could to make this project perfect. By noon, half of the barn was finished, as well as most of the high gables on the ends. The women excused themselves to get some dinner on the table, while the men cleaned up the brushes and closed the paint buckets. Everyone was hungry but very satisfied with the job well done.

Dinner was great. Sarah sat next to Terry and had paint on her hands just like he did. It felt good. She was as much help in setting up the food as anyone and she grew more confident. Not only did she feel as though she had done her part, others recognized it too, and gave her encouragement.

After dinner, Harry Linderman took Terry aside and told him some news he had heard from his brother Otis. "Otis has located your mother and found out that she works in the accounting department of a large law firm. It struck him that she might be the person we were looking for to manage the financial records for the new ranch. Otis didn't say it was settled, but that it was an impression he got when he talked with her. So Otis wants to know if you would object if she were to come to Somewhere and live at the BarJ."

What could he say? He didn't want to hurt his mom. Nor did he care about where she was. He had very little emotional ties with her anymore, so if they believed that was what they wanted, then it was fine by him. Terry had wondered what it would be like to see his mother again, and his brother and sister too. But he didn't really feel much like they were family. Not nearly as much as Jess and Molly had become. A strange thought came to him. *Is God's punishing me for leaving the way I did?* Terry would need to explore that with someone who knew better than he did, but for now he just wondered.

The barn painting was finished as the sun slipped behind the hills to the west. It looked great. It felt like it belonged. The ranch was taking on a ranch feel again. Terry decided that tomorrow he would try to put the horses and the cow in the stalls. It might be a challenge since the last time they were in a barn was during the fire, so he was planning a little surprise treat for them when they got to their places in the barn.

A few men stayed and finished up the last bit of painting. Terry helped with clean up and keeping the paint moving between the painters. The paint was nearly gone in the last bucket when a shout of triumph went up from the painters: "Done!" It was good. The barn was finished.

If only Jess could see it now. It just may be that he would see it sooner than anyone thought. Because right at that moment, Jess opened his eyes and smiled at Molly. Tears ran down her cheeks as she kissed him.

CHAPTER 62

Jess continued to get stronger day by day. The doctors at Cody Hospital took tests and did all kinds of investigations to try to figure out just what caused his condition. Their best guess was that he had been infected by some kind of insect bite, and it hit at a vulnerable time so that the toxin caused a severe reaction. It was frustrating to the whole Cody staff that there were no good answers. Doctors from all over the western United States were also doing their best to help with the diagnosis, but nothing conclusive was discovered. All the information was being collected so that future incidents could be compared and hopefully a treatment could be developed.

The bright spot was Jess's continued recovery with no apparent detrimental effects. Physical therapists moved and manipulated every part of his body and lab researchers continued to ask questions and more questions to collect information. Tests were done every day on his strength and mental alertness. Everything was showing a normal recovery. No one was disappointed.

One morning Molly was walking outside by the garden when one of the doctors saw her and approached. They talked about Jess and what he was like before the incident. Nothing unusual seemed to have happened the day before or during the night. The headache had been first noticed that morning at the breakfast table. As quickly as things could happen in Somewhere, Jess was taken to the hospital.

"What did Jess eat the night before," the doctor asked as if he had an idea.

"Nothing different. We all had mashed potatoes and gravy with some leftover vegetables from lunch. We always had some kind of meat, but I don't remember what it was that night. Maybe some hamburger; I don't recall. Nothing unusual and no one else got sick from it."

"Just a hunch," the doctor said. "I just feel we are missing something here but haven't found it yet. We will just have to keep looking. I think Jess will be able to go home early next week with the progress he is making. We will want to keep in touch as much as possible, but I understand there is no phone service at home."

Molly chuckled. "That is an understatement. We have no outside communication unless we drive twenty-eight miles to Meeteetse."

"We may have to work on that," the doctor said. "These emergencies could be fatal."

When Doctor Brandt saw Rob that evening, he asked what it would take to get some phone service in the Somewhere area. Rob didn't know but agreed that it was a project worth thinking about and he thought he knew just the person to get the ball rolling. John Linderman would want that kind of a project challenge.

CHAPTER 63

Sheriff Parks got the call from Cody and let out a shout of praise. Jess was coming home today by ambulance and would be coming through town. The sheriff organized a welcome party without equal. They would have a caravan to accompany the ambulance all the way to the Martin Ranch. There wasn't a person in the whole town who didn't have a part in praying for Jess Martin. Even school would be let out in time to meet the ambulance. Sheriff Parks sent word to John Fisher what was planned and was sure that there would be no work in the field today for any rancher in the Somewhere area. This was a big deal. And it was also an opportunity to celebrate something good in Somewhere Valley for a change.

As the ambulance neared Meeteetse, Jess asked what all the cars alongside the road were for. No one knew, but as they passed, each one fell in behind and turned on their flashing lights. The sheriff in town met the caravan with his siren wailing and lights flashing as they turned off toward Somewhere. Nothing was familiar to Jess until he saw Terry's S10 with all the family in it. He asked the driver to stop. As he did, Molly signaled to Terry and Sarah to come and ride with them. One of the other men drove the S10, and the family reunion in the ambulance was the most exciting part of the trip so far. Molly couldn't imagine it was happening, but as she saw her neighbors along the road with

236

lights flashing, she began to cry tears of joy. The driver and the EMTs could hardly believe it. They also had tears in their eyes. They could not remember such a welcome home.

As they turned into the gate at the ranch, Molly stared in unbelief. Where did that barn come from? Terry began to explain how it had happened and what the neighbors had said about the Martins and, "how you had help so many others, they couldn't think of not helping you."

There was no spot in the yard that didn't have a car parked in it. Terry had some of the visitors drive on down toward the pasture to make room. This homecoming was the most exciting event of the year. When everyone had finally arrived, the sheriff used his patrol car's loud speaker to give some remarks. "I can't think of anything I have seen in my lifetime that means so much to me and this community. We cannot express our joy and gratitude to God enough for bringing our friend and neighbor Jess Martin back to us. I think it would be good if we were to praise God by singing an old song we all know, 'Praise God from whom all blessings flow. Praise Him all creatures here below. Praise Him above all heavenly host. Praise Father, Son, and Holy Ghost.' Dear God, we don't even know how to give You enough thanks for what You have done for Jess and Molly and for our community. So all we can say is thank You. Amen."

A cheer went up that must have been heard in Meeteetse. The EMTs carried Jess into the house and got him settled in bed so he could rest. As they left, they were met by a line of people shaking their hands and thanking them for taking care of their neighbor and friend, including folks from town in the line of well-wishers.

As the ambulance left, Molly stood on the porch, gazing at the new barn. Joy and gratitude whelmed up so powerfully she couldn't say anything. Sarah came and hugged her. Terry put his hand on her to comfort and encourage her too. It was a good day.

One by one, the Meeteetse folks began to leave. All the ranchers thanked them for their care and their expressions of support. Pastor Hastings was last to leave. He gathered all the Somewhere ranchers and gave a prayer of thanks and encouragement. It was a good day.

That evening, the Martin family spent extra time in the room with Jess. It was good to have him home again. Terry and Sarah told the story of their ranching experience with a lot of laughter. They told how the barn had been given to them by grateful neighbors and how everyone helped putting it up. They didn't tell about their discovery of each other as the days dragged by, but Molly noticed something different in the way they looked and acted. It was good.

Sleep came slowly for Jess and Molly that night. "I just can't believe what has happened," Jess shared. "Terry and Sarah have grown up so much in these three weeks. The barn is just amazing. How can we ever repay all the others for their generosity?"

"We can't," Molly answered. "But I have to tell you that we can give thanks to God for more than just the stuff of life. During your time in Cody, I found out what it is that makes Rob and Lottie so different. Their whole lives are filled with the assurance that God is making them into special people. They live to please Him and to bring others to know that too. I have found what they have and have given my life to God for His purpose and His glory. Lottie helped me see what that means and I wanted it with all my heart. God gave it to me when I asked. So you and I, too, can live that way."

"In all the time I couldn't tell anyone what was going on in me," Jess explained, "I had an awareness of a special presence asking me to trust Him. When I began to wake up, I knew it was God talking to me and just said, 'I do,' and that was the turning point in coming back. I remembered a time when Rob had talked to me out in the corral while I was milking the cow. He shared what it meant to have God as a companion and Savior, but it just didn't make a lot of sense then. This whole unexplainable mess is just what the heavenly Doctor ordered and I know God lives in me now. I just want to live for Him. He built that barn. He healed me and He brought us together again. He gave us Sarah and Terry. I will never again think I have been able to do anything without Him. We have a treasure that only God could give. I'm not sure what the future holds, but I am confident it will be what God wants for us. I love you, Molly Martin, more than ever because I have a different kind of love in me to give to you!"

"We better try to get some sleep," Molly finally said.

CHAPTER 64

The reality of ranch life was apparent the next morning. Jess was able to get up slowly and come to the breakfast table. Terry brought in the milk and Sarah was fixing the eggs and bacon for breakfast.

"I didn't get much milk this morning," Terry said. "I don't know what is going on. I hope the cow isn't sick too."

"I'm sure she isn't," Jess said with a chuckle. "She is drying up to get ready for an addition to her family. I expect she will be better off if we don't try for much milk now. Let's just keep giving her a good ration of grain and hay. Are the horses and the cow in the barn yet?"

"I haven't tried putting them in yet," Terry said. "I was hoping they would get used to seeing it there before I tried. I hope they don't remember the fire too much, but I was going to try leading them through today. If they aren't too afraid, I may put them in a stall for the night."

"Good thinking," Jess replied. "You are really a rancher at heart."

"That's what I have been telling him for the last two weeks," Sarah said. "I'm not sure he believes me yet." Everyone laughed, including a red-faced Terry as he personally enjoyed every minute of it. Especially since it had come from Sarah.

"And you are becoming a good cook, but you won't accept it either," Terry retaliated.

"I can vouch for that," Molly interjected. "I barely had to do anything this morning. Sarah took care of it all."

Sunday morning was bright and clear as Ronnie Moore came up the driveway and climbed the steps, knocking on the door about 9:30. Jess answered and Ronnie nearly hugged him, he was so glad to see Jess up and walking.

"I can't stay long, but we are going to have another meeting in our barn this morning. Sheriff Parks will be speaking to us. He said he wanted to share some of his thoughts about the recent events. We will meet at 11:00 and have a potluck afterward. Everyone else knows, so don't bring any food, but we definitely wanted the Martins to be there since you are home again. I better be going. Remember, don't bring anything but yourselves. Everything is already planned. We just want you to feel loved and welcomed back home in a special way. I got to go. See you there," Ronnie called as he drove away.

Not only were all the ranchers from Somewhere Valley there, so were some folks from town, Sheriff Parks and Beulah and Harry Linderman and all the workers at the BarJ were there. The barn was filled with an air of expectancy.

Ronnie got up and announced they would sing songs that La Verne had copied. It didn't matter that the music wasn't there, everyone could participate any way they could or wanted to. As they sang the first song, "What a Friend We Have in Jesus," those who knew the tune led. Soon it was as though everyone had sung it all their lives.

Jess and Molly were especially touched by the hymn. They kept looking at each other to see if the meaning captured the other too. Terry noticed their glances and began to think more about the words.

241

Yes, he wanted Jesus to be his friend too. He wanted to know he could pray to Jesus without wondering if He were there. Could Jesus really take his sin away? He wasn't completely sure, but he surely wanted it to be. He remembered the conversation with Rob, and he was even more convinced that it was true.

They sang two or three songs. Then Arny Parks got up to say a few words. He made a comment that right now he was not sheriff but a friend and a man who had found the peace that God offers through Jesus. He explained how God could forgive everyone because of Jesus dying on the cross. "What that means for us is when we realize it, we can enter into God's forgiveness by believing He made it possible for all who will believe and accept."

He said a lot of other things, but the rest of it was lost to Terry. He quietly told God he wanted to have His forgiveness because of what Jesus did on the cross. No lights flashed in the sky, but Terry felt the weight lifted that he had carried for a long time, and he knew that God had heard his prayer.

Sarah knew more than she told. Veda Mae had talked to her when she visited the Fisher ranch. She, too, realized that what God offered she wanted. It wasn't clear how that would happen or how it would feel, but she knew that God had heard the cry of her heart, and she became a new creature in Christ Jesus.

CHAPTER 65

The BarJ ranch house was nearly complete. It needed some doors and windows and a lot of inside work, but the fire in the fireplace made it feel like home to Harry Linderman.

Harry took a calendar and realized that October was half gone. He decided that there would be a Christmas celebration at the BarJ by the middle of December. Everyone in Somewhere Valley would be invited. There would be food nonstop and music and a great celebration. There was a guest list to prepare and send out, so he started with all of the Linderman family. The next was Janet Lund and her entire family—Mary, her daughter, and her son, Will, and Terry, her other son, who he had come to consider a very good friend. All the Somewhere ranchers would have to come—McNernys, Youngs, Fishers, Moores, and especially the Martins with Sarah. No one must be left out. Sheriff Parks, Pastor Hastings and his family, Ike the surveyor. The list grew to fifty people. He nearly forgot Rob and Lottie Evans, but they must come for they would be the guests of honor for all they had done to get the legal papers in order. It would be a marvelous party with marvelous news and gifts.

Nothing would be spared. The construction crews had long since left, except for a carpenter and his helper; they were on the list too. It would be a marvelous time. Harry began dancing around like a child waiting for Christmas. There would be gifts, but there would be more. There would be love spread around the whole Somewhere Valley.

"It will be glorious!" Harry shouted. He just wished he had a woman's touch to put it all together. The only one he could think of was Molly Martin. She would know what to do. So he decided he would steal her away some afternoon on a false pretense to see if she would do it for him. He would like to bring Jess, but he also would be a guest of honor, so he couldn't have him plan his own party.

"All set," Harry shouted. "Let's do it!"

In the next few days, most of the outside windows and doors were in place and stained perfectly. The hardwood floors gleamed, and the fireplace kept the whole house warm. Inside trim and precision work were progressing nicely. The kitchen was nearly finished with the feel of an old-time farm kitchen but with modern appliances and fixtures. The old ranch house never had running water, but the new well and the all-weather system supplied the house with good, cold, fresh water. The generator kept all the electrical appliances, the lights, the carpenter's tools, and the fans running just like in Cleveland. Nothing was left out of Harry's planning.

There were other matters to deal with, and part of that was taking care of the cattle and yearlings Harry had planned to buy from the ranchers. So Monday morning he set out to make deals and plans for purchasing and shipping the yearlings in the valley.

It was a beautiful day to be out. A cool breeze reminded Harry it was fall. He saw the barn as he passed the Maftin's ranch and said a quick thanks to God for his provision to the Martins.

Everyone was excited to see Harry drive in. The deals were made, and the calves separated into pens for purchase and shipping. There was no taking advantage like Harry was accustomed to encountering in his business deals. It was so easy that by noon he was nearly done. As he drove into the Martins ranch, he was struck again by the miracle of the barn. Jess came out on the porch to greet him. They sat on the steps and talked about what Jess wanted to do with his stock.

Terry listened quietly. When the deal was struck, he offered to bring the herd up to the corral to be sorted. Terry thought Sarah could ride Jess's horse, and he would use Buck for cutting and separating. It was decided that next Thursday, Harry would have a truck come and pick up the younger stock. Then in a couple of weeks, he would come back for all the other stock they wanted to sell.

CHAPTER 66

After all the cattle were moved and each rancher received a check for the cattle they had sold, Harry Linderman looked over his new herd. The yearling heifers he purchased and put in his corrals at the home ranch gave him hope that this would indeed be a working cattle ranch again. He felt good and believed that in a couple years, the whole valley would have the best stock in the area.

With that done, he began in earnest to plan for the best Christmas celebration in the whole Meeteetse country. First he went to the Martin ranch and asked if Molly would be able to come to the ranch on Wednesday's to help him with curtains and furniture selection for the newly completed ranch house. She was more than eager to help and said she could do that if Sarah could come along too. So it was decided, and plans began to take shape.

At breakfast the next morning, Terry announced he could no longer sleep on the porch and would like to move into the tack room in the new barn. "I could get a heater and put a short chimney out the side of the barn. We can put all the tack in the grain room, and I maybe wouldn't be so cold in the mornings," Terry said.

"I think that is a good idea," Jess said. "I think we have a potbellied stove out in the old bunkhouse and enough stovepipe to do the job. Let's get that done this morning. Whatever else we need we can get tomorrow when we go to town for groceries."

Molly shared information on the job she was taking for a few weeks at the Linderman Ranch. She also thought that Sarah could go along to help. "Harry Linderman is going to pay me a little to work there for the next few weeks. I am anxious to see the house. It must be huge the way it looked when we saw it being built. Who knows. It may take longer than a week to get everything in order."

Jess and Terry went to work as soon as breakfast was over. Jess wasn't up to hard work yet, so Terry did most of the lifting and carrying. It felt good to work together again. The tack room project progressed nicely, and by noon, Terry's cot was moved from the back porch into his new home, complete with table, lamp, and potbellied stove. Jess was right, that everything they needed had been in the old bunkhouse.

After dinner, Jess and Terry saddled up and rode out to look at the cattle. It was the first time Jess had been on a horse after his illness. He was a little shaky but settled down as they rode silently. Jess enjoyed every minute and it felt good.

"What was it like in the hospital?" Terry asked. "Did you know what was going on or able to hear anything? It must have been terrible."

"I am not sure what I remember," Jess replied. "I wasn't always sure what I heard or what was happening, and everything just seemed like it was all dark, so I couldn't see at all. There were times when I felt very much afraid and other times when it felt like someone was right beside me, holding my hand or telling me it was going to be all right. When I started to come out of the coma, I could hear voices and sometimes someone humming a tune, which I later found out was Molly. She told me she was there all the time."

Jess hesitated as Terry looked up and saw tears in his eyes. He looked away quickly and pointed to the cows. "There they are. It looks like they are enjoying the cooler days. And the cold nights don't seem to bother them either. "We need to move them over into the hayfield for the winter. It is closer to the house, and there is plenty of feed until the snow gets too deep. Maybe next week I will feel up to it, but we better go back now," Jess said wearily. "I think we will need to get a better house by next winter too. I don't know how, but the one we have just isn't much to keep us warm. And we don't have a lot of firewood put up for this year either. There is just so much to do … and I just can't do it."

Terry noticed the despair and reassured Jess that he was there to do the heavy lifting and could probably get the cows moved alone. Jess looked up in surprise. He had heard how Sarah and Terry had kept the chores done, cows checked, and generally kept the ranch in order while he was in the hospital, so it seemed that what Terry said could work. But Jess wanted to be able again, and it was taking too much time.

Riding into the yard, Jess stopped and looked around like he had never seen it before. "How did this barn get built, Terry?" Terry told the story again about how all the neighbors had come, measured, put in posts, and how the semi had trouble getting in the gate but made it after all. He told again how the work had been done in just a few days; the men and women of Somewhere pitched in and made it happen. Harry Linderman was the foreman and had everything working like a clock, and they put in the last nail in just two days. And everyone painted.

"It was like a miracle," Terry said.

"Well it was quite a surprise to me when I first realized what had happened and saw it the day I came home again," Jess said. "I knew we had good neighbors, but this is above the level of good."

"People from Meeteetse came out to help too. Sheriff Parks was as busy as anyone and said it was just what the county needed to come together in a new way. He thought that things would never be the same around here from then on," Terry explained. "I think he is right about that."

At supper that night, Molly wondered if it would be a good thing to get out the old Bible and begin reading some of it every day. "I think we need to find out just what God is really like and how He wants to be with us all the time. We could start by reading about Jesus and go from there."

Everyone was enthusiastic about the idea. So nightly around the kitchen table they began to read. Mathew, Mark, and Luke. They began to realize more and more of the miracle of God's great provision. It was exciting to begin to understand more about Jesus on earth.

Terry was having trouble keeping awake and announced he was going to try out his new room. Saying good night to everyone, he caught Sarah's look that made him wonder just what it meant. But like someone he had heard about, he kept all these things in his heart and just wondered about them.

Lighting the lamp in the little room made him feel right at home. It felt good, and Terry said so. He didn't stay up long, but he couldn't get to sleep right away either. Just what is it about Sarah that bothers him. He really liked his accidental sister, but he couldn't put his feelings to rest about her. *She just seems special,* he thought as he drifted off to sleep.

CHAPTER 67

Terry woke with a start when he heard the horses and sat up. He couldn't figure out where he was in the dark of his room. Finally figuring it out, he found the lamp and a match. He opened the door and looked out. The sun was already high in the sky, which made him anxious. He dressed quickly, opened the door to the barn, and saw Jess feeding the horses. It was good to see him, but he felt guilty for not waking up to get the chores done as he had all these weeks now. Then he realized that he needed a window in his room, or night would go on all the time. That was the schedule for today.

Jess greeted him with a chuckle. "Good afternoon, sleepyhead. I wondered what happened to you. Night in your room is a lot longer than it is outside, isn't it? There's an old window we took out of the old bunkhouse, so what do you say we try to put that in this morning?"

"Good idea," Terry said. "I don't want to sleep my life away. When did you think we should move the cows?"

"If we can get the window done this afternoon, tomorrow morning would be a good time. We would have plenty of time so wouldn't need to try to hurry the herd. And that should make it easier."

The window project went smoothly, and it did cheer up the tack room lodging. Terry still like to call it the tack room. He thought it made it a little classy, so it was named The Tack Room Hotel. With that done, Jess and Terry drove out to the hayfield to check the creek that ran through the corner to see if it still had plenty of water. Finding a good flow made it an easy decision to move the stock the next day. On the way back to the house, Terry asked Jess if he could go to town tomorrow afternoon to get gas and a few personal items.

"That's a good time to go, after we get the cows moved. It shouldn't take a lot of time to do that, and I will send a list of other supplies we need here too," Jess said.

The cattle drive went so smoothly, they were done before lunch, so Terry left soon after. As he drove up to the General Store he noticed a pickup he had not seen before. Entering the store, a man approached him.

"I'm Jim Evers, and I noticed you're driving an S10 in excellent condition. The paint is faded, but it looks like you took good care of it. Would you be willing to sell it? I have been looking for one for a while, and yours looks as good as any I have seen."

"I hadn't ever thought anyone would want such an underpowered, overrated truck as an S10 Chevy anymore. It is four-wheel drive, and I am pretty fond of it. But what did you have in mind?" Terry asked.

"Well you see my truck out there?" Jim asked. "I would give you my truck and $500 to boot if what I see is what I get. Would you like to drive it? Then you would know what you are getting in to? I know it's a Ford, but it gets pretty good mileage for a 4X4, and it has around forty thousand miles on it, mostly on the highway. What do you think?

"I hadn't thought of selling, but I'll take a look," Terry replied.

Both men went for a ride in Jim's truck and returned to the store. They sat and talked for some time.

"How long is your offer good?" Terry asked. "I would like to think about it some. It seems too generous. Where did you say you were from, and how would I get in touch if I decide to do business?"

"I'm from over in Powell, but I drive by here at least two times every month. Think it over, and maybe we can get together. Here's my card with a phone number. Think about it," Jim said.

"Thanks, I'll do that," Terry replied as Jim Evers left the store.

"Do you know him?" Terry asked the clerk

"He comes in here once in a while. Seems like a nice guy. He runs a car dealership in Powell and does a lot of trading. I think he wants your S10 as a collector's item. I hear he has a quite a few vintage cars too."

"Well I will have to think about it. I like my little truck, but it is more than fifteen years old and has a lot of miles on it. You can't even buy a 4X4 S10 anymore, so it may be worth more than he is offering. Do you think he is trustworthy?" Terry asked.

"No reason not to from what I hear of his dealership. Seems like a square shooter," the clerk said.

Terry made his purchases and left for home. On the way he decided that if he could get something besides the Ford, he might consider the trade. Not that he was against a Ford, but it wasn't what he had always had.

Jess thought it might be a good chance to upgrade for him, too, after Terry told him about the conversation. "You don't suppose he would want an old Suburban for trade do you?" Jess said and chuckled.

"I have his business card," Terry said. "You could call him from the General Store."

"Well if it takes any extra cash, I won't do it. We need a new house sooner than we need a different vehicle. We will see just what happens," Jess said matter-of-factly.

CHAPTER 68

Life in Somewhere Valley settled into a fall routine. The nights were getting colder and the days shorter. Molly and Sarah went to the BarJ a couple of days a week. The routines just happened, quiet and comfortable.

One afternoon when Molly and Sarah came home in the Suburban they burst into the house laughing and in an especially good mood.

"What is the matter with you two?" both men asked almost together.

"Wouldn't you like to know?" Molly said, and just stood there smiling. With that she held out her hand with a piece of paper in it. Jess reached up to take it. What he saw made his face turn white, and his breath came in short pants. He nearly collapsed again right there, but this time it was not from illness but surprise and gratitude.

Molly had handed him a check for $400 for her work these last three weeks. It was more than Jess had seen in one piece since they sold the cattle.

"What is this for?" Jess asked quietly. "What is Harry trying to do with so much …" But he couldn't finish with the tears coming to his eyes.

"We worked hard," Molly said sternly in a slightly angry tone. "I earned every penny of that, and I intend to use it for the family.

So just cool down and be thankful! We will be helping with a few other things from now until Christmas since the whole Linderman family will be there for a great celebration. What do you think of that? And I can hardly believe we will be doing our work for nothing either!"

"I got paid too," Sarah said quietly. "It is more than I expected, but I am thankful for every penny. I have ideas how to use it too."

Jess could not contain the tears. They seemed to come easily since his time in the hospital, but he didn't care today. They were happy tears, and nothing could take away the joy of being home, having his wife there and the special blessing of two wonderful teens. Well not exactly since Terry had turned twenty. But it felt good. He got up, went over to his wife, threw his arms around her, and told he how much he loved her and how happy he was and all she meant to him. No one even breathed. But that wasn't all. Jess took Sarah in his arms, gave her a passionate hug, and told her how much she had added to the family. And how much he loved her. Terry watched in disbelief until Jess lunged at him and caught him by surprise in another passionate embrace. No one had ever told Terry how much he was loved, no one had ever hugged him with such strength and tenderness, no one had ever said they were glad he was part of the family, but it felt right and good. Tears were flowing all around the kitchen before Jess finished his round and was again standing beside Molly, drawing her close. No one said a word, but the love and oneness in that small room was so overwhelming that no eye was dry and no voice could have spoken if they had wanted to. God looked down and smiled!

At the supper table, Molly told Jess and Terry what the BarJ ranch house was like. "It has eight bedrooms, and two other rooms that have foldout beds in them. The curtains and the decorations are just amazing, western and yet quite modern. The kitchen has every modern appliance you could imagine, even a microwave oven.

"Harry said the emergency power plant would be in this week, and the REA thought they might have power by next summer. The corrals were complete with a complicated system for sorting cattle and feeding. The barn is four times larger than ours, but it fits in just like it was supposed to be there. The 'door yard' as Harry called it, was landscaped with grass and native shrubs from a dealer in Cody who did all the work. It really did feel like it was a home.

"I feel very privileged to be helping make it a home," Molly continued. "Harry is a kind, generous man who can't wait for all the families to gather for their first Christmas celebration. I got the impression, but am uncertain, that every one of the ranchers and families from Somewhere are to be there, too, and Sheriff Parks will bring some people from Meeteetse. This will be some kind of Christmas celebration! The great room has a thirty-foot ceiling, and he said he intends to have a huge Christmas tree in it for the party. So Sarah and I are supposed to help send out invitations and buy all the things needed to make it the best ever seen around here. I am so humbled by being in such wealth, but you would never know it from Harry."

Joy glistened in Sarah and Molly's eyes and everyone was silent. How had they been chosen to be included? What was it like to be a guest of such a wealthy family? Well, they were about to find out.

CHAPTER 69

Terry called the car dealer and told him he would rather have a Chevrolet. Jim said he had at least four trucks on his lot that could fit the description he gave for what he wanted. If Terry could get to Powell, Jim was sure they could make a deal.

Wednesday afternoon, after spending the morning gathering logs for firewood and having a huge pile, Terry mentioned he would like to go to Powell and why.

Jess was full of curiosity and asked if he could ride along. Terry was glad for the company and perhaps for the wisdom in making a deal with Jim. Molly and Sarah would not be home until late that evening, so the men left a note on the table and headed to Powell.

The Evers' Dealership was on the highway just outside of town. Pulling into the parking lot they saw all kinds of beautiful new trucks and could not help but look at them more thoroughly. As they wandered among some of the used pickups, Jim saw them and came out. He was a friendly man, introduced himself to Jess, and told him how glad he had come along.

"You know these kids of ours need our wisdom when making deals, and I want both of us to feel good about the deal we are going to make. I just know we can come up with something that will be just right for your son and I know Terry will be happy with."

Slightly embarrassed, Jess said, "Terry isn't really my son, but that is a long story. But I wouldn't let anyone take advantage of him just like I would for my son, if I had one."

"Well you won't be disappointed," Jim told him. "I have a son, and I feel the same way! Let's look at something I have in mind that will be able to fit into the offer I made to Terry in Meeteetse. Over here I have a half-ton, 4X4 with twenty-one thousand miles on it. It's only two years old. I took it in on a trade last year and just haven't felt like parting with it until now. So Terry, what do you think of this as a trade for your S10?"

Terry didn't know what to say. It looked brand new. No scratches or broken glass. No holes in the seats. It had an extended cab with extra room. *There must be something wrong with this truck,* he thought.

"Could we take it for a ride?" Jess asked.

"Of course. I'll get some plates for it and you can drive it as far as you want. But you have to be back before six because that is when we close." Jim laughed.

Driving out of the dealership, Terry felt like a king. He couldn't find anything that didn't scream, "Take me," about the truck. "I don't know why I wouldn't take the offer," Terry told Jess. "He offered a straight across trade before but paying me $500 to boot. What is going on?"

"I don't know either, but your S10 is rather rare. Maybe it's worth more than you think, not to you but to a collector. We should find out," Jess answered.

Turning in at the dealership about 5:00, they spotted Jim talking to someone else. They parked and wandered through the lot, looking at other trucks. But none was like the one they had driven.

When Jim finally came over, Terry asked, "Why do you want my S10 so badly? It isn't in real good condition anymore, has a lot of miles on it, and the paint is faded. It can't be worth much."

"I expected to have to explain, but I collect classic vehicles. The S10 was one of the first mini-pickups and was also a very durable utility truck. Your pickup is in great condition. It isn't all banged up. You must have taken good care of it, and it is worth a lot if it is restored to somewhat original condition, maybe even $15,000. I can't buy it for that, but I sense you could use a newer truck and a little more room. That's why I made you the offer the other day. It isn't often we see this kind of vehicle out this way either. So what do you say? I will trade you straight across for your S10 and throw in $1,000 bonus for making the effort to come and see me. I got this truck from a very wealthy man who wanted a new one so badly he could taste it and nearly gave me the trade in. So …"

Terry didn't realize it, but he was standing with his mouth open, not able to believe the offer that was being given. "I'll take your offer," Terry finally said. "On one more condition. When you get the S10 restored, I would like to drive it just once, if I'm still around here."

"You got it," Jim said and shook Terry's hand. "Do you want to take the new one home tonight or …"

"Can we?" Terry asked.

"You sure can, and you can bring me the S10 papers as soon as you can. Let me get this truck gassed up and checked, and you are on your way." Calling one of the mechanics to get on this right away, they went inside to sign some papers and wait.

"You wouldn't be interested in a Suburban, would you?" Terry asked.

"What do you have?" Jim countered.

"Well it is about as old as the S10, runs good, pretty solid body. Why don't we just drive it over, and you can take a look when we bring the papers for the S10?"

"That would be great. I have been looking for just such a vehicle, but I can't make as good a deal as for the S10."

"Let's just see what happens." Terry left it there.

While they waited for the pickup, Terry said to Jess, "I figure that nothing like this could happen unless God has a hand in it. I have heard of stuff like this but never thought I would live to see it. Who knows what is in store for us now?"

CHAPTER 70

It was dark by the time they pulled into the yard. A light was on in the house, but as they got closer, it went out. Getting out of the truck, they were confronted by a loud voice, "Just leave the lights on, and get in front of the truck so I can see you. This 12 gauge isn't picky who it tears up, and I won't hesitate to give it its head if need be."

Jess chuckled and told Terry it was Molly and to do as she said. So they came around into the lights with their hands high. A gasp of relief escaped from the "guard," and it was a great homecoming after all.

"I couldn't imagine who was coming in that pickup. I just thought of the rustlers. And Sarah is on the other side of the house with the pistol in case there is real trouble." She sobbed. "You scared us. How could you do such a thing, and where did you steal that truck?"

"It's a long story," Jess said. "Let's go in, and Terry can tell you all about it."

The joy that everyone felt was so real as the story unfolded. Sarah nearly cried for joy. Terry wanted to hug her and let her know that she could ride with him anytime she wanted to. What was he thinking, telling a girl he wanted her close to him? What was going on? He didn't understand, but it felt good and right.

"We have more to tell," Jess said. "Jim, the car salesman, said he was looking for a Suburban in reasonably good shape and may be able to make a good deal on ours for something newer and maybe more useful on the ranch. I told him we would come up when we brought the papers for Terry's truck."

"We can't afford a new truck," Molly announced in no uncertain terms. "We will *not* be in debt."

"I didn't promise anything," Jess explained quickly. "I just said we would let him take a look at the Suburban when we came back. We will just have to wait and see what happens after that."

"Well okay," Molly answered sternly. "But we have news for you too." She winked at Sarah. "We are invited, along with all the other families in Somewhere, to a Christmas party to end all parties at the BarJ Ranch on December 15. I can't imagine that it will be a little family gathering. All of the Linderman family are coming from back east, and Harry said they were bringing a couple of friends along. Fact is, someone is coming in next week who he hired to keep the books at the ranch. He is sure this person is overqualified for the job but is excited to have them. He hates keeping accounts but likes to use his wealth to make things happen, and I think he has plenty of that. He wants the ranch to be an example of honesty, integrity, and profitability. I think he will succeed without even breaking a sweat. That's a phrase he uses often, but it is descriptive and accurate. So what do you think of that? Sarah and I have a job as long as we want it, and we will, I'm sure, be paid well for doing it. Not that the privilege isn't really enough. So if we are going to take the Suburban to Cody, we will have to do it on a day we aren't need at the BarJ," Molly finished. No one spoke for fear of losing the good feeling.

The days got cold quickly as October faded into November. There was snow on the western mountains, and they expected it would be in Somewhere soon.

Sarah and Molly weren't needed at their job on Thursday, so

they took the Suburban to Powell, expecting to drive it home again.

Jim was glad to see them and finished up the paperwork for Terry's trade, including a check for $1,000. It was overwhelming, but Terry kept control as he and Sarah watched the title being signed over.

"If I were you," Jim offered, "I would go to the bank and open a savings account that lets you write some checks on this money. It won't gain much interest, but it will be safer than in a box at home. And a check isn't easy to spend a little at a time. But that is what I would do. You also may want to talk to Rob Evans, over in Cody, about making some investments that would earn a return. He is pretty good at it, and it could be a great start for you. Anyway, thanks for making my day. It has been great getting to know you."

Coming out of the office, Jim went over to Jess. "Did you find something on the lot you would be interested in for a trade?"

"There are a lot nice units out there, but the price tag is way out my reach," Jess replied.

"Let me drive your Suburban around a little. Then we can talk about what may be possible," Jim said, taking the keys from Jess.

"I'll be back in about a half hour, so make yourself at home. Better yet, let me get you a loaner, and you can get something to eat while you are waiting."

Jim came back after pulling a pickup up to the door. "Take this, and go up to the Broken Wheel Cafe. It's the best place in town. I left a map on the seat for you."

When they returned to the dealership, Jim met them in the showroom. "I want to make you a proposition. I like what I see, but I want to take a better look at the frame and the engine. So how would it be, if your vehicle is worth what I think I need to offer, I give you a pickup to go home in, and I can check it out the

Suburban? I don't want to give you false hope but it looks pretty good. So what do you say?" Jim questioned.

"I guess that would be okay, wouldn't it Jess?" Molly said tentatively. "When would we need to be back?"

"I would send up a couple of men to make the switch if it looks good for me to take this unit. Or we could just say that you could come back in two weeks and finalize whatever agreement we could make. Either way, you need to be getting home soon. It is supposed to snow, and sometimes it gets pretty bad out in this country, as you know."

"I think we would be okay with that arrangement," Jess said. "And we do need to get home.

So it was settled, and they climbed into a two-year-old, crew cab pickup for the trip home. It seemed like luxury with a radio that worked and a heater that didn't make any noise. Molly looked through the instruction book, trying to see how to make everything work. The miles went by more quickly and quietly than they had ever known since they moved to Somewhere. It was a strange feeling that this could happen from someone who had their best interests in mind, but they couldn't figure out just what it was. And God smiled.

CHAPTER 71

—⟨∞⟩—

Winter came with a bang. The Suburban had been traded for the very truck they rode home in with very little extra to pay for it.

Molly and Sarah had been very thankful for the four-wheel drive a few times in getting to work at the BarJ. The Christmas celebration to end all Christmas celebrations was planned, and some of the people were arriving. The new accountant had been on the job for a couple of weeks and was getting the computer up and running with the information Harry needed to make financial decisions for the ranch. The calves he bought were in the corrals with enough hay to keep them happy and heathy. The hired foreman did his job well and made the whole ranch his responsibility. It would run right or he would fix it was how he saw it. Harry loved it!

Jess and Terry were busy feeding and making sure there was enough water for their cows. They looked forward to the party but didn't have any time to see the BarJ during the next three weeks. The new pickup sat beside Terry's amazing deal. The cost had surprised Molly as they were able to pay what Jim wanted in cash.

One cold morning John Fisher drove into the yard. He had a mission. He and Veda Mae just got back from Cody for a medical checkup and had talked with Rob Evans. Rob had told them that the trial of the rustlers had gone as expected, and the entire ring had been broken up. The Cattlemen's Associations in two states had put up a large reward for their arrest and conviction payable to those who were instrumental in catching the gang. He didn't know how much it would be but thought it would be substantial. This was good news for everyone. The year had been hard, and winter was using up their resources faster than planned.

Jess thanked John for letting them know. And as John drove away, Jess found himself thanking God for this and all the other special things that had happened that fall. It didn't surprise him, but it made him think that it wasn't just the other stuff but the inner stuff of life that had also changed in him and his family. Could it be that he, Jess Martin, really believed in God and had given his life to Him? That is exactly what he thought and again thanked God.

When Molly drove into the yard that evening, she just sat in the new truck and thought about her own life and what had happened to her. She saw things so differently, and she didn't really know why. She was more patient and even more ready to help others. "I don't know what has happened to me, God, but I like it and want You to know that You can make any other changes You want. I am a much better person because You have made all the difference."

Glancing to the side, she realized she had been talking aloud, and Sarah had been listening. So she said to Sarah, "You are one of the most precious changes that have come to me in this journey. You and Terry are God's good gifts to me and to Jess. I think we have all changed and have God to thank for it. You are so much different than at first. No longer angry about everything, or afraid, but loving and kind. And don't think I haven't seen how you feel about Terry. And if I don't miss my guess, he about you. God has brought us together to be His trophies, so we can show others how to live to please Him. And Harry, well if God isn't evident to anyone who has been around him for a while, they are blind and deaf. He is singing hymns all the time, and he never uses bad language. I am so full of joy I can't help it."

The women fell into each other's arms. And God smiled a big smile!

There was a knock on the pickup door. Jess yelled, "What is wrong? Are you having trouble?"

Opening the door, Molly explained, "We were just trying to understand that God has come into our family and made us so different, and we are so thankful, and we—"

"Well," Jess interrupted, "that's nice, but it's getting cold. You better get inside before God has to thaw you both out." They laughed all the way into the house. The warmth of a good fire in the fireplace was welcome.

Supper that night was great. No one could have told you what the food was, but they would never forget the praise and thanksgiving that came from everyone around the table.

Molly announced that the Christmas party at the BarJ was set for two weeks from Friday. All the Lindermans would be there. Some from Meeteetse would be there. All the ranchers from Somewhere Valley were to be there too. Rob and Lottie Evans were coming down from Cody. It was going to be the most exciting party ever in that part of the country for a long time. And it would be talked about for a lot longer.

CHAPTER 72

The Martin's new truck rolled into the BarJ yard, the first of the local ranchers. All week Molly and Sarah kept secrets about all the excitement that the coming of the Linderman clan was causing. They knew other things about which they had been sworn to secrecy. They were anxious to see how everything would turn out.

They were directed to where to park and started to the house. Terry felt an excitement he had not had since he was very young, and his father had come home with some marvelous gifts, and they were all together. As he entered the house, he was overwhelmed by all the decorations. He just stared at the tree with its special trimmings. The house was extravagant but so inviting. Someone asked to take his coat, and as he took it off, he realized who it was.

"Mom?" Terry whispered. Tears filled his eyes, and his mother held him close. Neither could speak; nor did they want to. Terry had never felt the love his mother was pouring out to him just then, and he didn't want to lose it again. They blocked the doorway for a long time. Finally they moved into one of the side rooms and shared their apologies and their joy. Mrs. Lund—Janet—poured out her sorrow for not being a better mom. Terry countered with apologies for not caring what she thought or how she might have missed him after he left. Nothing was unconfessed and nothing was left of their bitterness or regret when they realized that God had made it possible for them to be together again.

"I got a call from Otis Linderman about a job as an accountant a while ago. I couldn't figure out why he would call me and he didn't tell me at first either. After I talked with him and he looked at my credentials, he offered me this job. He said he thought I would find it rewarding and satisfying. He didn't say I would find my son again, but he knew all along. I'm sure of it.

"Your sister has not talked to me in more than a year, but your brother is here with me. He is helping out on the ranch and is going to high school this winter in Meeteetse. Neither of us knew you were around here at all. But it is so wonderful to know you are."

"Mom," Terry had not called her mom in a long time, I'm sorry for the pain I caused you, but I couldn't have become who I am there in Cleveland. You won't believe all the things that have changed about me, all for the good I hope. I have thought lately about trying to find you again, but it must be a God thing that you are here. This is really a great Christmas!"

As they came out of the side room, Terry took his mom around and introduced her to all the ranchers. He saw Rob and Lottie Evans and took her over to let them get to know her too. No one was left out. But he couldn't find the person he most wanted her to meet, Sarah. He was anxious about it but tried not to let it show. And so the evening went on.

Otis Linderman asked all the guests to take their seats at the tables. There were so many they went from the kitchen down the hallway. He tapped on a glass, stopping all the talking.

"Everyone here is special to our family." He introduced all the Linderman clan. It took so long, Terry wondered if he would ever finish. Then Rob Evans stood and introduced all the ranchers to the Lindermans. But Sarah still was not there.

"Now we have a special treat," Otis Linderman announced. "We found out that one of the rancher's daughters sings a lovely song. So without any more waiting, Sarah, come and sing "Silent Night" for us before we get this dinner started."

Every jaw dropped as Sarah stepped to the head of the table and sang three stanzas of the beautiful Christmas carol. She sang as though she knew who she was singing about, and it was true. She knew the One who lay in the manger and gave her the new life she had come to live for and treasure.

It was silent after Sarah finished. No one moved. Lottie Evans stood and prayed for the gathering and gave thanks for the food and the feast of thanksgiving they were about to take part in. It was beautiful and everyone echoed the "Amen." The dinner was good, but the look Terry got from Sarah was enough dinner for him.

After the dessert, Rob Evans stood and called for attention. He shared how he had become involved with the Martin family from Somewhere. How he had been contacted by John and Otis Jr. to help with the legal work in setting the ranch back in order and making sure all the small ranchers were protected.

"I have a packet for each rancher and each member of the Linderman clan." Everyone laughed. "In this packet," he continued, "you will find a description of your property, corrected by the surveyor and approved by the county clerk's office. Every rancher will have to build some fence since the existing boundaries are not the legal boundaries. Harry Linderman will give you assistance next spring and summer to make the necessary changes. All you need to do is file the deed that is included in the packet with the county clerk's office in Cody and pay the registration fee."

Stunned silence met the announcement. Timidly Jess asked, "Does that mean we have more land than we thought we did and that it is now legally in our names on verified deeds?"

"It does mean that," Rob replied. "You no longer need to worry about anyone questioning your right to your ranches. Now there is one other item in your packet, an envelope addressed to each family. Before you open it, I want you to put your arm around your wives. You will need each other's support when you open this envelope. Got that? Now the both of you open the envelope."

As the envelopes were opened, there were gasps of surprise and tears of joy. Rob explained, "The Cattlemen's Associations had posted a reward for information leading to the conviction of a rustling ring that spanned three states. The reward was $50,000. Since every rancher in Somewhere Valley was involved in the capture of the rustlers, it was divided five ways, and each family holds a $10,000 certified check in your hand."

"I have one more announcement to make. Somewhere Valley has had so many tragic and near-tragic events this past year. All of you have had to make a dash for Meeteetse more than once to get medical help or Sheriff Parks. Well Otis Linderman has—"

"That's Otis Linderman Jr.," Otis corrected.

"Yes," Rob went on, "has decided he wants communication here at the ranch, so he is looking into investing in communication service through a local telephone company. It is hoped this will be operational by spring. It is one of my fondest dreams too," Rob added. "I have worried many times about your welfare, and this is great news!"

A cheer from all the folks at the tables went up, and the dessert was served.

No one spoke. Joy and relief came from everyone sitting around the tables, including the Linderman family. No one could have guessed what was to happen at this celebration. No one but God knew how to make it the celebration He wanted it to be.

EPILOGUE

As the evening progressed and the dinner was cleared away, the guests became friends with people they could never have met anywhere else but in Somewhere, Wyoming.

Terry stood in a doorway between the large room and the hallway. No one noticed him there by himself and he was glad no one tried to engage him in conversation. His day had been so full he couldn't hold any more. His life here in this remote place had taken so many unusual turns he could not have planned. Here in this quiet place on the fringe of the pleasant, marvelous evening, Terry Lund renewed his promise that his life and heart belonged to the Savior who had been chasing him all these years. He felt that nothing could make him any happier or match his quiet joy.

Across the room another person watched the party process. She was not involved but felt she was a real part of it. She felt the fullness and love of those in the Somewhere Valley and especially of Jess, Molly, and Terry. She, too, had found the Savior who had pursued through the terrors of slavery, abuse, and rejection. Then she saw Terry. By himself, and she knew. She moved slowly, mingling with others around the room. Soon nothing was between them. Terry had not seen her, as she appeared in front of him.

Looking into his face, she knew that what she felt and what he felt at that moment. "I love you, Terry Lund," she said softly and leaned toward him, kissing him gently.

Terry enveloped her in his arms and knew that the future included them being together in God's ever-changing plan.